MW01516015

the
SALTBOX OLIVE

the
SALTBOX OLIVE

Angela Antle

BREAKWATER
P.O. Box 2188, St. John's, NL   Canada   A1C 6E6
WWW.BREAKWATERBOOKS.COM

COPYRIGHT   © 2025 Angela Antle
ISBN   9781778530517
                9781778530524 (EPUB)
                A CIP catalogue record for this book is
                available from Library and Archives Canada
COVER ART: Julie Liger Belair
PAGE LAYOUT: Nadine Hodder

ALL RIGHTS RESERVED. No part of this publication may be
reproduced, stored in a retrieval system or transmitted, in any form
or by any means, without the prior written consent of the publisher
or a licence from The Canadian Copyright Licensing Agency
(Access Copyright).
For an Access Copyright licence, visit www.accesscopyright.ca
or call toll free 1-800-893-5777.

We acknowledge the support of the Canada Council for the Arts.
We acknowledge the financial support of the Government of Canada
through the Department of Heritage and the Government of
Newfoundland and Labrador through the Department of Tourism,
Culture, Arts and Recreation for our publishing activities.

PRINTED AND BOUND IN CANADA.

Breakwater Books is committed to choosing papers and materials for
our books that help to protect our environment. To this end, this product
is made of recycled materials and other controlled sources.

Canada Council   Conseil des arts
for the Arts   du Canada

Canadä

Newfoundland
Labrador

MIX
Paper | Supporting
responsible forestry
FSC® C103567

For Eli and Veronica

chapter 1

THE OLIVE

This is the Broadcast News of Newfoundland for February 6, 1940. Governor Sir Humphrey Walwyn will issue a proclamation today, calling for volunteers to form an artillery unit.

Arch sits up in bed.

Men between the ages of twenty and thirty-five, who weigh at least one hundred and twelve pounds, stand no less than five feet four inches tall, and are of sound physique and good eyesight will be accepted. The first four hundred can sign up at the CLB Armoury tomorrow.

For weeks, rumours have been forked over wharves with codfish and passed over merchants' counters with tobacco. And now here it is. The call. Arch throws off his eiderdown and lets the icy February air prickle his thighs and stomach. His future has finally arrived. The stove door creaks. Min is striking the first match to light the day. She'll get the tea stewed, the bread in the oven, and might even read through a few pages of her mystery before Skipper comes in from fishing.

Arch swings his legs over the edge of the bed, pulls on the vamps he discarded the night before, and plucks his teeth from the bowl on the washstand. Otto would've heard the same news and will be soon hooking up his dogs to give Arch a lift to the station in Heart's Content. In the kitchen, Min is punching down the dough. He kisses her cheek and says, "I might not have time for tea. Otto is on his way."

"You'll have to make time so I can read your leaves."

They both know her fortune-telling is complete fiction, but he gives in. The dishes from last night's surprise visitors dry on the counter. It was strange to see the two Tucker women sitting primly in their front room. Mrs. Tucker and Anna brought his last tutoring pay packet. Without algebra and history, Arch and Anna had very little to talk about. He caught her looking up expectantly every time someone entered the room. She didn't know. He whispered that Garl had taken off. Gone underground. Probably in North Sydney. She wiped at her eyes with her mitten, leaving fuchsia threads tangled in her eyelashes.

Sipping her tea, she asked him if he didn't think an almost-priest becoming a soldier was a bit odd. He laughed, admitting he was glad to be going somewhere, to see something, instead of spending the rest of his days in a leaking dory. She turned to him on the chaise and hugged him close. Her curly blond hair tickled his lips. What to do with his arms? She said she would miss him and thanked him for tutoring her. He tingled all over. He'd never been that close to a girl. A girl that his brother was stringing along. She let go when she heard her mother's footsteps in the hall.

Arch melts an O on the window with his breath. He scratches his index finger through the frost to make a peep hole. Curt hiss. Boiled water contracts the cold metal snout. Otto will soon round Turk's Head. The ballycaters near shore will no doubt slow him down, giving them a few minutes for their tea. He pulls his chair out and Poirot jolts awake from her frayed quilt under the table.

"When did Skipper go out?" he asks.

"He didn't. He wants to say goodbye."

Skipper proudly tells anyone he meets at the community wharf, on the church steps, and in the store, that Arch is joining up. A soon-to-be-soldier son is a lot less shameful than an almost-was-priest. Skipper can be slyly charming, funny even, like Garl. Arch used to pray that he would carry on like that at home, but as soon as his father was alone with them, he'd turn as sour as a dog that bites the hand feeding it.

Min says, "You know, Arch, you don't have to go with the first batch."

He's been waiting for this. "Min, this way, I'll get more training, get a salary from day one to pay off the teeth, and I might even find Garl."

She withdraws a smooth purple beach rock speckled with fool's gold from her apron pocket and presses it into his palm. "Tell them when you're signing up, about your inventions."

"C'mon, that's just tinkering."

"You know it's more than that," Min says. "Make sure you mention it."

Poirot's nails click across the floor. Otto's dogs are drawing close. Arch burns his throat as he swallows the tea. Min swirls the remaining liquid and a frown settles with the leaves.

"Off to become a real man, are ya?" Skipper fills the door frame in his stained undershirt and long johns. "Got your fine china out, Minnie. Nothing but the best, for little Archie."

How long has he been listening? Poirot scratches at the back door. Min ignores her husband and stands on her toes to look through the O. "He's here. Otto's here."

Arch knocks the table when he stands and tips the cup. Leaves spill into the saucer. His reaches for Min's hands, brushing the nub of her missing thumb as he kisses them. He hugs her and tries to memorize her scent: witch hazel, birch smoke, and the tang of salt fish and brewis soaking in a nearby bowl.

"Write. Tell me about all the places," Min says.

"I will. I promise."

He gives Poirot one last scratch behind the ears before nodding goodbye in Skipper's direction. Duffel hoisted over his shoulder, he pushes the storm door through a knee-high snow drift that accumulated overnight.

When Otto's dogs jerk the komatik out over the bay, Arch doesn't look back at the grey saltbox clinging to the rocks, but he imagines the sound of Min's last china cup smashing.

———

He joins the nearest line and stands as straight as he can. In the last war, they only accepted soldiers who were five-eight and taller, but as the death tally grew, the height rules fell. After thirty thousand casualties, they even accepted men who were Min's height, five-three. He's not sure what to make of the fact that the height rules this time start at five-four.

A squirrely young man, with a mop of dirty-blond hair and a smattering of acne, nudges Arch. "Going in for gunner?" He's young enough to be one of Arch's former students.

"I'm a Slade from Salmon Cove." He thrusts out his hand. One of his eyes is turned.

Arch says, "Fisher. Turk's Cove." He hopes the other enlisters are older and have good eyesight. A group of young men in camel wool coats and shiny brogues bust in through the CLB's double doors. They're charged up and acting like they know everyone and everything. His young friend sneers. "Friggin' townies."

"Don't mind them, they're just pretending they're not nervous," Arch says. "I certainly feel better knowing that we're artillery and not infantry this time round."

"B'y, it's a job to say which is best. Sitting duck with a twenty-five-pounder or charging forward with an Enfield," says Slade before he spits on the polished floor.

Arch is unnerved by Slade's eye. While one casts northeast, the other peers straight on, piercing into Arch's soul. What kind of aim could he possibly have? Slade draws his hand across his throat and says a little too loudly, "Just give me a gutting knife, and I'll straighten out Adolf myself."

Arch is relieved when they're called to separate desks. An ancient Great War soldier with a handlebar moustache squints at Arch. "Name?"

"Archibald Fisher, sir."

"Age?"

"Twenty-three."

"Special skills?"

Arch hands over a letter from Captain Tucker with the address of the Winterton fish plant stamped on the top. The old soldier elbows the clerk next to him. "Says here, he built an aeroplane. Too bad we don't have an air force!"

Remembering Min's advice, he speaks up. "Yes, sir. The parts were all there in the woods, where it crashed, and I put it back together so it could fly again."

He doesn't tell them that Garl crashed the plane, after gloating to Anna that he could fly better than Charlie Lindbergh.

"So, you trained as a mechanic?"

"I worked as one. I also make radios, repair locks. I used to l-look after Archbishop N-Noel's carsss," says Arch.

He hopes they won't ask him why he's no longer fixing the cathedral fleet.

"Mechanic's certificate?"

Arch shakes his head. "No, sir."

"Highest level of education?"

What's the use of telling them he only did three and a half of the seminary's four years? He looks at his feet. "Grade ten, sir."

The clerk stamps a card and scribbles on a dotted line before handing it over. "Your regimental number is 970408. You best memorize it, Private Fisher."

If Min had been here, she would've kept talking until Arch got officer stripes. But he's gotta do this his own way. He doesn't want anyone in this new life to know about his failure in the last. He's in the army now and he's not sure priestly types are welcome. Not wanting to make a misstep that will set him apart, he salutes the old soldier, hoping he used the correct hand and tries to sound pleased. "Thank you, sir."

————————

Caroline senses she's being too intense and attempts to dial it back with a sip of coffee and a deep breath. "There was a woman photographer. American. Lee someone? There's a famous picture of her taking a bubble bath in Hitler's tub, with her mud-caked boots on his bathmat. She did more than that, but that's the image that pops to mind." Dry cereal crumbles out of Viv's mouth. "Mom, no one cares. It was so long ago."

"Not that long ago. They were your age and they risked everything." Frantic scratching at the back door.

Viv ignores it and says, "The prof didn't mention women."

Caroline gets up to let the dog in. When she comes back to the kitchen, Viv is playing Candy Crush. The conversation forgotten. Walker lopes in, takes bacon and eggs out of the fridge, and turns on a burner. "What are you two arguing about?"

"Not an argument." Caroline looks at the bottom of her coffee cup and hopes she can top up before Walker empties the carafe. Viv says, "Mom is just explaining how we don't appreciate what women did in the war."

Walker drips yolk down the front of the stove. "Jeez, Mom. Not every conversation is about femini—"

She cuts him off by reaching for the carafe.

"Um, I haven't had any yet," he says.

"Don't worry, us feminists only want half." She pours and says, "The bravery and curiosity of those women are still moving culture forward."

Viv rolls her eyes and roughly packs up her schoolwork as her father comes downstairs and announces his intention to go for a run. "I'm finished the essay now," Viv says, "and it won't make any difference if I add in some stuff about random women."

Caroline turns on the hot water and sluices soggy cereal and coffee grinds off the dishes. Water sprays up on the window. More to clean. No wonder the world is in a state. How will we ever tackle climate change, the war in Ukraine, Gaza, if a nineteen-year-old won't acknowledge those who've gone before? Leo shoots her a "cool it" look.

"Your mother is right, Viv," Leo says as he's lacing up his shoes. "It's important to tell women's stories."

Walker scrambles his egg. "Yeah, Viv, it's all on you."

Viv makes a face at her brother as air brakes squeal in their driveway. Caroline turns off the tap. "At ease. I'll tell him he's got the wrong address."

She opens the front door to a burly man in a wolf sweatshirt and India Beer ball cap.

"Caroline Fisher?"

"Yes. But I'm not expecting anything."

"It's from Turk's Cove. We put it on the truck this morning."

Caroline's great-grandmother, Min, lived in a saltbox in Turk's Cove for over nine decades. Since her death, any number of first, second, and third cousins, aunts, uncles, nephews, nieces, boyfriends, and girlfriends have used her place as a shelter from life's storms. She no longer bothers to ask her mother about Min's and who's refusing to talk to whom over the grass, the clapboard, the septic, the roof, and the starlings nesting in the eaves. The mover looks back over his shoulder and gives his buddy a nod. "Missus, I'm hauling for tonight's ferry. All I knows is that it's some sort of tree."

"The tree? The tree is alive?"

"I'm not so sure 'bout dat, but it do weigh a friggin' ton."

Curtains twitch up and down the street as the men lower a massive clay pot onto their dolly. Caroline flicks knapsacks, shopping bags, dog leashes, boots, and sneakers out of the way to clear a path through the front porch. When she looks up, a busted assembly of dry twigs and cracked branches shimmies towards her.

Leo asks, "What is that and where the frig are we going to put it?" For once, Walker agrees with his father. "Mom, there's no room."

Caroline ignores them. Their house is at least four times bigger than Min's saltbox and her great-grandmother loved this tree, spritzing and watering it with spring water she warmed on the wood stove.

"Viv, turn up the heat."

They called Min's house Chianti because she kept the temperature "on cremate" to replicate the tree's natural climate.

The movers leave a trail of curled, brittle leaves through the house before sliding the pot off the dolly with a thump. Everyone stands back. Wolfman scratches his belly. "So, tell us, what in the name of Christ is it?"

"It's my great-nan's olive tree," says Caroline.

"Big martini drinker, was she?"

He laughs at his own joke as Caroline looks for her purse to tip him. "Who hired you?"

"Some dude from California. Moved here to surf, can you believe that?"

"I don't understand."

"Me neither! You couldn't pay me to get in the water."

"No, not that. What does he have to do with the olive?"

"It was in a house he was renting. Listen, we had to saw some branches off to get it out the door, but they were dry as bones, not a bit of life in 'em. Anyways, buddy said he had to go home for the winter. He sent it to you because he didn't want it to freeze."

Caroline follows them out. Just before the driver hoists himself into the cab of the truck, he says, "There's a book too. A family book or something. There's a note in it that the tree was yours."

"The family bible? Did he give you that?"

"Just the tree. He locked up the house after we took it out and went straight to the airport. His name is Hunter, Harpo, something like that. Said he'd be back to surf in the spring. I told him, 'Buddy, we don't do spring in Newfoundland, come back in July.'"

Before he leaves for his run, Leo says they may need another post in the basement to support the pot's weight. Caroline sifts through the dry, grey soil, unearthing ancient cigarette butts ringed in coral lipstick. Definitely not Min's colour.

The front door closes and the lock beeps. Leo is gone for his run. Viv's in the shower upstairs and she can hear Walker laughing at TikTok videos in the basement. She flips open her laptop to find the crowd on Facebook who grow their own veggies, keep bees, chickens, and goats. It's a lively page where a racket can break out over compost acidity. Backyard gardening? No. Backyard farmers? No. *Backyard Farming and Homesteading*. That's it. Today's hotly debated issues are how to grow potatoes in hanging bags and how to diagnose a chicken illness, complete with gross photos of green poop. She posts a couple of shots of the olive, confident that most members would rather see a dead tree than a chicken's arse, and asks if anyone has experience growing olives in Newfoundland. She's unprepared for the immediate flood of responses. *Do you really think you can bring that thing back? That's firewood. That's not an olive. You did a shit-job with the pruning; it's the worst time of*

*the year to be at that. Olives won't grow in Newfoundland; we don't
have enough sunlight.*

She shuts the laptop. The last person is wrong. Min's olive is at
least twenty years older than Caroline. She sees Min's floury hand
over hers on an upturned glass. They're cutting tea bun circles out
of dough patterned with olive leaf shadows.

Caroline's mother calls a few nights later. CNN booms in the
background.

"Mom, can you turn down the TV, please?"

"I can't, Caroline. I can't stop watching the thing in Ukraine. Putin
bombing children and women at the train station. Heartless. They're
saying, the experts, that the whole thing is about oil. Imagine! Killing
people over oil? That reminds me and I hate to change the subject,
I want to pay for a tow truck to bring my car into town."

"Let's wait to see what the snow-clearing situation is at your new
place, Mom. Remember, we talked about that?"

"Yes, yes, I remember. What's this about Min's tree? You didn't
say anything about that when I called last Sunday."

"Yes, I did. I told you he was American. Californian. Must've been
renting Min's place."

Her mother changes stations.

"The movers said he has the family bible."

"He couldn't possibly have that, Caroline. Your grandfather
burned it all with the letters."

"Right. Why haven't we ever talked about that?"

"I don't know, girl, there's nothing to talk about."

"Mom, it's pretty dramatic, burning your brother's wartime letters.
Why? Why did Pop burn Arch's letters?"

"I don't know. It never made any sense. Felt guilty, I s'pose."

"Guilty? About what?"

"Because he came back, and Arch didn't. He'd never talk about
it. You know that."

"Why don't we ever talk about it?"

The familiar wail of a trumpet. "Gotta go, Caroline."

"But you just called. What did you want to talk about?"

"*Coronation Street* is starting. I'll think on it later. Gotta go. Love ya."

The drone of disconnection.

Caroline spends the rest of the evening studying olives. Greeks taste olive oil in wine glasses and Italians believe if an unchaste woman plants an olive, it will die. There are living trees with names that are thousands of years old. But there's little information about caring for potted olive trees in northern climates. Leo bounces onto the bed.

She says, "When we were in Florence, in art school, I read something about—"

"Trinity Bay olives?"

"Not exactly. It was an article about a father and daughter who saved old fruit trees. Strange-shaped pears, stripey apples, purple plums; fruit they saw in old paintings and frescoes. They'd go to the exact convent garden or village where the artist worked to find the actual tree. To save that variety."

"And you want to find this detective duo?"

"The father has probably passed, but she might still be alive. She's the only Italian tree expert I know of."

Leo speaks into his phone. "Hey, Siri, woman who saves trees."

Caroline lies back on the pillow. "I don't know if we'll find it. I read about them long before the internet."

"Remember tearing up the Lonely Planet Italy book into provinces so we only had to carry the section we needed?"

Leo snuggles into her.

"C'mon, stay focused."

They eventually find the article. Caroline recognizes the photo immediately. Father and daughter, Isabella, posed nose to nose as if they were painted by Uccello. Her father has died, but their outfit is now on Facebook. The Arboreal Archaeology Foundation.

On the page, there are images of frescoes and still-life paintings alongside baskets of the real fruit: pear-shaped apples called Ox's Nose, twisted gourds, and purple-fleshed peaches. She taps out a message to Isabella and closes her laptop.

Leo says, "Remember the guy at the market who would match our pears and apples with the right cheese?"

"Is there a wrong cheese?"

She reaches for him under the sheets. "Remember our first taste of"—she slips her hand under the elastic of his briefs—"tartuffi?"

He kisses her neck and unbuttons her pyjama top. "Si and carciofi."

"C'mon! They're more like melanzani."

"Mmmmmelanzaniii."

He kisses her breasts. "And midnight walks for gelato?"

She takes his shirt off. "Si, si, pistacchio and mirtilli."

"Or my fave." He slides her pyjama pants over her hips. "Fichi."

After sex, Caroline falls asleep thinking about those walks in the dark Florentine streets. The city was a miracle at night. No tourist lineups. No Vespas, buskers, or tour bus exhaust. No pickpockets. No tour guides with little flags yelling at their charges, just stars and cobbles, sometimes the clatter of cutlery and glimpses of crystal chandeliers and painted ceilings through open second-floor windows. The Arno's murk slithering under Santa Trinita. Oltrarno. The winding paths at the Pitti Palace. The olive groves of Maiano. Min leans a ladder into the crook of an olive tree. She's wearing trousers under her skirt, and she kicks off a pair of red suede shoes before climbing the wooden rungs in bare feet. Halfway up, she reaches back for Caroline's hand.

The next morning, Caroline is spritzing the dry olive branches when her phone trills. "Ciao, Caroline. That is quite an old tree you have."

"Ciao, Isabella. Grazie for your quick response. Do you think it's still alive?"

"The olive, it never dies. We have trees that were planted before the Crusades. How did you get it? I am looking at your location and you're quite far north."

"I might have the only olive in Newfoundland. I don't know where it came from, but it has a connection to Italy. My grandfather and great-uncle were there in the war."

"Dove? The Canadians were in Ortona, yes?"

"They were British Army. I'm not sure where they were stationed."

"We had British soldiers near here during the war and Indian soldiers too. If this tree is one of our olives, it will regenerate. The first thing you need to do is get it out of the pot. Be very gentle handling the old roots. Bathe them in warm, not hot, water, and leave the root ball in the bath, immersed in water for twenty-four hours. Somehow, you must keep the water warm. While it is having its bath, you will put all new soil in a much larger pot. I'll send you a recipe for the soil. You will see, your tree will wake up."

Caroline thanks Isabella and sends a small donation to her foundation. She texts Leo: *No shenanigans tonight, we're bathing the olive.*

Embarrassed that she couldn't answer Isabella's questions about where Pop and Arch fought, Caroline borrows *The Fighting Newfoundlander* from the library. The text describes major battles at the Sangro River, at Cassino, and a winter in the Apennines. There's a crude map, with no camp locations. No information about their day-to-day reality. She starts zooming in and out on Google Maps wanting to know precisely where they walked, drove, slept, and ate. She wished she had bugged Pop for stories when he was alive. When she was a kid, her parents drove from St. John's to Turk's Cove at least once a month for Sunday dinners. By the time they arrived, Min's kitchen windows would be dripping with steam from the boiling potatoes, turnips, pease pudding, and cabbage. Caroline has one memory of asking Pop about the war and he changed the subject. When she pressed, he handed her a Time-Life book about D-Day and said she should read about the A-Team. She still doesn't know what he meant by that.

They ate their Jigg's dinners below the two oval soldier portraits in Min's kitchen. Pop looked serious and proud of his officer stripes. Arch was only a private, but he's laughing in his photo.

When Min died, Caroline was in Florence, studying art. She led a rowdy wake at the Irish pub near Santa Maria Novella with her student friends, Leo's rock-climbing buddies, and some stray Aussie backpackers because she couldn't afford to fly home. If she can bring Min's olive tree back from the brink, it would be a way to honour what her great-grandmother meant to her.

—————

Clutches of women blow their noses into embroidered hankies outside the CLB. Arch walks through competing clouds of perfume. It's as if he's walked onstage for a play that's already started. He looks around for Garl. Maybe big brother signed up today as well. A boy, about eight years old, is chewing a giant wad of gum. His eyes are closed with the effort. The men in camel coats shake hands and chat easily with each other's families. Min knit him a new sweater, but he's still wearing his fishy logans, and the same threadbare pair of pants he had on when he joined the seminary. A huge man with thick red eyebrows and tufts of red chest hair protruding from his collar horses around with a mob of kids. He flexes his enormous forearms like a circus strongman. Two boys clasp onto each bicep and he easily lifts the foursome off the ground. The boys squeal, pedalling their feet in the air. The man's chin dimples when he laughs. He gently brings the boys back to earth to lead a circular march. He lifts his legs stiffly and pumps his arms like a windup soldier. "Watch it now! No goose-steps!"

Nine kids of various ages imitate the man's moves, marching in circles and banging into each other until the smallest girl, a little redhead of about two, trips and skins her knee. The giant scoops her up. She loops her arms around his neck and kisses his cheek with fierce devotion.

There's a sudden, sharp whistle and the men scramble into a rough lineup. The giant hugs a short, wide woman holding an infant and slides into line behind Arch.

"Christ, the youngsters will be crying soon if we don't get going. I'm Tom Walsh. I work . . . worked at Cook's."

"The marble works?" asks Arch.

"Yeah."

"I'm Arch Fisher."

"B'y Arch, I feel like I've seen you before. What do you do?"

Arch doesn't want to step into his new life with a lie on his conscience, but he says, "Uh, fisherman."

"Every second man fall out!" is bellowed from a bull horn. Their first command. Chatter rises as the men step sideways in a tattered attempt to form a parallel row. With Tom walking alongside, Arch's stride lengthens. There are photographers from the newspaper, even a movie camera on a tripod at the bottom of Long's Hill where it meets Queen's Road. Arch tries to hold his head high and stop worrying that someone from the church will recognize him as the line of Newfoundland volunteers surges forward.

chapter 2

MULLEYSTONE

Big Ben strikes as Lucia joins the queue at the Grosvenor post office. She stands under the sign for European packages and unfolds Papa's letter. *Tia Ester and Tio Ronaldo have come down from Bologna to take the waters.* She doubts very much that her well-heeled aunt and uncle are swimming in the cow's water tank. *If any more relatives visit Spa Moo, they'll be sleeping in the barn and eating hay! Write to us soon. We miss you and Cosi as always. Love Papa and Mama.*

His humour signals that all is well, save the extra mouths to feed. Why are her city relatives on Monte Sole? Perhaps they got tired of listening to her father brag that it's the perfect place to safely ride out the war, close enough to Bologna for supplies, but barely a dot on the map. The postmark is almost two months old, which has become the norm. At the wicket, she returns the envelope to her purse and retrieves the postal slip. "Good afternoon, sir, I'm here for a package from Italy," she says.

The clerk pushes the slip back without looking at it. "No packages from Italy. Next!"

What an ass. He wouldn't treat her this way if he knew she spent the morning embroidering a gown for Princess Elizabeth. She refuses to budge. "Sir, I work at Hartnell's, and that package is for the atelier."

Even postal clerks know Hartnell has a Royal Warrant. His jaw clenched, the clerk gets up from his stool and checks the slip against the shelves. Her heart leaps when he grabs a long metal pole to loosen a bundle from a high shelf, deftly tipping it over the edge and catching it in his free hand. As he walks back towards the wicket, he brazenly holds her gaze and rips the package open letting the contents drag on the dusty floor. She is shocked. He flings the ripped paper, broken string, and fabric through the grill and says, "Trying to smuggle in contraband? If you work at Hartnell's you know very well that silk is subject to government rationing and there's a customs fee of fifteen pounds. Your master has thirty days to pay up."

Her ears burn as he stamps the customs slip and nods to the next person in line. She stuffs the slip, the fabric, and its torn paper shell into her bag and hurries outside. How can she possibly give Hartnell a gift and a customs bill at the same time? To make matters worse, she's now late.

Before she can remove her coat and sit at her station, Mrs. Price summons her to Hartnell's office. She hands her tea in a gold-rimmed porcelain cup and saucer and Lucia's stomach falls. The British always give you tea in a cup and saucer before they tell you bad news. A few minutes later, Hartnell sweeps in and lays *The Times* down on his desk with a front-page picture of Churchill facing her. The headline reads, *Collar the Lot!*

"Have you read the papers today, Lucia?"

She shakes her head. Hartnell sits, crosses his legs, and lights a cigarette. He takes a long draw and blows the smoke over her head. "They, and by they, I mean the war office, seem to think your man,

Mussolini, is now the enemy. I mean, he has been flirting with the Germans all along, hasn't he?"

The old dread of Fascists rattles her cup in its saucer, but she doesn't dare lay it down on the polished walnut surface of her boss's desk. He stubs out his cigarette in a crystal ash tray and stands. "A few days ago, he and Adolf made things official with something they call the Pact of Steel. What malarky! Unfortunately, as soon as they put their pens to paper, you, your son, and all the Italians here in England became enemy aliens. The rag trade will be absolutely devastated."

All day long, Lucia and the other women in the atelier stitch their worries into Hartnell's frocks. Nerves frayed by nights in bomb shelters and fears for menfolk in France and North Africa pierce seams and hems. Lately, they've been sewing frets over a rumoured German invasion into buttonholes and darts. It's been the perfect cover for Lucia. Not one of the Fascisti in London would ever look for the co-founder of Stella Rossa in a place that made royal frocks. Her mother and grandmother taught her to sew because they imagined her life would be as limited as theirs, but every stitch she makes is just a mark in time until she can get back to Paolo's side and lead Italy into the future. The news that Mussolini and Hitler have joined forces is not news to her.

"Mr. Hartnell, Cosimo and I are British citizens. We've been here almost ten years."

"No logic to it, my dear. Even the Italians who fought with us in the last war are being rounded up. The tabloids are calling it spy fever. Can you even imagine?"

He looks back from the window and says, sotto voce, "Lucia, you are one of my queen bees. If you know anyone in the countryside, out in Dorset or Norfolk, you should go there, keep your head low, and wait it out. After all this drudgery is over, there'll be an explosion of creativity. We'll have the most fabulous fabrics and be able to use as many buttons and embroidery stitches as we like. But today, right now in fact, you've got to go. At the Club, I heard that ateliers are being raided. It might be this afternoon or tomorrow, but the police are coming."

The ripped brown paper. Now she understands the postal clerk's sneer. She unclasps her bag. "Mr. Hartnell, this is from my village. It was to be a gift, but unfortunately there are duties."

He holds the crumpled silk up to the window's light. Despite the dirt from the post office floor, it shimmers. "Thank you, dear Lucia. Here I am letting you go and you're giving me a splendid gift. If only I could use it."

"The worms don't work for Mussolini," she says.

He laughs, leans in and asks her what she knows about silk. She tells him her family kept worms and she looked after them as a child. That everyone in her village did. He lights another cigarette then whispers that he has an idea. She should collect Cosimo from school and pack a few things in a grocery bag. No suitcases. He will swing by to pick them up at six. She can tell no one and must exercise extreme caution walking home.

Lucia crams her legs behind the front seat of the convertible while Hartnell winds a white silk scarf around Cosimo's neck. When they pull away from the curb, she looks up at her flat's windows for what she hopes isn't the last time. Cosimo is so excited to ride in a motorcar, he hasn't even asked where they're going. It's a good thing, because she has no idea. Once clear of the crammed city streets, docklands rubble, army checkpoints, and ammo factories, they eventually drive down narrow tree-lined roads that cut through green pastures. They drive for a couple of hours, past woods and villages that look like places from fairy tales until they stop at a stone building with ramparts and a turret. Cosimo sits up in his seat and says, "Nice castle!"

"My dear Cosimo," says Hartnell, "that's just the gatehouse. Wait until we go through the keyhole."

They drive through the archway, and up a pebbled drive lined with moulting white peonies. The house is an expansive, stone, three-storey affair. The evening light casts long shadows from a Gothic church and graveyard on the western side of the lawn. Hartnell parks and turns to Lucia. "I don't know if my friend can take you in, but I didn't want to risk asking her over the phone, so leave your things in the boot until I've had a chance to ask her properly." He turns to Cosimo. "Now, young man, you must pay attention to me. This is very important. Once you get out of this car, you cannot speak Italian to your mother. Lady Haskell has staff, and anyone could turn you in, do you understand? I will introduce you as Lucy and . . . what English name would you like to take?"

Cosimo unwinds the scarf. "David?"

"Ah yes, Michelangelo's favourite."

He turns to Lucia. "Can you pronounce his new name?"

"Of course. Davidee."

"Try cutting off the last 'd.' Just think it, don't pronounce it."

"Davide."

"Oh my. Call him Davey and I'll tell the staff you're Swiss."

A blond woman in a blue skirt and white blouse waves from the terrace. There's a scent of scorched hair. Cosimo's nose crinkles and the corners of his mouth turn down. Hartnell waves back and as he ascends the stairs, kisses the woman on both cheeks, and sweeps his arm towards them. "Allow me to introduce you to my Swiss travelling companions. This is Lucy, one of my finest embroiderers and a silk weaver, and this is her son, Davey. Friends, I'd like you to meet the incredible Lady Haskell."

Not a hair out of place. A silk scarf knotted just so. "Welcome to Mulleystone, Lucy and Davey and please, do call me Zoe. Would you like tea or a lemonade?"

Lucia's face flushes. How does one sound more Swiss and less Italian? "We'd love some lemonade, thank you very much, and Davey would like to stretch his legs."

Zoe's eyes sweep over the two shopping bags of clothing in the back of the car. "Of course. There's a lovely path along the river. Join us when you're ready."

Zoe leads Hartnell into the house and Lucia follows Cosimo along the river that runs through the garden. He asks her about the smell.

"Your Nonno called that the smell of money." It strikes her then that she has no way to let her parents know where they are and that there'll be no more letters from home.

Cosi interrupts her worries. "Lady Zoe burns money?"

"No, silly. That's the smell silkworms make when they're about to spin their cocoons. When I was your age one of my jobs was feeding the worms. See these trees along here. They're mulberries. It's the only thing silkworms eat. 'Moro,' in Italiano, but you heard what Mr. Hartnell said, no more Italian."

"Mama, are we staying here?"

Lucia pulls him close, "Let's try it out for a while . . . Davey." He squirms out of her arms and asks if there are stables. As they're crossing the garden, an aeroplane drones overhead. Cosi shoots at it with an imaginary gun.

———————

Empty British Army tents line Mulleystone's lower garden. The cook says the Army is building a mock airfield to lure German bombers away from London. Officers come and go from the house at all hours. Lucia keeps her head down and avoids speaking. It's not like she has time to chat anyway, she can barely keep up with the ravenous worms. She's ripping leaves and sprinkling them over the plump, writhing bodies when she hears Zoe coming up the back stairs with a man. Not recognizing his voice, Lucia turns back on to the door and continues feeding her charges. Zoe and her guest enter the adjoining worm nursery. Lucia peeks and is relieved to see the man is not in uniform but remains vigilant because of Lady Zoe's formal manner. "Mr. Thistle, meet the worms that will make your maps."

"The smell is quite something, isn't it?"

"Oh. I barely notice it. There are over twenty-five hundred worms in these two rooms, and very soon they will produce a pound of the world's finest silk."

"Only a pound?" he asks. "That's very unfortunate, Lady Haskell. My project will need ten times that."

Undeterred, she explains that if the number of worms is to increase tenfold, she can call back a few employees and restart one of her spinning machines. But he refuses, citing the project's top-secret clearance. Then he admits they're comparing Mulleystone silk to American synthetics from an outfit called Dupont. Lucia hears the irritation in Zoe's voice. "Mr. Thistle, forgive me, but something mixed up in a vat will not help us win the war."

"Perhaps," he says, "but it's all part of Churchill's charm offensive to bring the Americans onside."

After Thistle leaves, Zoe joins Lucia to harvest leaves. "I would've introduced you to Thistle, but he's secret service, and could make trouble. His silk map project is quite top secret."

Lucia wonders why Zoe is telling her about it if it's so secret. "I won't speak of it. But, why maps on silk?"

"Waterproof. Easier to smuggle behind enemy lines than paper."

Noises from the fake airfield grow as they enter the lower garden.

"He's having a problem with the dyes. We can beat the Americans if we can come up with some way to make the contour lines and rivers crisp. Do you have any experience with silk dyes?"

"Not really, I just fooled around with beet juice and crushed flowers when I was a child."

Zoe stops and takes Lucia in as if seeing her for the first time. "Oh, my dear, I am so sorry. Here I am going on about Thistle's project, when you must be missing your family terribly. When was the last time you heard from them?"

Surprised by this sudden interest in her well-being, Lucia's eyes fill with tears. She clears her throat and says that it's been over a year. As they walk, she fights the urge to let her fears spill out. The limbo of knowing she could be arrested and deported any day, the fear of enemy planes dropping bombs on Mulleystone, the worry over what her family may be facing, that Paolo will be assassinated or betrayed or that her family will be punished for their connection to Stella Rossa, and worst of all, the fear that Cosi will never meet his father.

They round a corner into the lower garden and there's one, two, five soldiers on ladders in the mulberry trees. Sawed-off branches litter the ground. Zoe drops her basket, kicks off her high heels, and runs. "Stop that, young man! Stop that right now!"

chapter 3

CWAC

Bright red lipstick. Pristine smocks. Kitten heels and berets tilted just so over chignons. Barbara unbuttons her knobby cardigan and tries to hold her head high as she walks past the girls in the OCA lobby. Without asking, she knows every single one of them is applying to painting. Why that is more acceptable for young women than photography, she'll never understand. All around the edges of the gym, young men watch her and whisper. Pretending not to notice, she waits and when it's her turn she steps up to the bearded prof at the Industrial Design table. He looks right through her to the next male in line. Barbara stares at the space between his eyes, just like her father taught her to do when hunting moose. She lays a brown envelope on the table between them and speaks slowly, doing her best to imitate the Ontario drawl. "Hello, sir. I'm here to interview for photography."

He frowns. "It's a technical course. You need knowledge of lenses and chemistry for the baths."

"Yes, sir. I develop my own photos and assist my father in his darkroom. He owns a studio in St. John's."

"St. John's? The one in Newfoundland?"

Bullseye. She tips open the envelope and shakes the photos out.

"You're a long way from home, Newf."

He paws through her capelin and icebergs and pauses on her father's salmon line arcing over his favourite pool. He holds up her still life of miners' helmets and lamps.

"This is good. It reminds me of the summer I worked in Sudbury and I bunked with the Newfs. They were a riot and the showers were always free."

"Sir?"

"Either they didn't wash, or they didn't know how plumbing worked. I always had the showers to myself."

Barbara's cheeks redden. How she would love to tell this arsehole off.

"You use your father's camera for all these?" he asks.

"I have my own Rolli, sir."

He glances around the gym and scratches his beard. Her cheeks are getting hot. He sighs and scribbles on her papers. "Take these to the admissions wicket."

She stuffs her prints back in their envelope and mumbles thanks, only checking the papers when she's back in the lobby. She's in. Accepted. An Ontario College of Art photography student. Tonight, she'll call her father and share the good news. The papers state that darkroom supplies and access are free and her father has given her a suitcase full of recently expired but still usable film.

The next morning, she greets the caretaker, Mrs. Donoghue, as she's turning the key in the front doors. Hours before any other students or profs arrive, Barbara is happily sliding her Kensington kids and Spadina shopkeepers into and out of baths with tongs. Her photos capture scenes of women sharing gossip and haggling over the price of chickens. Rotten vegetable wars between rival kid gangs with elaborate fruit-crate forts in alleyways and stolen portraits of tired commuters lost in thought.

As the semester progresses, she experiments with stories on the back of her prints. Chatting with her subjects alleviates her loneliness, but the professor refuses to read the writing, dismissing it as "bad art and worse journalism." His words sting and she stops attending lectures. Instead, she studies the compositions of the student prints drip-drying on lines strung through the department. By the glow of the red safety, she learns to push herself, experimenting with dodging and burning. Cropping and deepening shadows to make her images more dramatic.

She is shooting a series of commuters reflected in Chinese restaurant windows when she spots her friend, Patsy. She almost doesn't recognize her in her army-type uniform. Patsy says it's for something called *see wack*. "When Canada joins the war, the Canadian Women's Army Corp will be ready to be useful," says Patsy. "I'm on my way to a meeting now. Come with me, you can take pics."

When they arrive at the Shaw Street Shul, four sewing machines are going full tilt. Bolts of khaki wool are stacked on the gym floor. A truck motor is hauled in on a dolly. Socket wrenches are lined off next to gauze bandages and a gurney. Half the women are in uniform. Barbara snaps photos of others being fitted. Over the rat-a-tat-tat of the Singers, Sergeant Boon calls them to order. There are upcoming Morse code exams, first aid courses, a letter from the Ottawa CWAC group, and a new mechanics course. A young brunette puts up her hand. "Sarge, my mother won't let me out of the house in my uniform. She says the neighbours will think I'm trying to get myself a soldier."

Boon claps her hands to quiet the rising chatter and says, "Just say, we're supporting our men in uniform, not advocating for women to fight. We volunteer so that the men can be freed up for tactical and combat roles."

By meeting's end, four more women leave in uniform and Barbara has two rolls of CWAC photos.

The following week, she arrives early as Boon is laying out envelopes, stamp rolls, and porcelain stamp moisteners. She tells Barbara that they've been writing politicians at all levels but have yet to receive a single response. Barbara shows Boon the prints she developed from the previous meeting and tells her she'd like to approach *Chatelaine*. Boon agrees and lends her a uniform.

Walking down College Street, she understands how CWAC members could be accused of playing at military roles and making up ranks. The fitted wool jacket and neat skirt feel great, but also draw wolf whistles and raised eyebrows. She ignores the unwanted attention, focusing instead on calming her nerves. This could be her first national photo spread. Exiting the elevator, she walks past mail slots and a wall of enlarged covers to a seating area dominated by a raised, curved desk. The blond receptionist wears a telephone headset. Barbara approaches. "Hello, my name is Barbara Kerr, I'm with CWAC, the Canadian Women's Army Corps. I'd like to meet with an editor."

The receptionist twirls the headset's wire with a manicured index finger. "Funny, I've never heard of see . . . what did you call it?" A button on her desk lights up and she presses it. "*Chatelaine* magazine, how may I help you?"

Once the call is forwarded, Barbara jumps back in. "We're lobbying the government to create meaningful wartime roles for women."

The receptionist stands and, opening a file drawer, says, "No one wants to go to war."

"Of course not," Barbara replies. "But we should be prepared." She unzips her portfolio and the receptionist glances dismissively over her photos. "Do you have an appointment with Miss Enstrom?" she asks. Barbara admits she doesn't and asks if she can leave her portfolio on spec. The receptionist refuses, but on her way back to the elevators, she slides the portfolio into Enstrom's mail slot.

———————

The June 1939 *Chatelaine* photo spread, with Barbara's glamorous portraits of CWAC mechanics, truck drivers, Morse code technicians, and nurses, changes everything. So many young women show up at the next meeting that some activities are moved outdoors into Trinity-Bellwoods Park. Express letters arrive from the British Columbia Women's Service Corps, the Women's Volunteer Reserve Corps of Quebec City, and a group in Halifax. More importantly, Ottawa can no longer ignore them. Boon says every MP's wife, daughter, secretary, and mistress must be reading out loud to them from their copy of the magazine.

In September when Canada finally announces it is joining the war effort, Barbara quits OCA and becomes a full-fledged CWAC member. She applies for every job opening at the newly formed Canadian Film and Photo Unit, but weeks go by without an interview. Leaving the cinema one night, Patsy points at the marquee and asks, "How do we know what Joel McCrea does in this film?"

"It *is* called *Foreign Correspondent*."

"Yeah, smarty pants. He's also wearing a trench coat and has a press pass."

"What are you suggesting?" Barbara asks. "That I put a little card in my hat?"

"No, silly! You need a portrait. Just like the ones you did for the campaign."

"A photo of a photographer taking a photo?"

"Exactly! Meet me tomorrow on the steps of City Hall. Bring your tripod and two cameras."

"Why two?"

"One is a prop. Photographers carry cameras."

With Barbara's help, Patsy snaps her portrait. She's wearing a helmet, her CWAC uniform and holding her flashy Speed Graphic tilted just so. The prints make her feel silly. War photographers do not wear lipstick. Patsy encourages her to include a print in her next job application. Despite her reservations, it works. The Canadian Film and Photo Unit wants to use her portrait to lobby Ottawa for more money and, in return, they'll hire her as an archivist.

The job is not difficult, and it gives Barbara insight into life in the field as a war photographer, stoking her ambitions. Eventually, she starts notching her desk with a nail file every time a job applicant walks past the archives. Mostly they're young guys straight out of high school or college, only a few have newspaper or film experience. She knows this because she pre-screens them by telephone while flipping through their meagre portfolios. Some even have the nerve to ask why a woman is calling and not the boss. When the notches reach the other corner of her desk, she puts her thick portfolio on her boss's desk.

A few minutes later, he's in her office shaking her thick portfolio. "Have you got the number for this guy?" he asks. "He's really good and has tons of commercial work and newspaper credits. Find him and have him call me. I'm free all afternoon."

"So, he's good?" she asks.

"Best I've seen so far!"

He goes back to his office, and she counts to twenty before walking down the hall.

Her boss looks up. "You found him that fast?"

"Yeah."

"Great! When can he come for an interview?"

She folds her arms over her chest. "He's already here, sir. He's me. They're my photos. I've applied for the last eighteen openings, but you haven't given me an interview."

He slumps in his chair and lights a cigarette. "Babs, we can't hire you."

"Sir, you said these were the best photos you'd seen. I've published photos in *Chatelaine*, the Eaton's and Sears catalogues, *The Globe and Mail*, and the *Toronto Star*."

"Fashion and social snaps are not the kind of experience we're looking for."

"I've done more than that, sir. I'm familiar with the workings of the unit, and I've been developing film since high school."

"Look, Kerr, we can't send a woman into war. It just wouldn't fly."

"Think of the fabulous PR, sir. The first Canadian woman war photographer!"

He sucks air through his teeth. "You'd be thrown in with a gang of wolves."

"Wolves?"

"The other photographers. And their wives would be writing letters to their MPs demanding they cut our funding."

"Sir, you don't know that."

"I can't send you into the field, Kerr. There are no latrines for women."

"What?"

"That's right. There are no ladies' rooms in war and besides you're the best archivist we've had."

Her arms fall to her sides. "I'm the only archivist you've had."

That night over beer, Patsy says, "You'll never get to be a war photographer if you stay here. Come with me to London."

"London? In England? Doing what?"

"Filing clerk. The Army is flying me over and putting me up. There's tons of jobs and"—she winks—"they must have ladies' latrines."

chapter 4

A JAM

Someone in the crowd had pushed an orange into Arch's hands. He sits alone and peels it slowly, breathing in its bright scent. The last time he ate one was in the seminary. He'd like to retreat into a book. It would be the perfect respite from all the forced revelry, but he doesn't want to set himself apart from the men he'll be spending the next months, maybe even years, with. Men who all seem to know each other already. Card games have formed, and bottles and cookie tins are being passed around as the elms and grand houses of the Waterford Valley recede into the evening. Just as the moon rises over Doe Hills, a tumbler of whisky is placed on the table in front of him.

"How are ya, Archie?" Tom Walsh lifts an armrest and jams himself into two seats.

"I'm all right, Tom. Was that your wife seeing you off?"

"You can call me Tombstone. Yes, that's the captain. She'll be keeping the troops in line while I'm gone. What about you?"

"I'm on my own," Arch says. "No wife, no girlfriend."

"Well, b'y, don't expect me to be kissing you goodnight." He holds the amber liquid up to the light. "Father says Golden Wedding got him through the first war. He hid it in my duffel while the captain was distracted. Archie b'y, I just can't shake the feeling that I've met you before."

Arch wants to leave the past behind on the tracks. All of it. The shame. The fear. Skipper. Father Tobin. Failing. If he can avoid being connected to the church, he just may have a chance to become someone else. Someone Tombstone would want to be friends with. Someone who is outgoing, brave, even funny. Then it hits him. Tombstone's wife might've been one of the confessional weepers. He takes a sip of whisky to mask his guilt and steers the conversation to Tombstone's children.

"Yup, ten, and another one on the way," Tombstone says. "I was going for a dozen until this friggin' war got in the way."

Most seminarian Saturdays were spent sharing a cramped confessional with Father Tobin. Sliding open the divider to listen to exhausted female penitents with ten, twelve, eighteen was the record, children. Once the sniffles subsided, Tobin would remind them that contraception was a deliberate violation of natural law. For the truly desperate, he'd suggest Onan in Genesis 38, leaving it up to the women to grasp his inference to coitus interruptus. But he was too much of a coward to suggest the technique to their husbands knowing they'd likely pull back the divider and give him a limbing.

"They're my pride and joy. Where you from, Fisher?"

"Trinity Bay, a little place called Turk's Cove, near Winterton."

"Turk, eh? So, you're a pirate?"

"Not the kind with treasure."

If there was any pirate gold in Turk's Cove, Arch and Garl would've found it. They overturned every rock in every cranny and crook above and below the waterline. Arch made a metal detector from a discarded magnet and a broken scythe handle. Using that and Garl's pickaxe, they probed the cabbage, potato, and turnip gardens, the blueberry patch, both beaches, all the caves at low tide, the graveyard, and the dump. The only treasures they found were some hand-forged nails, broken pieces of china, a rusty buckle, a silver fork missing two tines, and a giant hook that Garl claimed the mysterious Turk used as a hand.

More nuisance than a mysterious X on the map, Turk's Cove was known up and down the coast as a place of wet feet and frustration. A rocky stream intersected the main road and forced travellers to alight from their taxi, cart, or sled to wade through the freezing cold water. An unwanted baptism at the only Catholic toehold that side of Trinity Bay. Curse words flowed into the cove every day especially if another vehicle was not yet idling on the opposite side to complete the journey. Unknowing travellers might sometimes walk into the cove to size up the maze of riddle fences hemming in half a dozen silvered saltboxes, red ochre barns, sheds, stages, and wharves built and occupied by Fishers, Ryans, Antles, and Conways. Most visits would be cut short when the weary traveller spied the tiny Catholic church that doubled as the school. Once they understood they were in enemy territory, they'd hightail it back to the road to sit on their trunk, drying their socks and shoes until their ride came along.

———

Raindrops mottle the kitchen windows at Mulleystone. Lucia is waiting it out, taking her time with breakfast. Marie, the cook, holds two pots of jam in front of her. "Taste these two, will you, and tell me which is better." Lucia spoons a red dollop onto her toast. When her palate makes contact, she is transported home. Her little sister's purple-stained milk teeth. "Marie, this is like my mother's jam. It's lovely."

"Here then, try this one, and hurry up. Thistle's here for tea."

Lucia spoons an identical-looking lump of jam on the other end of her toast. It's too sweet. It reminds her of teatime at Hartnell's. "This one tastes like the city. Like it is store-bought."

Marie nods in agreement. "Yes, it has pectin in it." She mops her forehead with a silk handkerchief. "Number one it is, then."

She stomps off with a platter of scones and jam. When Lucia stands, she knocks the jammy knife onto the white tablecloth and is scrubbing at the stain when Marie yells down the hallway, "Lucy! Lady Hartnell needs you in the sunroom."

———————

The train whistles for Windsor Station. Those not used to hard liquor are already puking out of windows and others are sprawled across the aisles. Cursing and accusations of cheating erupt from rambunctious games of Growl. The conductor, a doughy man with a lisp, is not impressed with the so-called soldiers. When he leaves their car, Slade, the young man with the wonky eye, jumps up and re-enacts the man's passage. "Ticketh pleathe! Ticketh pleathe! You in d'army? Hand over your ticketh, tholdier!"

Prancing up the aisle, Slade leans down into card games, and punches pretend holes in imaginary tickets. His eye makes everything funnier. Men are soon shrieking with laughter and Slade is so pumped up with the attention he doesn't notice the conductor's return. Arch is laughing so hard he's holding his hand over his mouth, so his teeth don't fall out. Tombstone's giant arms are crossed over his chest. He may be the only one not amused. He whispers to Arch that Slade was locked up in his Majesty's for theft and only got out because he signed on. Arch stops laughing. Slade's comment about gutting Hitler now seems more sinister.

The conductor's face is scarlet by the time a man named Jackie grabs Slade's shoulders and turns him around. The car goes quiet. Slade rears back then recovers and bows. "Oh, there you are! I was just getting everybody all sorted out for you." He hustles down the aisle and dives into Arch and Tombstone's seats. Tombstone rolls his eyes and makes room. Arch doesn't want to be stuck up but considers moving, not wanting to be associated with a criminal.

———

Thistle claps his hands and stands when Lucia enters the sunroom. Zoe speaks to her in a formal fashion that makes her stand up taller. "Dear Lucy! My apologies for calling you away from your work. We're comparing two maps and need your assistance. Marie will hold hers up to the window, and if you could hold this one up at the same level, our hands will be free to have a good look with the magnifying glass."

Zoe and Thistle go back and forth between the two maps, talking contour lines and dye bleed. Every time Thistle asks Lucia a direct question, Zoe answers. Lucia thinks she may get out of this without saying a word until Thistle suggests switching. He and Lady Haskell will hold the maps, while Lucia and Marie tell them which dye lot they think is crisper. Zoe interrupts. "Thistle dear, Lucy is quite behind schedule. We're going to have to excuse her."

"Lady Haskell. I do believe you're trying to cheat!" he says. Zoe flinches. "You had Marie here look at both, and she likes your map the best, and now you're dismissing Lucy before she's had a chance to look at mine."

Lips pursed, Zoe motions for Lucia to examine Thistle's map. The magnifying glass trembles as familiar rivers snake through childhood mountain contours.

"Look familiar, dear?" asks Thistle.

She composes her face and lies. "No, sir."

"Never been to Italy?"

Zoe says, "Lucy is Swiss."

Thistle ignores her. "Lucy, I'd love to hear you tell me in your own words which map is better."

Lucia carefully studies both pieces of fabric and composes her response. She says, "The lines bleed on both maps."

"Yes, you're correct. Given that there's no difference, and it is far faster, we will manufacture the maps on American nylon, not Mulleystone silk."

Zoe grips the back of her chair. "Thistle, have you truly exhausted every possibility?"

"Yes, I'm afraid so. These samples are the best, and yours is simply not good enough."

Lucia knows that their food and board depends on Thistle's contract. She swallows hard and asks, "What about pectin, sir?"

They stare. Did she pronounce it correctly? "Let me show you."

She leads Thistle, Zoe, and Marie back to her breakfast table, loads a spoon with the sugary jam and drags it across the woven silk tablecloth. The colour bleeds into the weave looking like a furry red caterpillar.

"That's jam with sugar. Now, jam with pectin."

Zoe looks like she's holding her breath as Lucia creates a parallel red line. The pectin jam sits up like a hedgerow. It maintains its shape. They wait, but the colour doesn't seep into the cloth. Zoe claps her hands. "Lucy, this is wonderful! This could be the solution. Mr. Thistle, you must try pectin in the ink!"

Thistle shakes his head. "With all due respect, Lady Haskell, this is more than a mere matter of household science. There's no guarantee it will work with our dyes."

"Surely you'll try it before giving up on our silk. Imagine our POWs trapped behind enemy lines. A map made of British silk will be much more meaningful than a limp nylon one."

Lucia takes a step towards the basket she uses to collect mulberry leaves. Thistle looks up. "Miss Lucy, could I see your papers, please?"

Zoe attempts to soothe him. "Phillip, that's not necessary. I know Lucy is from Switzerland. I looked at her papers when she first came here."

"And when was that? Who brought her here?"

Zoe hesitates. "I came with my son, sir, a little over a year ago," Lucia says. "I'll get my papers, but may I harvest the leaves first? If the worms don't eat soon, they will perish."

Thistle follows her into the garden. The repetitive action of plucking the leaves is soothing, despite the headache gathering in her temples. She calms herself with thoughts that she'll soon see her family.

––––––––

When the ferry arrives at North Sydney there's not a spare second for Arch to check the phone book or ask around about Garl. They run over the tracks, their duffels bumping against their backs, with just minutes to spare before the departure of the Saint John troop train. The cars are packed with Nova Scotian soldiers decked out in spiffy new Canadian uniforms. By contrast, the Newfs are still wearing their motley and worn mix of civvies. Some reek of vomit, others of rum, and a few are picking fights with the herring chokers. The only thing holding them together is what sets them apart: their accents, clannishness, and overall lack of sophistication.

Slade announces in the packed train car, "The crowd from Nova Scotia can think they're better than us now, but once we're across the pond, they'll be BEF, and we'll be lording it over them as full-on British Army."

Arch makes sure to sit far from Slade. At New Glasgow, a couple of Newfoundlanders get off to find beer and haven't returned when the train starts pulling away from the station. Slade unlatches his window, leans out, and yells, "Stinky! The train is leaving!"

The car erupts in a chorus of "Stinky! Stinky!" Two women across the aisle from Arch and Tombstone hustle to the next car, latching the door behind them. Stinky and his buddies round the corner of the station running full pelt. With a rollie hanging from his bottom lip, Stinky is making good time despite the wooden crate of beer tucked under his arm. Miraculously, his buddies catch up with the caboose and manage to grab on, but Stinky doesn't want to let go of the beer. As the locomotive ascends a grade and slows, he attempts to grab the handle with his free hand but misses, trips, and drops the crate in a yeasty explosion. His cheering section boos and sits down. The train starts picking up speed and the space between Stinky and the caboose is widening. Slade is leaning out of his window with both arms extended. Tombstone tut-tuts. "What does he think he's going to do? Pull him in?"

Two conductors hustle down the aisle just as Slade pushes both shoulders and his chest through the gap. His skinny hips are balanced precariously on the window's ledge and, just before the conductor can grab his belt, Stinky latches onto Slade's outstretched hands and pulls him clear. Everyone stands to see Stinky kneeling over Slade's crumpled body. He gives a thumbs up before the Saint John troop train trundles on. The Newfs have their first casualty. Even though he's annoying as hell, Arch wonders how Slade will make it across. Tombstone cracks his gigantic knuckles. "Good Lord," he says, "they'll never turn this crowd into soldiers."

#970408
Private A. Fisher
166th (Newfoundland) Field Regiment RA
██████████████ *February 10, 1940*

Dear Min,

There's not a breath of wind out here on the Banks, but birds! There're birds of every kind: bully birds, gulls, puffins, terns, shags, it's quite something. We got our ship in ███████ ████████ *, where the streets were swarming with Canadians. Their uniforms must be from the last war because they smelled of mothballs, but they all had shiny new boots. I hope ours are half as nice. There's still no sign of our gear. The townies in line for officers' stripes are poisoned and will complain to anyone who'll listen. If it wasn't for Tombstone (Tom Walsh a stone carver who worked at Cook's) we'd still be in Canada. The* ████████████████████ *tried to leave without us. We were standing on the plank when she started pulling away. Tombstone bawled out, "Johnny Canuck, cut the goddamned engines!" Thankfully they listened. We scurried on board like rats while the Canadians made fun of us. But we had the last laugh. Someone at home or in Britain had arranged for every single one of the first-class cabins to be assigned to us! We may not have uniforms, and we certainly don't have tuxedos, but we've got a standing invitation to drink brandy with the captain every night! An invitation I'll be taking up as there's only one, armed* ████████████████ *assigned to protect the whole convoy of about* ████████████████ *. By the time you read this, we'll (hopefully) be across.*

Flocks and Flocks of Love, Arch

———

Buzzed on Calvados, Arch's stomach heaves with the waves. He runs his fingers over the rivets by his bunk. Who were the men who drilled and tightened them? Men who knew what tool to use and how much force was required. Men who cut the metal and bent the pieces to fit it all together. Like the workers who built the new bridge at home. They told him about Marconi, helping Arch imagine life beyond the cove. Told him how the Italian tied a key to the line of a kite and sent his assistants out into a snowstorm to keep it aloft while Marconi sat inside listening for days. Waiting for something only he believed would come. Willing the metal arm on his device to move. Waiting until it finally vibrated. Once. Twice. Three times. "Dot, dot, dot." The tale hit Arch like a bolt of lightning. A famous inventor received the first transatlantic wireless message in Newfoundland. When he told the story to Tobin and admitted he wanted to go to university, the priest had him. He promised to pay for Arch's grade eleven spot at St. Bon's if he entered the seminary after graduation. Grateful to get away from Skipper, Arch agreed and told himself he'd take Min to live with him on his first posting. How foolish to think he could become an inventor while training to be a priest.

The new bridge changed Garl too. It made him into a performer. The surface was smooth enough for a scuff. Arch rigged up a record player to an old tractor battery and Garl played the mouth organ along with the records until his lips swole up. Kids from Winterton, Hant's Harbour, Heart's Content, and New Perlican ran over the coastal path with 78s tucked under their arms for the Fishers' illicit dances. Illicit not because of what they got up to, but because they were mixing. Sally Anns and Anglicans danced with Methodists and Catholics and vice versa. The intermingling of faiths added a frisson of the taboo to their chaste steps. That's where they first met Anna Tucker. She was a few years younger than them but made up for the gap in years with the haughty confidence that comes from being a fish-plant heiress. While all the other girls bobby-pinned their manes to their foreheads, Anna wore her untameable cloud of blond curls loose and sometimes with a crown of wildflowers. She was beautiful and kind, but Arch knew better than to let on that he thought so.

chapter 5

BAPTISM

Plunging his hands into the bone-cold murk, Arch feels around for the cod trap, coveting the free-flowing warmth of the tap in the cathedral's garage. Sunlight soap letters bordered in grease, radio warbles from the *Grand Ole Opry*, and the intoxicating scent of the future: motor oil and gasoline. Arch could see the path in there; good work, good food, books to read, and eventually your own house in a parish far away. Even though his only true vocation was to the internal combustion engine, all he had to do was wear the cassock, keep the fleet in working order, pretend to believe in the Holy Ghost, and put up with their ways.

Skipper hawks into the drink. "You haven't said how you managed to screw up."

Feet straining against the dory's ribs, they're drawing up fathoms of nothingness.

"It wasn't as g-good as you think . . . You . . . you weren't th-th-there."

"Nope. No one's ever handed me anything."

Water curves: the trinity of gravity, surface tension, and buoyancy is unravelling. The net is impossibly taut and his gutting knife skitters up the gunnels. The creatures plummet, and off balance, Arch splays, face-first, into a cloud of brine. Wild wetness. Cold grates the back of his throat as the dory smacks down hard behind him. Windmill arms. No one swims. The cold will get you in minutes. Heaviness claws at his shins like the cassock, tripping him up, dragging him down. Pinpoint gull eyes watch him sink back to that day. The edge of Tobin's ring grating his knuckles as he pulls Arch's hand under his robe. Hemmed in by the confessional walls, alarms ringing in Arch's ears. The old priest's mouth is open. Arch pushes against him. Scrabbles to his feet and stumbles out, running past the painted posies under Mary's pink toes. Her perfect, plaster feet.

Water pulses, pushing him under the shadow of the dory. His logans sink into the ripped-open cod trap and bubbles ripple through his pinched lips. The weight of his skull tips him over, after the creatures. What a life. Bump dories, rip nets, sleep suspended in the sea. The whale jolts his shins, pushing him up hard and too fast. Puncturing light, his eyes burn as lupins wave from the faraway shore.

When he stepped out of that shameful puddle of black cloth for the last time, pure relief washed over him. The others were in the chapel for vespers, but Arch still took the back stairs as a precaution. Stepping over the day's milk delivery, he smacked right up against the one and only. Just his frigging luck. "Father? Father Tobin. I was just l-l-looking for you. I've decided to g-g-go."

"Where's that, Fisher?"

"H-h-home. I'm going home."

"Home?"

"It's time to g-go."

"Mere weeks, man, and you'll have your own parish."

Tobin extracts his silver cigarette case. He places a cigarillo in his thin lips. "Perhaps we should go to confession?"

Without the cassock, Arch can kick at the shame. "Unlike you, I have nothing to c-c-con-confess."

Tobin snaps the case shut. "You'll regret that."

––––––––––

Skipper's gaff pierces the slippage between this world and the whales'. Arch throws his numb arms forward, but the rusty tip jabs into his chest bone. Sunlight sputters and he tops up with galloping gasps. The underside of the whale's tail flashes below his pumping feet. The hook flays open Min's handiwork, releasing Arch from the weight of water-logged stitches. He sinks, but his sweater stays suspended.

––––––––––

Tobin exhaled smoke into Arch's face and his fists just shot out. The priest stumbled backwards over the day's milk. Clattering cages. Shattered glass and black legs pedalling in pooling white liquid. Instead of tearing out of there, Arch let the shame leak away. He placed one foot in front of the other, walking purposefully away from a life he never craved. Power from speaking Latin and living with sly men who mocked their parishioners while sucking up to merchants and politicians. He leaves the metal gate clanging in the wind as he crosses Military Road and steps onto Garrison Hill.

He'd run to catch up with Min on these same double-wide stairs over a decade before when he was about eight years old. For every single, determined stride of hers, he had to take two and jump a bit. He was trying to draw her attention to a black fox back then. It was floating over the hill behind them, but she wouldn't look at the magic. Her jaw was set. They were going back. Back to the train station. Back to Turk's Cove. Back to the saltbox and Skipper. Arch had been happy on the train. Maybe happier than ever before. It was just the two of them and Garl would come later. That was her plan until she saw the damn cathedral on the way to the boarding house. Its heft convinced her to seek the bishop's blessing. Once she told him about the insults, fists, and broken bones, she thought everything would be grand. Instead, he ordered her to go back home with a daily penance of ten Hail Marys and one Our Father, as if the sins were hers.

When they tiptoed into the saltbox later that night, it already felt like someone else's place. Holding hands and whispering about bedclothes, they were trying not to disturb the dog, but never got past the table. Skipper reared up in the darkness, his palms smashing down sending empty moonshine jars crashing to the floor. Garl's lantern light slicing through spindles. The crunch of splintered glass and the dog whimpering. Skipper's accusations. Min assuring Garl she planned to send for him when Skipper no longer needed help with the fish.

––––––––––

Arch stops to get his bearings. Rubs his face to forget that night. Three boys are playing ball on Queen's Road, dodging cars and horse carts. Drivers shake their fists from open windows. He could stay in town and look for a job, but the Catholic garages wouldn't want to hire him any more than the Protestant ones. Just like Min all those years ago, he's got to go back. He's got no choice. The haughty pride he felt for pushing Tobin has already soured. He sets his shoulders against the biting wind from the Narrows and heads towards the tracks out of town.

Garl was alongside Arch at the kitchen window when Skipper dragged Min to the woodpile. She went along to calm him, beseeching him to not wake up the whole cove. Why didn't someone come to help? Did she think Skipper wouldn't do it? Arch's tears rose with the axe and spilled over and pooled in his collarbone as it came down. She was too mortified to scream, but she knelt in the sawdust, with her eyes shut like fists, for a long time. Skipper flicked the top of her thumb to the gulls like it was nothing. Said he'd lop off the rest if she ever left again. Min staunched the bleeding in the barrel of winter flour. The blood turned the stuff at the top into a rosy paste. Min slept in the kitchen after that, leaving Arch upstairs with the old man snoring in the next room. Garl wasn't more than ten, but he lit out into the spruce and built a camp somewhere, only coming home for food when Skipper was away. Arch envied him.

His lungs unfurl as he surfaces in a water-devil of beaks and flapping feathers. His mouth gaping open just like the black backs and terns circling his head.

Walking home from the cathedral took three days on the rail lines. Being alone with his thoughts was harder than the hunger and the cold, but the time allowed him to move through pride, anger, and most of his fears. When he arrived at the back door, Min jumped up and squealed, holding him tight and weeping while the kettle moved from grumbling through to whistling. Even though they were stained blue from the berries, she marvelled at his teeth as steam haloed their heads. Skipper was still fishing on the Labrador, so for a few weeks, they talked, walked, baked, made jam, turned soil, picked potatoes, pickled beets, and lugged seaweed up from the shoreline to her drills. She never once asked why Arch left the church. Maybe she knew the answer. One night by the wood stove, he admitted his only regret was not staying long enough to get his own priest's house. He'd dreamed of a remote place with brass locks on the front door, books, a grandfather clock that chimed the hours, and a warm kitchen for her. She could cook for him there and parishioners would hire her to make their christening, wedding, and anniversary cakes. Just her cakes, she'd have to give up the fortune-telling. She grinned and agreed it wouldn't look good for the priest's housekeeper to be practising the dark arts. That was the only time he asked her if she felt guilty about making up stories when people offered her their palms. She said, "Stories? Stories are how we tell people we love them."

———

Baleen scissors the water and both whales offer up their rough, impossibly pink tongues. Arch would love to slide down their gullets just to get away from Skipper and Tobin. Through the foamy lop, he sees Skipper's back. He's leaning out of the dory. Jabbing at Arch's sinking sweater, poking holes in him like he always has.

———

When Skipper came home, the squid were running, but they didn't take part. He didn't want to discuss his son's failure with boatloads of nosy neighbours. Until Tobin's letter arrived, with the engraved tasselled coat of arms, Arch was able to avoid joining his father in the dory. But that envelope lit up the whole shore with the worst kind of talk. Some surmised it was a summons from the Pope, because he'd broken a promise. Others were convinced he'd stolen silverware or crystal. No one would believe it was just a bill for his goddamned dentures. It also contained a veiled threat in the form of his seminarian portrait. A pocket-sized reminder of Tobin's perversion. How he told Mr. Tooton he wanted to change Arch's pose. With his back to the camera, he caressed Arch's hands before rearranging them on the bible. The photo captured Arch's flush of shame.

When Arch told Min the amount due, she put her hand over her mouth and said it would cost a summer and a half of fortune-telling and moonshine sales. Hadn't Skipper just shingled Tobin's church? Hadn't she carried her own rocking chair down the road to the tiny clapboard building, every time he wanted to hold mass or confession?

———————

The whale's snout nudges Arch up and over the gunnels, spewing a salacious twister of fishiness from her blow hole. The smell stuns Skipper long enough for Arch to climb back in the dory and grab the gaff. Shocked by his son's resurrection, Skipper scuttles forward to the forecastle. His silence betrays his murderous intentions. Arch stands and pushes the gaff into the papery skin of his father's throat. The dory, the sea, the whale, the birds all drop away and it's just him and his tormentor.

"You tried to f-fucking drown me."

"You learn them blue words in the seminary?"

"I'm your son!"

"Your mother's a schemer," Skipper croaks. "How do I know you're mine?"

The gaff's point releases a pinprick of blood. No one would blame him. The whole cove knows. Min would finally be free to live in peace. His muscles tense. Fishermen drown all the time. He could. He should. Fear flutters across Skipper's face and Arch just can't. Skipper will throw his cowardice back in his face the first chance he gets. Arch exhales against the pounding in his chest and says, "That I'm standing here wanting to murder you is all the proof you need. I carry your evil in my veins. But I'll never give in to it."

The cow and calf exhale together and glide away with their squawking attendees. Arch sits, the gaff within reach, and points at Skipper. "But if you ever lay a hand on Min again, I will kill you."

Hauling for shore, he decides to bring eggs to Captain Tucker in Winterton tomorrow. They say the line at his fish plant needs mending and Anna needs a math tutor. He'll make enough to get to town and sign up. Fighting in the war will be a brighter future than staying here in a bay named after the holy mystery, where he might become as bitter as his old man.

Big Ben signals the end of the newscast as he drips into the back porch. Arch dries his hair and arms with a cloth before facing his mother. Will he tell her about the whales? It's too foolish for words. She'd embellish the tale so much; she'd have the mother and baby coming to his rescue and telling his future. He grabs an old shirt from a hook and is buttoning up as he sloshes into the kitchen. Before she can ask him why he's wet, he says, "I'm going to see Captain Tucker tomorrow about the tutoring. Hopefully, he won't hold it against me that I'm Catholic and an ex-almost-priest. I might even make enough to pay off the teeth before I sign up."

She'd been making a frame out of driftwood and lupin seeds for his seminarian portrait. A hairy lupin pod catches on her cardigan sleeve as she reaches for him. "Oh, Arch."

He holds her and says, "This time we'll be artillery. We'll have the big guns to back us up."

She tries to speak, but nothing comes out. He follows her gaze to the wharf where Skipper is beheading and gutting each fish with a chop and a rip, flicking the brown and purple entrails to the birds and hoarding the livers and tongues for himself.

"But the Brits . . ."

"They won't be able to send us in ahead this time, Min. We'll be mixed in with them. We'll be British Army."

chapter 6

DEPORTATION

Dawn lights up the mildew-stained cover. Since they've been sleeping in the lifeboats, Tombstone has not been waking up yelling about torpedoes. The sea's low grumble has given way to long, crisp slaps. The ship's engine churns slower. Arch peeks out. The horizon is cut in two by a wall of sooty squares. "Tombstone, wake up. We made it! We're in Liverpool!"

———

"There she is, Miss Lucy, the *Star of Inis Mor.*" The ship is frilled in curls of barbed wire, its dull grey hull is slashed with rust, but Corporal Buley is grinning. "When we sailed to Norway for our honeymoon, she was bright white with red stars on the funnels, and a wide red ribbon all around." Lucia has a hard time imagining its former glory, but Buley is lost in the past. Cosimo kneels up to get a better view. "Are we going to Norway before Canada?"

Buley draws a map in the air with his free hand. "You'll sail from Liverpool, up the coast of Ireland, and across the Atlantic to Newfoundland. You'll dock in St. John's, I imagine, before sailing onto Montreal. From there, I don't know. Train?"

Cosimo's mouth falls open. "Newfoundland? Will we see polar bears?"

Buley chuckles. Lucia is grateful that he's making the trip feel more like a Sunday outing than a deportation. It also helps that Lady Zoe insisted he transport them in her Bentley. Liverpool looks ready for an invasion. Soldiers are stationed on every street corner and on rooftops overlooking the docks. Tanks are walled in behind sandbags, ground floor windows and doors are boarded up, and barbed wire is everywhere. On the next pier over, a troop ship has docked and there are hundreds of men on deck waving and shading their eyes from the morning sun. A Salvation Army band plays "God Save the King."

Deportees hustling towards the *Inis Mor* peer into the Bentley's white leather interior, eyeing Lucia and Cosimo. She's hoping she won't know any of the Italians on board and would like to get out and stretch, but Buley suggests they stay put until the gangplank lowers. He turns on the radio and the car fills with the voices of the Andrews Sisters singing "Bei Mir Bist du Schon." Despite their situation, the song lifts her mood. She watches men on the next pier over, throwing their hats in the air. The deportees outside the car pick up their pace. Buley strains to see what's happening and says it's time. Lucia takes a deep breath and steps out of the car, crosses her handbag strap over her chest, and fetches her battered suitcase from the boot. She dressed simply, politely turning down Zoe's offer of a fur stole. They'll need to blend in. The ship will be full of Fascists. While they lived in London, she was able to avoid them, but one slip about their surname or the mountain region where she grew up could put them in danger. Cosimo lifts his kit bag out of the boot and shakes Buley's hand, thanking him for a pleasant drive. Buley says, "Miss Lucy, I hope you and David will be much safer in Canada."

She smiles for Cosi's sake, but both adults know the dangers of crossing the Atlantic. Buley gets back in the car, salutes them, and reverses along the pier, honking the horn every few seconds to part the stream of deportees. They are soon swallowed by the crowd. Lucia's suitcase knocks against the backs of legs. At one point, Cosi is lifted off his feet. She squeezes his hand tightly, fearful that the whole lot of them will pitch into the oily water between the ship's rusty hull and the pier's edge. Cosi asks, over the voices, how many nights it will take to get to Canada. Lucia doesn't answer, she's looking for someone, anyone with a clipboard who can order everyone to slow down and be safe. Cosimo yanks his hand away. "Mama. My spells! I forgot my book of spells! It's in the car!"

She reaches for him and says, "It's too late." Before she can grab hold of him, Cosi slips through the crush of bodies. Lucia turns. Panic rises in her chest. The forward thrust of the crowd causes her to stumble, but she holds her suitcase up as a shield and pushes against the tide of bodies. She spots Cosi's blond head bobbing through the sea of deportees. If they get separated here, they could end up in different countries. A man pats her bottom, and she swats him away, stretching up to full height to watch her son duck past bent nonnas, mothers, packs of children, priests, nuns, and sailors carrying bleached white duffels. She loses sight of him for a beat. Two beats. Longer. She yells, "Cosimo, torna qui imediatamente!" She plunges in, "Scusi!" What if he falls in the water? "Scusi." Someone elbows her hard in the ribs. "Scusi. Scusi." She ignores curse words and insults and keeps pushing away from the ship. "My son. I've got to reach my son." A flicker from the Bentley's headlights. Why can't she see his head? Her suitcase is wedged out of her grip. She doesn't look back. She can move faster without it. The crowd thins as she reaches the car. The driver's door hangs open. Buley is kneeling. Cosimo is lying on his side. His face is twisted in pain. "What happened?" Lucia drops to her knees.

Buley says, "Miss Lucy, I'm so sorry." She cradles Cosimo's head in her lap. "I had my head turned to reverse." Cosimo moans. "There was rapping on the window. I didn't know it was David. It happened so fast. I'm so sorry. I ran over his foot."

They lift Cosi onto the back seat. Blood is seeping through his white sock and when she tries to take off his shoe, he groans, "Fa male!"

The ship's horn lets out a long drone. The nosy deportees who'd stopped to watch the drama pick up their parcels and hustle away. Thistle's threat that they'd be sent to prison if they don't get on the ship rings in Lucia's ears. "Buley, there must be a hospital nearby."

He says he'll ask at the guard house. Cosimo whispers, "Mama, my book?"

She places the book under his head to comfort him while Buley speaks to the guard. Lucia can't hear what they're saying, but she can see that Buley is pleading. The young guard looks at the Bentley and shakes his head. What if he sends her on to Canada while Cosimo stays here alone in hospital? She dips her head out of sight and wipes some of the blood from Cosi's sock onto her cheek and nose. The guard walks around the car and opens the back door jostling Cosi's foot. The boy screams out in pain. Real tears stream through the blood on Lucia's cheeks. Flustered, the young guard apologizes and scribbles on their deportation orders. Buley gets back in the car and reports that they're going to the Royal Infirmary for an X-ray and must return immediately.

The matron at Emergency scans their deportation papers and declares that the hospital has no obligation to treat enemy aliens. A pregnant woman and her husband glare at them before moving to the far side of the waiting room. Speaking her mother tongue on the pier has loosened something inside Lucia. The deportation, Cosi's injury, and the unknown. But she will not cry in front of this nasty woman. Buley fibs and says he's a guard on the ship and has been sent by the captain to get the boy's foot X-rayed.

"Is that right, Sergeant?" says the matron. "Who is your captain then?"

Lucia says, "Moulton, Captain Moulton. He sent us here. He told us we would get the best care in Liverpool in this emergency department."

The matron does not acknowledge Lucia, but replies to Buley, "Yes, and a fine Liverpudlian he is too."

The X-rays confirm broken bones and the need for immediate surgery. The nurses who prep Cosi are much kinder than the matron. They tell him when he wakes up everything will be fixed. Lucia paces in the waiting room until Buley whispers that she should sit, and he should stand because he's the guard. She does what she's told and hands him money for the canteen. "Are you going to get in trouble with your unit?" she asks.

"No, it's okay, I'm on leave."

"Oh, Buley, I've ruined your leave."

"Miss Lucy, this is all my fault."

"It was an accident. Don't say another thing about it. I'm grateful for your company and your kindness."

He returns to the waiting room with sandwiches and tea, just as the surgeon arrives to tell Lucia they set the major bones but to close the wound they had to take skin from Cosimo's thigh and graft it onto his foot. Buley checks his watch and asks how soon he can bring them back to the ship. The doctor removes his mask. "Sergeant, these people are not going anywhere. Tell the captain to call me, and I'll explain. The skin graft may not take and there's a high risk of infection for the next forty-eight hours. He's up on the ward now but he may not wake until tomorrow night."

In the hallway, Lucia suggests Buley go to the nearest barracks for the night and they'll sort out a plan for the next deportation ship when Cosi wakes. Grateful to be off duty, he agrees. Lucia tries to get comfortable in the chair next to Cosi's bed, watching the night nurses carry out their duties.

In the night, she's startled by a loud noise. A bomb? Bedpan? Lucia sits up. Her heart is pounding. The night nurses are calmly knitting in silence by the light of their desk lamp. It must have been a dream. She caresses Cosi's cheek, shifts her body in the chair and tries to settle back into sleep.

The whoosh of blackout blinds wakes her in the morning. Sunlight fills the ward. There's a young nurse standing on the other side of Cosi's bed, holding his wrist and counting along with the watch pinned to the front of her smock. "His pulse is fine. He should wake up soon and please, if you're hungry, feel free to get yourself a cuppa and some toast from the nurses' kitchen."

Lucia stands and stretches at the window. There's open water at the pier where the *Inis Mor* had been docked. Buley arrives with a Thermos of tea and some buns he liberated from his mess hall. "I called Mulleystone this morning, to tell Lady Haskell why her car is delayed. She wanted me to relay that you should write her. She'll take care of any bills here but asked me to drive her car back today."

"Please thank her for her kindness. And look, I promise that when Cosi is released, we'll get on the next ship."

He hands her their deportation papers and winks. "Miss Lucy, as far as Lady Haskell, Thistle, and I are concerned, you and Cosi are sailing across the Atlantic on the *Inis Mor*."

Lucia whispers, "You did an excellent job guarding us. Thank you."

Dr. Grimes arrives at lunchtime. He takes Cosi's pulse using the clock on the wall and shines a small flashlight into the boy's eyes. Before speaking to Lucia, he flips through the chart at the end of the bed.

"Mrs . . . My apologies, there's no names on this chart."

Lucia tries to clip her words. "I'm Davey's mother, Mrs. Buley."

He scribbles their names on the chart while speaking. "Mrs. Buley, David is fine. Children sometimes take longer to get over the anesthesia. He'll come out of it, at the latest tonight. I'll check back."

———

In a Quonset hut at their training camp. A soldier issues Arch a thin mattress that folds into three *biscuits*, and a cardboard respirator. By five a.m., the two key biscuits have separated, and his back is in contact with the cold metal springs of the cot. He's squirming around attempting to get comfortable when someone shouts, "Wakey, wakey, Newfs! Hands off cocks, hands on socks!"

Captain Joy is a short man of about forty, with crow's feet, a barrel chest, and an enormous mouth. Slade dubs him Rasputin. He orders them out onto the parade grounds. They're a motley crew. Tombstone's shirttail is out, Slade's mouth is hanging open, and some of the townies are pulling on overcoats as if they're expecting rain. They're all hatless, having thrown their headgear in Liverpool Harbour when Miss Penelope Moore said she'd look after them. When Rasputin turns to assess his new charges, his arms stiffen at his sides and the corners of his huge mouth turn down. "Attention! Noooo-fen-laaaaanders!" Arch draws up his shoulders and Slade sucks in his stomach.

"Why aren't you in unifoooorm?"

Slade steps out of line with his palms out. "Listen, b'y, it's not our fault, they've been promised to us at every turn."

Rasputin's disbelief soon turns to anger. "Fall in, Private!"

Slade continues. "Someone shagged something up, Captain, because they just haven't shown up."

"Shut uuuuuup!"

Rasputin is enraged. "In the British Aaarmy, Private, you only speak to a superior officer when asked a direct question!"

Arch figures it won't be long before Slade is locked up again. Joy orders the lot of them to run around the parade ground five times. The grounds are immense and hopping with snazzy uniformed units from all over the Commonwealth. Arch thought they'd be training in a farmer's field or somewhere far from civilization, but the three-storey Woolwich barracks overlooks the Thames and seems to be in the centre of London. Lorries, cars, motorbikes, and double-decker trams rumble by outside the gates. Breathless after their third time around, and with no sign of Joy, the men wander off in twos and threes to find grub.

———

After dinner, an evening newspaper is delivered to the night desk. Nurses and orderlies from other wards come by to read the contents. There's a lot of whispering and concerned expressions. Lucia is curious about what they're reading, but daren't speak in front of all those people. When a young night nurse comes by Cosi's bed to roll down the blinds, she asks about the paper. The nurse whispers, "Oh, it's terrible. It's the *Star of Inis Mor*."

Lucia's mouth goes dry. "Is that a ship?" she asks.

"Yes, full of deportees. It sailed from here the other night and sank off Ireland."

Lucia grabs Cosimo's hand for comfort as the blood drains from her legs.

The nurse continues. "The papers say it was a U-boat. Hundreds have drowned. Whole families."

Cosimo cries out, "Mama, basta!"

"What did he say?" the nurse asks.

How can Lucia remind him not to say anything more in Italian? She speaks in her best clipped English. "Davey, darling, you're awake.

You must be hungry?"

Confused, Cosimo looks from Lucia to the nurse, blinking. What if he says something about the ship? The nurse fusses with his bedclothes and asks if he would like some toast. He nods. "My foot still hurts, and now my thigh."

The nurse says, "Yes, it will hurt for a while, your mother will tell you all about it."

chapter 7

ROYAL RHODYS

Trumpets sound and in five-foot-tall letters, the newsreel title card announces: *Breaking News—Dunkirk Evacuation.* The reel opens with aerial footage of the English Channel peppered with boats.

For days and nights, ships of all kinds have plied to and fro across the channel under the fierce onslaught of the enemy's bombers. Every kind of ship crammed full of tired battle-stained and bloodstained British soldiers. A warship lists with the weight of thousands. *Transport officers count the men as they come ashore, no question of units, regiments, even nationality. French and Belgian soldiers who fought side by side with the British in the Battle of Flanders arrived as well.* Now Arch knows why he heard French spoken at breakfast. *All of them were tired, but the most amazing thing was that practically every man was reasonably cheerful, and most of them managed to smile.* The soldiers' faces are completely at odds with the hyped-up patriotism of the narrator's delivery. *Even when a man was obviously on the verge of collapse from sheer fatigue, you could still tell by his eyes that his spirit was irrepressible. And that is a thing that all the bombs in Germany will never crush.*

The men share a haunted, spent look and the reality of what they're strolling into comes home for Arch. Up to now, his only worry was that he'd fail at being a soldier. Now he's worried that he'll succeed. What does he see in the eyes of the giant men on screen? What are they trying to tell him? They look like they've discovered they've been lied to.

After the movie, Slade hurries ahead to the barracks and Arch is grateful for a quiet walk back without the young shagger who seems to have glommed onto them. Tombstone is talking about some news or other from home and doesn't seem as worried about the faces of the Dunkirk men. The barracks are quiet when they arrive, but when they try to get into their bunks, their sheets have been shorted, and springs detached. Both end up on the floor trapped in twisted bedding cursing Slade. .

#970408
Private A. Fisher
166th (Newfoundland) Field Regiment RA
██████████████ *Barracks, May 28, 1940*

Dear Min,

I got your letter and package dated May 3rd. I've sent two letters since then. I hope you got them. Thanks for the tobacco and the cookies. They were devoured and appreciated. If you find the time, can you knit me a few pairs of vamps? The heels are already worn through in the army-issue ones that came with our uniform. Aside from hole-y stockings, we finally look like real soldiers even though Captain Joy disagrees. He lords it over us with daily or twice-daily inspections, just so he can punish us for not being up to snuff.

What a rigmarole! Slade, Tombstone, and I have come up with a scheme to beat him at his own game. When we're in barracks, we wear our socks on the outside of our boots, so we don't mark up the waxed floors, and we don't have to mop for inspections (prob why the heels are worn). At night, we sleep next to, not in, our bunks. You might think this is foolish, but it takes forever to make the beds correctly and display the firearms and kit for inspection. You have to drape your gas capes, just so, and top it all off with the steel hat. It takes longer than putting up a Christmas tree! And we figure sleeping on the floor is toughening us up for the front. We won't have perfectly made beds there. The bathroom scheme is similar. We only use one toilet, sink, and shower stall out of four. That way there's only one to clean. Joy has vowed to find out how we're so much faster than everyone else.

There are air raids every other day, but no one seems to pay them any mind. I was in a coffee shop yesterday and when the siren sounded, everyone stopped for a second, and then went right back to sipping their tea. The band didn't even miss a beat. I wanted to crawl under the table, but I would've been the only one down there and I was in uniform. Did you get the portrait? I thought about waiting until I got the rank of gunner, but with Joy, who knows when that'll be. There were soldiers from every country lined up to have their picture taken. You're not supposed to smile, but just as the shutter opened, Slade broke wind, and I couldn't help it.

Love from your soon-to-be Gunner, Arch

PS. There's a second-hand bookstore near here. They have loads of Agatha Christies. If you send jam or molasses, cigarettes, anything, I could easily trade it for books. I've had

*my pay sent to you. Once I make Gunner, it'll be 17s 6d. It'll
take no time to pay off the chompers.*

――――――

When Rasputin finds a day-old turd in one of the off-limit toilets,
their scheme falls apart. Slade vows to find and punish the rogue
shitter, but Tombstone says it was probably Rasputin himself. Arch
hopes they won't find out it was him. As every day passed and the
pressure rose from Joy, he felt increasingly uncomfortable with their
dishonesty. He can't shake the thought that the more commandments
they break, the more likely they'll die. Once they've cleaned all the
Newfoundland toilets with toothbrushes as punishment, they sneak
out to a pub called To Live and Let Live. Despite a crush at the
bar that is four or five uniforms deep, Slade attempts to worm his
way through. He pushes one guy too hard and gets a well-deserved
shove backwards.

"Jeez, b'y, I'm just trying to get a beer!" Slade says.

"That's what we're all doing, mate. Go to the back of the queue."

Tombstone tuts from the back as Slade gets another shove.

"Look, chap, I don't want to fight you," says a red-haired Brit.

"Why?" asks Slade. "You a friggin' coward?"

Tombstone yells, "Slade! Get back here and wait your turn."

A Scottish private tells Tombstone, "That's Ginger Saad! He's
Britain's middleweight champ. He don't want to get into it with him."

Tombstone springs forward and hooks Slade's arm just as he
hauls back to throw the first punch. "Slade, that's Ginger Saad!" he
says.

"I don't care if he's a ginger snap!"

"He's a boxer, you nimrod. Want to get us in more trouble?"

Leading Slade outside, Tombstone tells him it's his mouth, not
his shagged eye that's going to get them all killed. Arch volunteers
to get their beers.

Slade is already arsing around with a crowd of Scots a few tables away when Arch puts the tray down.

"I figured out where I've seen you before," says Tombstone. Arch braces himself. Tombstone wipes suds off his upper lip. "I believe you were wearing a priest get-up."

Arch is jolted back to the vestibule at St. Pat's, the smell of boiled cabbage clinging to the women's wool coats. Tombstone surrounded by his slew of youngsters. He doesn't want his new friend to know he's a flop.

"You still a priest?"

Arch says, "No, I got fed up with it and left a few months before the call."

They watch the tugboats and barges putter in the Thames. Arch wonders what's next. "You left the tipoff turd in the terlit though, didn't ya?" asks Tombstone.

Arch is grateful Slade isn't within earshot because he'd never hear the end of it. "I was feeling guilty, I guess, about lying."

"Jeez, b'y, you're going to have to get over that," says Tombstone. "We'll have to break more than a few commandments to get through this madness."

Arch braces himself for anger or judgment, but instead, the big man points at the barrage balloons lifting into the sky. "We must be getting visitors again tonight."

We. Acceptance. "No more secrets, hey, Arch? It's not lies that will get us killed, it's keeping secrets from each other."

On the way home, Slade puts on a pommy accent and says, "Pip! Pip! I heard at the pub that the King will be training us on the guns at Sandringham."

They're so used to Slade's bullshit by now, they just roll their eyes.

———

Arch never imagined he'd get to drive through the gates of the Royal Estate at Sandringham. Their gun training CO is a Major Hawkins and, unlike Rasputin, he's looking for less work, not more. He takes one look at Tombstone and makes him Number One. Arch is pleased to be named his Number Two, operating the breech and ramming the shells. Slade is Number Three—ammo layer, which Tombstone says is appropriate given the amount of crap he lays down. Spruce is the loader—Number Four. Whelan is Number Five, and Jackie is Number Six. He's second in command and responsible for ammo prep and operating the fuse indicator, when he's not cooking their grub.

At the training gun, Hawkins slaps a riding crop on his thigh. "Private Walsh, the orders have come in from a forward observation officer that the Huns have been found, you've fired a ranging round to see if it lands on or near the enemy. Keep in mind this also alerts the enemy to your position. Now you must act fast lest you're blown to bits."

Tombstone straightens.

"Should we try a second correction to neutralize the enemy, or should we ask the director to plot the next shell?" asks Hawkins.

"Plot it, sir."

"Good decision, Number One. Now, Private Fisher, you're the stick."

Arch catches Tombstone's eye. Neither of them knows what the stick does. "Please explain, sir," says Arch.

"You put two shells in the gun at a time. Shove them up into the muzzle and get out of the way to avoid kickback."

Arch shoves the heavy shells into the muzzle, almost nipping his fingers in the chamber. When the gun fires, his ears clang and temples ache. The major's mouth moves. He's pointing at Arch's feet. What is he saying? Frazzled, Arch steps back just as a red-hot shell casing falls out. Somehow, he gets another twenty-five-pound shell in the gun for the next round. His forearms are already aching.

Out of sync with the gun's heavy metallic dance, Arch is envious of Tombstone's easy grace as he swings the barrel into position. But no single soldier could work this thing alone. Not even the big man. They are all necessary and will have to rely on each other's strength, coordination, and aim. Especially when one of them has a turned eye. Hawkins slaps Tombstone on the back and tells him a good Number One trains his men in all aspects of the gun. Arch can barely feel his fingers and is hoping for a rest when Slade drops a live shell. Everyone runs for cover as it rolls across the gravel driveway and comes to rest against the front tire of the major's Rolls. There's a collective intake of breath and a silent countdown, but somehow it doesn't blow. Hawkins reams Slade out, orders him to retrieve the shell, and threatens to make him a moving target at tomorrow's exercise. Arch has seen what the shells can do to a stack of hay bales and wonders if even that could straighten out Slade.

———————

Shouts ricochet up the main stairwell and chair legs worry the floor. One of their ward nurses piles file folders into a wheelchair. Lucia looks out the window and sees people streaming out of the hospital. Nurses holding babies, doctors and orderlies leading patients. Some are pushing hospital beds or pulling cribs, others walk gingerly, arm in arm with patients gripping IV poles. A matron comes in and claps her hands three times to be heard over the growing din. "We are evacuating. Everyone remain calm! There is a bomb. Threat. Just a threat! It's a threat! If you have family or visitors who can help you leave, please do that. If you're able to walk yourself, just get up and go. The rest of you will be done in order. Nobody runs and nobody panics."

Lucia gathers up Cosi's book of spells, Zoe's letters, and their clothing. She hands over his crutches and drapes Cosi's wool coat over his shoulders. As they emerge into the morning sunlight, the reason for the hasty evacuation hangs above them in a copse of elms. Suspended from a tangle of ropes, broken branches, and ripped parachute silk is a bomb the size of a London taxi. It's only twenty feet or so from the ground. Cosimo leans on his crutches. "Holy smokes, Ma! A parachute mine! That could blow up the whole block!"

Ambulances and trucks speeding into the circular driveway stay well clear of the device. Lucia catches sight of the nasty matron from Emergency overseeing stretchers being loaded into ambulances. She turns away, hoping the woman hasn't spotted them. A nurse from their ward says, "Mrs. Buley, thank God! Can you and David go to the park three blocks over to help Sister Elizabeth with the children? I've got to get the babies. Oh, and this is Norah." A little blond-haired girl in a red and white flannel nightie and bare feet reaches for Lucia's hand. The nurse's voice drops to a whisper. "Probably best not to pick her up, she has scabies."

When the nurse leaves, Lucia picks up the little girl and a bobby leads them across the road. In the ward, she worried Cosi might not be getting the hang of his crutches, but out here in the sunshine, she's relieved to see him moving with ease. They find Sister Elizabeth and the children playing Ring-Around-the-Rosie. She puts Norah down on the grass so she can join in and whispers to Cosi that they should go back.

"To defuse the bomb?"

"No, silly. We should walk down that side street and catch a train back to Mulleystone."

"We'll get Lady Zoe in trouble."

"Thistle thinks we went down on the *Inis Mor.* Zoe wrote to tell me when you're strong enough we should come back. The train station is only a few blocks away, do you think you can make it?"

Cosimo flicks his left wrist. "I'll say one of my spells so we can fly."

———————

Major Hawkins gives them a break from the gun with an ammo pit competition between crews. As soon as he leaves, Slade starts bitching about the heat and claims Hawkins and his buddies are off somewhere drinking Pimm's, laughing at the colonials digging bough whiffens. Arch hands Slade an axe and suggests he find some wood. When he's gone, Tombstone wipes sweat off his brow. "Jesus, he whines likes my youngsters. You got any brothers and sisters, Arch?"

"One older brother, Garland."

He gives Tombstone the basic details as they work. Eighteen months older. Born out of wedlock. Even Father tormented Garl about that, as if it was his fault. Arch says he's such a shit disturber, he may be working with the Germans. He tells Tombstone how Garl lost the family house in a poker game.

"Three men from Western Bay came to collect. I was teaching at St. Bon's and father was fishing off Labrador, so Min faced them down alone. They had crowbars, axes, and a cart and were riled up and ready to dismantle the whole works. She paid them off with moonshine. Gave them her entire summer stock and made them sign a paper promising not to come back."

Digging shoulder to shoulder, Arch tells Tombstone how Min was orphaned and met Father when she was just fourteen. How terrified she was nine months later when she gave birth to Garl alone in a trapper's hut. Trying her best to remember what she'd seen the midwife do with her own mother. Cutting the umbilical cord with a gutting knife she'd cleaned of fish scales the day before. By the time Skipper came back to Labrador to fish the following June, Garl was two months old. When he came ashore to clean his catch in the evenings, he refused to look at either of them. But every day, Min stood silently on the wharf above his dory, letting Garl wail. Skipper would fork a cod out of the dory with his gaff, hoping she'd take it and go away, but she let it slap and twist at her feet until it was still and flecked with flies. Only when Skipper rowed back to his schooner for the night, would she take the fish by the gills to her tilt to cook it. One evening, an English missionary tied up alongside and witnessed the scene. He spoke to Skipper's captain and married them the next day. Min and Garl arrived in Trinity Bay on quintals of salt cod in the hold of Skipper's schooner. She was so terrified of the sounds of the ocean and motion of the ship, her milk dried up. Garl and her held onto each other in hunger and nausea, pitching back and forth in the salt-crusted darkness. When they landed, Skipper complained about having to pay her passage as she stumbled down the road behind him holding a limp but still breathing baby Garl. Arch was born in Min's bedroom in Turk's Cove the following spring, giving Garl the life-long claim that his little brother had it easy.

Slade interrupts. His arms are stacked with thick, gnarly wood. "I know! I know! It's not straight, but it's not like they got spruce here."

Tombstone sizes up the curvy branches. "Where did you get this?"

"Some overgrown bushes, back behind our tents. Nowhere special."

"This didn't come from the garden?" asks Tombstone.

"No, numb-nuts. There were flowers on it, but it was back behind our camp, growing like a weed. Jeez, Walsh, a few days as Number One and you thinks you're the boss."

"I'm not the boss, asshole, just making sure you don't get us in more trouble."

———

#970408
Private A. Fisher
166th (Newfoundland) Field Regiment RA
Somewhere special, June 1, 1940

Dear Min,

April Fools! I got your March 20th letter yesterday. I feel like you missed one of my letters because you haven't asked me anything about this 'special' place. Still no sign of Garl, but we're finally getting trained on the guns. Their range is an impressive ████████████████ *, if you fired one off our back bridge it could probably flatten the Cable Station in Heart's Content! Watching the experienced crews is like watching a dance. I can't imagine how long it will take our crowd to learn all the steps in the right order.* ██████████████ *is our training officer here at* ████████████████. *The* ██████ ██████████ *is not in residence, and I wouldn't be allowed to talk about* ████████████████ *if they were. It's peaceful here, except when we're making a racket on the guns.*

The flowers pressed in here are Rhododendrons. I beg the censors to not take them out. Our crew won an ammo pit competition, but just as we were headed to the pub to celebrate, the estate's gardener showed up and threw a conniption. It turns out we (Slade) chopped down part of a 250-year-old Rhododendron! Of course, we didn't know it was that old or that it was the ████████████████ *'s tree. By that calculation, every tree in England is his.* ████████████ ████████ *had to drive back from his R and R. He cared less for the safe, dry storage of the ammo and the rumoured* ████████████ ████████████ *and was just as PO'ed as the gardener! Over a bush! As punishment, he ordered us all to march FSMO—Field Service Marching Order—that's where you walk carrying your complete kit, wearing respirators and gas capes. It was about 85 degrees and sunny. We marched three miles to the gardener's cottage to apologize. But we interrupted the old geezer's tea, and he was not at all appreciative of our sweaty efforts. On the way back, some of the boys got heatstroke and one vomited in his mask. Quite a mess as you can imagine. Tombstone stopped to lend the guy his canteen to help him clean up and* ███████████████████ *drove up and told them both off. Tombstone figures he'll get demoted for that. We all think the punishment is ridiculous, as everything we are doing is for the protection of England, the* ████████████████████ *family and all their bloody trees. The b'ys are bellowing out that supper is ready. I must go!*

Love, your not-yet-gunner, Arch

chapter 8

AUNTIE BABS

Barbara's desk at Merton Park is the first stop for film packets from the front. She carefully opens them with a nail file, checks the dope sheet for locations and subject matter, and holds the final frames up to the light to see if the photographer survived. Sometimes she must wipe blood off the cellulose before developing it. Still shots go to the newspapers, CP, and government, and she edits the film sequences for newsreels. Once the in-house censors give her a pass, she zips through the bombed-out streets of London on her Raleigh to deliver the footage to Pathé and Gaumont. If she pedals fast enough, her sequences can be on Piccadilly's screens that evening and if there's air transport, they could light up Montreal and Toronto's cinemas within a week, hitting the wooden movie palaces strung along the prairie rail line to Vancouver after that. Her father wrote that he's seen some of "her" newsreels at the Nickel in St. John's. It makes her so proud to know that her work, even if she's just the editor, is keeping folks up to date on the war. She's built a great network of editors, censors, cashiers, black marketeers, projectionists, and secretaries who source flashbulbs and film and help her get supplies to the front.

In her fifth month on the job, she's summoned to Major Doran's office. When she knocks, he's waiting at his desk underneath the notorious German propaganda image of Canadian soldiers lying dead on the beach at Dieppe. He tells everyone on their first day that it's the picture that persuaded the government to fund the film unit.

"Sergeant Kerr, come in. Close the door." He lights up a cigarette. "Look, I'll get right to it. I know you're buying stock on the black market."

She is taken aback. "Where did you hear that, sir?"

"One of our shooters sent me a letter thanking us for the steady supply of film and just last night at the club, the head of the British Film Unit was complaining that they've run out." Before she can say anything in her defence, he holds up his hand. "According to our official inventory, we haven't had stock in two months."

"Sir, they're risking their lives. They need film."

"Kerr. You know very well that marketeering is a serious offence, and I can't officially know anything about your activities."

She exhales and looks down at her black-market shoes. "Understood, sir."

Between them, on the desk blotter, are two bottles, one of Alberta rye and another of Quebec maple syrup. He asks, "Out of curiosity, how are you paying for the stuff?"

"I've got some savings."

"Kerr, that is very valiant, but you can't keep that up."

"It's just until we get more stock."

Doran says, "We won't be getting more stock and supplies are about to get scarcer. Look, I'm not going to punish you, but if I get an official complaint about your activities, I will have to follow protocol."

He motions to the bottles. "Now that we've got that out of the way, could you do anything with these? The consulate left crates of the stuff in the basement."

"I could definitely trade the rye, but the syrup?"

"Sugar rations are only eight ounces a week, Kerr. That's not enough to sweeten a pot of tea. Why don't you try Cyril? I suspect he's got a healthy knowledge of the market."

#970408
Gnr. A. Fisher
166th (Newfoundland) Field Regiment RA
█████████ *Algeria, July 29, 1943*

Dear Min,

Thanks for the bakeapple jam. We didn't even wait for bread, Tombstone, Slade, Jackie, and I just sat down in the sand and ate it with our fingers. It was almost as good as a trip home. The █████████████ *and some others who fought with us here have gotten leave, but we haven't heard a word. Please send more jam if the postage is not too expensive.*

Now that we've driven 'the Huns' away, we're at war with the bugs. Despite the netting over our beds, we wake up covered in bites. Quite a few of the men have dysentery and last week, we had a swarm of locusts. When I read about that in the bible, I pictured flying grasshoppers, but locusts are much larger, about the size of capelin, and add to that thorny bits on their legs and backs, flying in every direction. Kamikaze capelin with armour! When they came on, there were so many they blocked out the sun. Foolishly, Slade and I stayed outside to watch them limb the leaves off a tree. Then they got so thick, we couldn't get in out of it. We sat in the sand covering our eyes while they crawled up the legs of our shorts into our shirts, anywhere there was an opening. Tombstone was smarter. He hid in the latrine. It took a couple of hours for the cloud to pass and then we were ankle deep in dead locusts. Slade and I look like we've been in a prize fight. I've pressed one of the wings into this letter for you so you can get an idea of their size. That's what we're up to for entertainment. Locusts, and bingo.

We're hearing all kinds of rumours about where we're headed next and when we'll get reinforcements. We're not too fussy about where, we just want to get out of here. The heat is something else and all we do is drills. Slade worries we're going to miss the whole war. I'm hoping for ▆▆▆▆▆▆▆▆▆▆▆▆*, even though I've heard there's a lot of mud, but please God, it won't be as hot.*

Slade here. Mrs. Fisher, thank you for the jam and tea bags. Here's hoping Archie has some fine ▆▆▆▆▆▆▆▆▆▆▆▆ *posies pressed in the next letter. I appreciate you thinking about us.*

Back now. Slade wants to add a note every time I take my paper out. He's not getting any letters from his crowd, so I figure there's no harm.

PS. *If you send paper and envelopes, I can write more often. I got a letter from Anna a few weeks ago, but I haven't read it yet, knowing I've got something to look forward to helps with the monotony. I must beetle off to bed now, the mosquitoes are calling.*

Love, Arch

———

The brass bell above the door at Cyril's off-licence tinkles and he looks up from the meat counter. Barbara fishes the maple leaf–shaped bottle out of her kit bag and tells him what it is. "I always thought that was made up," he says.

"No, it's real. Comes from maple trees in the spring. Would you like to try selling some?"

"Barbara, my love," he says, "my customers won't buy tree sap."

The doorbell jangles. A woman struggles to manoeuvre a large pram into the store. Barbara lays her kit bag over the bottle to hide it from view and helps with the door. The woman thanks her and asks Cyril if he might have a little extra on hand for Charlie's birthday cake. Doran was right. Cyril either sells black-market sugar or he's willing to front the woman extra rations to take off her next card. He pushes his glasses up on his nose and says, "Let me see what I've got in the back, Lynne."

Alone with Lynne, Barbara admires Charlie who appears far too wide for the pram. "How old is the birthday boy?" she asks.

"He's turning three," says Lynne. "We've made him a little cake, and we've got some strawberries, but no cream and without sugar it's dreadfully bland."

Barbara lifts her kit bag. "You could try this. It's maple syrup."

She rips a corner of brown paper off the roll and drips syrup onto it. Lynne runs her finger through the plump droplet and tastes it. "Not leafy at all. That's lovely. It's like brown sugar."

Cyril is back, winded from his climb into the cellar. He's wheezing and holding out a can of Lyle's Golden Syrup. "I've been saving this, but you and Charlie should have it."

"Oh, Cyril, thank you, but I'd like to buy this maple stuff," says Lynne.

Cyril frowns. "Unfortunately, I don't sell it."

Barbara gives Lynne the bottle. "Please, my birthday gift to Charlie."

Lynne thanks her and invites them both to the party. When she leaves, Cyril's smile fades and he crosses his arms. "She'll tell her friends and there are severe fines for selling stolen food on the black market."

"It's not stolen."

"Fell off a lorry, did it?"

Barbara says as boldly as she can, "Either I cycle around London making deals myself with bottles smashing together in my kit bag, or you take it off my hands and sell it for twice what you pay me."

Cyril reluctantly agrees to try out ten bottles, but no more because he's worried about looters.

Barbara writes *Socks and a bible, Aunty Babs* on the customs slips of the maple syrup film. Partisans value the flammable film stock for fuses and the shooters have told her that British and American photographers will steal Canadian stock without a thought. Everyone wants the scoop. Barbara can tell the Americans stage some of their scenes. Their Hollywood shooters can't help but create a narrative and their newsreels end up looking more like silent films. The Brits are more likely to shoot wide landscapes of battles, with puffs of smoke and troops far off in the distance as if they're filming war games. In contrast, the Canadian shooters are jumbled in with the soldiers and while their death toll is higher, their vivid and dynamic sequences are more authentic. They are risking their lives and the least she can do is keep them in film stock.

———

Weeks of marching in sandy circles, digging latrines, lining up tents, and recalibrating guns in Algeria's searing heat with no clear idea about where they're going next is driving Tombstone, Slade, and Arch batty. Not even outings to Setif's canteens relieves their boredom. Complaining has become Slade's hobby. When the CO announces they'll have to ration their drinking water, Arch puts up his hand and volunteers to rig up a desalination machine. He's willing to stand in a hot tent, over a fire, with a welding torch for a few hours of peace. He might even find a quiet moment to read Anna's letter without Slade and the others looking over his shoulder and peppering him with questions. Anna has never written him before, and he's enjoyed imagining what might be in the letter. No doubt there'll be news about wartime St. John's, gossip about her instructors at teacher's college, books she's reading, movies at the Nickel, or maybe she's already teaching in some remote bay and she's writing about mischievous students and the grumpy widow who runs her boarding house. It's a small miracle her letter found him at all with most Allied forces already back in Europe. It sat in Mornag's tiny post office for a couple of months before it was forwarded to the 166th via Setif.

With sweat running down his back, Arch finishes welding the scavenged German radiator and sets the still up for a test drip. He sits, takes the battered envelope out of his chest pocket, and unseals the censorship tape.

Anna Tucker,
Salvation Army Teacher's Dorm
Springdale Street, St. John's, Newfoundland
August 24, 1943

Dear Arch,

I pray you are safe, and this letter finds you without too much of a delay. When we heard on the radio, in the spring about Rommel's defeat, I think all of Newfoundland let out a sigh of relief. Do you think the war will be over soon? I hope so, the Germans can't win, can they? What's it like there? Is the desert still and silent? Are there birds or is it empty? What does it smell like?

I miss talking with you. Not the sums, don't get me wrong! I miss your company and how you always helped me make sense of things. I have some great friends here in town and life is much more exciting than in Winterton. It's such a thrill to be somewhere where no one knows me, where I can eat cake for breakfast, ride the tram any time I want, and spend hours window-shopping or reading at the Gosling Library and no one gives a hoot.

I saw Garl in June. You were right about where he was. He came home from the mines in Cape Breton and was talking about signing up. Mother and Father had one eye each on me at all times, but Garl and I did manage to sneak away for a long walk.

I don't know how to tell you this, but I think of you as a true friend and know you won't gossip. I am pretty sure because of that walk, I'm in the family way. I don't dare go to the doctor and I don't really need to—I know what is happening. Just writing it out here makes it more real and now I'm crying, but I'm also relieved to tell someone. You're the only person who knows. It's not obvious yet, but once it is, in a month or so—certainly before Christmas break—I'll have to move back home. Once it is known, the college won't let me graduate, much less teach children.

Garl has never spoken of marriage, but he didn't know about my situation when he left and I'm sure he'll do the right thing. I've written several letters to him via the War Comforts Committee and asked for them to be forwarded, but he hasn't responded. I imagine mail is often interrupted. Are all the Newfoundlanders in one place? If not, do you know where he is training? Please tell him about my situation and ask him to write as soon as possible. I trust in your discretion.

In sincere friendship,
Anna

PS. Please don't be too disappointed in me.

The tent walls close in. How could Garl be so careless? Why won't he respond to her letters? He folds Anna's pages carefully, puts them back in the envelope, reseals the censor's tape, and secures it in his chest pocket. The dunes groan in the midday heat and a droplet of sweat from the tip of his nose makes a circle in the water pan.

———

Barbara's maple syrup film keeps the shooters in stock until the end of the North African campaign, the occupation of southern France, and through some of the battle for Stalingrad. The photographers send Aunty Babs letters of thanks stuffed in around the film canisters with tidbits about their daily lives. Their notes intensify Barbara's desire to join their ranks. When she gets wind that the Americans have hired half a dozen female war correspondents, she decides to approach Doran. Although not permitted at the front, the American women are shooting stories about nurses, USO performances, and whatnot. Work Barbara knows she can do with one eye closed.

One July morning, a Navy corporal brings her a Mae West held together with grimy medical tape. She takes it with trepidation.

"What's this?"

"From your friend Ron"

"McMahon? Is he okay?"

"Yes, yes he's fine. Says he got the biggest scoop of the war. He told me there'd be a bottle of rye in it if I delivered this to you as soon as I got back."

"Back from where?"

He holds out a yellow envelope. "It's all in the note."

Barbara reaches for it and he playfully pulls it back. "The rye?"

She gives him a bottle from the crate in her office and he hands over McMahon's letter. "Check the lining of the jacket."

Aunty Babs ONLY!!!!!—RUSH RUSH RUSH delivery. Untape Mae. I got the only film of the landing. It's all in the lining. She sticks her hands into the lambswool and finds four film reels along with the dope sheet. A few white pebbles fall out onto her desk. *This is a big upset and the first sign that things might go our way.* PS. *No film left. Not a frame. Not one of our boys has any. If we march through a larger town that hasn't been bombed, we may 'borrow' some. I hope London is a blast these days—but not that kind of blast! Your sweetheart, Ron.* Barbara hurries to the editing suite. One of the pebbles sticks to the sole of her shoe and scrapes the linoleum.

———

Water drips onto the toes of Arch's boots. How in the name of Christ will he find Garl? He runs his fingers along the tank's seams searching for the leak. He closes his eyes to slow his galloping heart. When he opens them, Slade is inches from his face. Arch jumps back and Slade says, "Jeez, b'y Arch, I thought you'd nodded off." He says there's a surprise for Arch in the mess. Finally. Min's package. They've been smoking used tea leaves rolled in bible pages for a couple of weeks now. Slade holds up Tombstone's Brownie and gets Arch to pose with his invention. They walk together into the blinding sunlight to the shaded mess. It takes a few seconds for Arch's eyes to adjust, and his stomach to flip-flop. Skipper? Here? His breathing catches. The figure moves. Not Skipper. Garl. It's Garl!

"G-G-Garl?"

A toothpick dangles from the corner of his mouth. Unhurried, pale, and tall, Garl is all angles and whip-straight hair, in contrast to the curly mane barely contained by Arch's side cap. Garl stands but makes no move to embrace his brother even though it's been over three years.

"Jeez, b'y, it's g-g-good to lay eyes on ya," Arch says.

Garl drawls, "Skipper sent me over to look out for you."

Slade slaps Arch on the back. "Arch? Sure, he's the one looking after all of us."

Garl says, "He wants to make sure you don't quit this too."

Battling the Huns, the heat, and the thirst, scrounging for food, coming together as a crew, getting over the desert's wide-open exposure, beating Rommel, and rigging up little doohickeys has helped Arch feel like himself, but Garl's arrival brings back the suffocating sense that his life will always be weighed down by fear and shame.

————————

Noting the location of Ron's shots and the names of the divisions on his reels, Barbara yells down the hallway, "No naps today, Patsy!"

Peeking out of her doorway, Patsy asks, "Who's hurt?"

"Nobody. They've landed in Italy!"

"No way. It hasn't been on the Beeb."

"McMahon's dope sheet says, 'Canadians posing at Sicily train station.'"

She threads the film onto her Steenbeck to excise the most dramatic scenes; visual proof that the Canadians are on Italian soil. She's got an hour to edit, get it past the in-house censors, and deliver it to the newsreels. She snips off shots of Canadians exercising on the deck of a warship and poring over Italian maps, cuts to an onboard prayer service, then edits in a wide shot of the armada at sea with barrage balloons. She adds guns firing from the deck of the destroyer. Smoking coastal batteries. Canadian infantrymen wading ashore. Small explosions on land. Ron must've been in the first troop carrier that rolled up onto white pebble beaches. Soldiers run to a line of trees, guns at the ready. She sticks these shots on the wall next to her desk with editing tape and uses the razor blade to slice through the celluloid capturing Field Marshall Montgomery on a seawall with the armada behind him. He's twisting a fly swatter in his hands as an Italian general in a white feather hat surrenders. She edits the shots together onto a new reel creating a minute-long sequence with a perfect ending: the 1st Canadian Armoured Brigade standing underneath a bullet-riddled sign at the Pachino-Noto train station. A minute is unusually long for a newsreel, but this is a whole new theatre of war.

———

Tombstone arrives with the day's mail. He lays a battered box in front of Arch and salutes Garl. Red ants march out of the package's worn corners as Arch stares at Garl's stripes. How the hell did he become an officer? He's anxious to tell him about Anna. Garl smirks. "I see Min is still spoiling you."

Arch introduces Slade and Tombstone to his brother. Garl nods at them both, slides his penknife under the twine, pulls up with a jerk, releasing the greasy cardboard flaps to reveal a partially flattened fruit cake wrapped in stained cheesecloth and crawling with Algerian ants. It looks like something from the infirmary. Garl cuts a fair-sized piece, peels away the gauze, flicks off the insects, and stuffs it in his mouth. Slade looks from Arch to Tombstone and back again. Arch had forgotten how Garl just takes what he wants without asking. Tombstone hands Garl a letter. The envelope is plain, but he'd know Tobin's handwriting anywhere. He nudges the still-crawling cake towards his friends.

———

At the censor's office, Barbara goes straight to Glenda's desk where she's stretching. "Hiya, kid! Just leave it in the basket, I'm going on break."

"I've got new footage from McMahon."

Glenda flinches. "Glad to hear he's still breathing."

Barbara is not the jealous type, but she makes a mental note to ask Ron about Glenda next time they meet. Maybe she should be keeping her options open.

Barbara whispers, "They're in Sicily."

Glenda isn't impressed. "Yeah, that's been in the works."

"Any chance you can look at it before your break, so I can make tonight's newsreels? A little good news for everyone."

Glenda frowns. "I'm not sure the war office wants the good news out yet. Who else knows?"

"Just me and Patsy."

"No one in foley?"

"No time for that. I covered it with music. I need to get it on the reels before the Americans get wind. You know what they're like, it's as if they're the only ones at war!"

Glenda sighs and puts her cigarette case back in her purse. "Who's in the footage?"

Barbara reads from the dope sheet. "1st Infantry and 1st Armoured, a shot of Monty and some bigwig Italian."

"No one else?"

"Not on this reel, it's just the bare bones."

Glenda takes Barbara's reel and goes to the head censor's office. She closes the door. Barbara checks her watch. Thirty-two minutes before the newsreel deadline. Through the censor's frosted glass window, she watches Glenda cradle the phone receiver in her neck as she threads the reel onto the censor's Steenbeck. He stands back on to Barbara watching with folded arms as Glenda talks into the phone. If Barbara can make it, Canadian newsreels will break the news on Piccadilly screens this afternoon and it could hit Broadway, Toronto, and Montreal as early as tomorrow. If she can pull this off, Doran will have to agree to let her work in the field.

Glenda strolls back to her desk and hands over the reel. "It's fifty-two seconds. We censored the shot of the train station."

"But that's the only proof they're there," Barbara says too loudly.

"Use your egg, Babs. We can't tell the enemy exactly where they landed."

Before she can argue her point, a long beep from the radio interrupts the clacking typewriters. *"This is a BBC news bulletin. The Allies have landed on Sicily. No further information at this time."* Barbara's shoulders fall.

Glenda picks up her purse and elbows her playfully. "Hop on your bike, Kerr. You've got the only footage in London. I was talking to the British censorship office and they don't have a thing."

She hugs Glenda, takes the edited reel, and runs.

chapter 9

ROOFTOPS

If Mama knew Cosimo was stealing food, she'd be angrier than the waiters, pigeons, and stray dogs he outruns for scraps. He walks the city's back laneways and side streets at night with his nose in the air, obsessed with what the Bolognese might be eating behind their locked green shutters. He hasn't smelled frying onions or even burnt toast, let alone roast chicken, but has certainly overheard lots of complaints about shortages of flour, soap, salt, and meat, as well as whispers that the Germans are gluttons. Since arriving in Bologna, he's been sleeping in an empty crypt knowing no good pilot would waste a bomb on a graveyard. Luckily, the giant tree shading his hideout is a walnut. The nuts give him a tummy ache, but they fill him up.

———

Arch leans on the troopship rail as they steam past the HMS *Nelson*. The enormous British warship is anchored crossways, blocking the entrance to Valletta's harbour. When they get around the hull, he sees why. The town looks like a sandcastle that has been kicked over, burned, and stomped on. The entire Italian navy is anchored here, right where they surrendered a month ago. Even with their guns pointed down, their gleaming ships are impressive. An Italian sailor in white cycles around the deck of his warship and nods at Arch. Slade joins him at the rail and tut-tuts. "Jesus, Mary, and Joseph, months of fighting the Eye-ties and now they expects us to kiss and make up?"

They've been looking forward to shore time in Malta. They're all desperate for a taste of British beer, Arch wants to buy a news-paper and paw through the paperbacks in the NAAFI, and Tombstone has a bundle of letters to send home. But now that they're here, it's doubtful there's a thing to eat or drink in the ruined town. They drop anchor in the middle of the harbour and small punts filled with baskets of fruit row towards their ship. Once alongside, the boatmen motion for lines. Slade obliges and watches the fruit seller tie the rope around a basket handle. Slade hoists up the fruit. He hands Arch a ripped-open thing, full of seeds. Tombstone says it's a pomer-granite. Arch can't figure out what you're meant to eat, and the red juice stains his hands and the front of his uniform. They throw a few coins in the basket and lower it back down.

Garl arrives. "No frigging shore leave," he says. Arch knows he's telling the truth because he can hear the waves of complaints breaking over the deck behind him. "We're to anchor here for the night and then go on to the boot."

Tombstone unbuttons his shirt. "So, it is Italy."

He hands Arch his packet of letters, kicks off his untied boots, and asks, "What's the point? Two months after we've invaded?"

He pulls his shirt over his head, drops his shorts, and places one foot, then another on the railing rungs and dives off the ship. Starkers. Slade gapes. "Jeez-us H. Murphy, red fur. Everywhere!"

Arch, Slade, and Garl lean over the railing as Tombstone's head emerges. He flicks the water out of his ears and dog paddles in the inky Mediterranean.

"Going to town without your small clothes, Tombstone?" asks Slade.

Tombstone yells, "Hold on to my letters, Arch!"

Slade strips and dives off the ship with a Tarzan yell that inspires twenty or so others to do the same. Arch is torn between wanting to join the fun and thinking about the last time he was submerged in salt water. Garl lights a cigarette. "You getting in or staying on mail watch?"

It's now or never. Arch asks, "You get many letters in training?"

"Who'd be writing me?"

"A-Anna."

"Anna who?"

"Who do you think? Anna T-T-Tucker, from home."

"Why would she write me?" asks Garl.

The swimmers are shrieking like youngsters and the fruit sellers are pelting them with oranges.

"You tell me, G-Garl."

"I didn't get no letters from the little miss. You and her pen pals?" Garl's eyes dart to the nearby railings as more men strip off and dive into the sea.

Arch says, "She did write me."

"I always knew you had the hots—"

"No, it's n-n-not like that. She wrote me when you didn't write her back."

"So what?"

"Did you even r-re-read her letters? She's in a spot of trouble."

"Why is she writing you about it?"

Arch looks around to make sure no one can hear him. "She s-s-says she's in the family way."

"Well, Jesus!" A muscle in Garl's cheek jumps and he slaps Arch on the back. "Congratulations, Father Arch. I didn't think you had it in ya." His face stretches into a wide smirk.

"Geographically impossible. I was in Aaa-algeria."

"Oh? Whose is it?"

"Whose do ya think? It's yours."

Garl undoes his belt. "Nah, b'y, she's really not my type."

"Garl, she said it happened on a l-lo-long walk."

Stripped down to his drawers, Garl climbs the rail. "That was all just a bit of fun, Arch b'y. You should try it."

Garl jumps as Rawlins rushes up to the rail. Their captain doesn't have to be told that Tombstone is the ringleader. He bellows, "Sergeant Waaaalsh!"

Arch knows Anna wouldn't lie. He'll let Garl stew for a couple of days and bring it up again. He can't wait too long because Anna might be showing by now.

Rawlins cups his hands on either side of his mouth. "The first one to touch the side of the *Nelson* and get back on board gets extra beer rations."

The school of Newfoundlanders turn and swim full tilt towards the dazzle camo'd hull. Slade is the first one back on board and he's called Lord Nelson for a few days until he gets up to some arseholery and loses the honorific. Despite not getting ashore and not knowing exactly where they're headed, dinner that night is celebratory. There are rumours of leave once they get set up on the boot and Tombstone has his hopes up. He wants to get home so the new baby can be christened. Arch catches Garl's eye, but he looks away. He might be standing at Garl and Anna's wedding if they get leave.

Their ship steams past Sicily as the dawn lights up the smouldering Mount Etna. Slade, Tombstone, and Arch are smoking Maltese cigarettes on deck. "What in the name of Christ are we going to do here?" asks Slade. "They've already surrendered."

Arch says, "G'won, b'y, the Germans are still holed up in Rome. Maybe we'll get to be part of the holy city's liberation."

"Ready for your papal blessing, are ya, Arch?" asks Tombstone.
Slade says, "I always wanted to see dat Sa-teen Chapel."

––––––––

Cosi bites into a chicken leg and the juice dribbles down his
face. The greasy dream wakes him, and he touches his chin.
Too hungry and cold to go back to sleep, he flicks his wrist and
whispers, "*Cuddiwch fi. Helpa fi I ddid o had I fwyd.*" Conceal me
and help me find food. Is it possible he smelled roast chicken while
sleeping? At dawn, he is lost in a Fascist zone just as everyone is
waking and shaking out their mops, but the spell holds, and he
escapes to a nearby rooftop. He is having a grand morning nap
against a water cistern when the sound of breaking glass wakes him.
Peeking over the parapet, he watches a Nazi patrol smashing up
an apartment. "*Gwna fi'n fach iawn.*" Make me tiny. The soldiers
bully everyone up from the dining table and down over the stairs.
They aren't very nice, screaming and pointing their guns until the
women and children are all crying. In the street, they rip open
everyone's suitcases and dump clothes, paper, and books onto
the dirty cobblestones. A lorry comes and they push the people
into the back. When it drives away, a couple of soldiers run back
upstairs. Cosi watches through a gap in the shutters as they empty
drawers, break chairs, and smash dishes. One meanie cracks a big
mirror with the butt of his rifle, and another shoots up a wall of
photographs.

––––––––

Caroline books her flights from St. John's to Bologna. She adds
on an additional regional flight to Pescara and back, sad that
she doesn't have time on this trip for trains. She has such fond
memories of travelling around Italy on the slow local trains with
Peter, their grumpy art history teacher. He took her class all over

the country to study frescoes, altars, sculptures, and mosaics. He knew, or made up, the most scandalous stories about the artists and their patrons, bringing those long-dead Renaissance art stars back to life. One of her favourite classes was in Ravenna, where he showed them church windows made from paper-thin alabaster. The caramel light through those windows gave the impression of sight.

————

The clothing and wrecked suitcases stay in the street all day. German trucks drive through the wreckage and the Bolognese give it a wide berth. No one dares touch anything or move it out of the way. Once curfew sounds, Cosimo descends from the roof, steps over the clothes, and tiptoes up the staircase. The apartment is still. The door hangs from one hinge and mirror shards and torn papers litter the floor. The cupboards are bare, but he checks the same places where Mama used to hide sweets. Ha ha! He lifts the lid from a pot and finds what the Germans were looking for: two hard-boiled eggs, a plum, and a pat of butter carefully folded in a ripped piece of waxed paper. He digs the toast crumbs out of the butter with his index finger and spreads it over his dry lips. If only he had some of Marie's Mulleystone jam. In case the people come back with bread, he refolds the wax paper and places the remaining butter back in the pot. He eats one egg in the dark, shattered room and puts the extra one and the plum in his knapsack for Mama. She'll be famished when she arrives from the border.

————

Caroline drives to Gander to meet Maddy Jenkins, a graphic novelist she's hoping to collaborate with on her undefined art project. Leo encouraged her to go to Italy to satisfy her curiosity about her Pop and Arch, assuring her she'd figure the project out once there.

Maddy invites Caroline to the Legion for lunch. It's the same place that housed Irish passengers during 9/11, a place celebrated in the Broadway show *Come From Away*. Caroline is not sure what she expects, but it looks like any other Legion; black and white framed photos, flags, dartboards, lino floors, plywood stacking chairs, and long tables covered with paper tablecloths. When they sit with their cold plates, Maddy introduces her to a dapper, older man dressed in a suit and tie.

"Caroline, this is Reverend Wesley Oake. He may be interested in our project. He served with the 166th in Italy."

Caroline's heart leaps. She didn't know any of the men from the 166th were still alive! She doesn't want to appear too eager but has a million questions. "So nice to meet you, Reverend Oake, my Pop and great-uncle served in the 166th. They were in Queenie Battery."

"I was in Queenie too. What were their names?"

"Garl Fisher was my Pop and Arch was my great-uncle."

Oake doesn't hesitate. "Of course, I remember your grandfather. He was a great singer and a good hand at recitations."

"Oh, I didn't know that. He didn't talk about the war."

"What we lived through in Italy was horrific." His blue eyes fill with tears. "We lost so many good men . . . boys, really."

Caroline is surprised that after all these decades, his memories elicit tears. "Do you remember anything about my Great-uncle Arch?"

Oake shakes his head and dabs his eyes with his napkin. "I'm sorry, my dear. Thinking back on that time near Monte Sole is heart-breaking. There was so much death and they forgot us up there. The brass. We would've starved if it wasn't for the Italians."

———

From the rooftops Cosi can sometimes track country people coming in through the city gates with food to sell. He's followed lorries full of cows and carts of broccoli, but they went to the German barracks. Today, he spots an old strega and a pig-nosed man coming in through Porte Via Issaia. They're cranky from carrying their heavy bags. If he knew an X-ray spell, he could see through the brin. When they finally stop and fold down the tops, bright green apples glow in the sunlight.

#970408
Gnr. A. Fisher
166th (Newfoundland) Field Regiment RA
Somewhere new, October 17, 1943

Dear Min,

I've got two letters on the go now. We're on the move and stamps are hard to come by. As soon as I find some, I'll post both and let them race across the Atlantic. Thank you for the fruit cake. It must've cost a fortune in postage. It was quite tasty for something that survived a few flights, at least one long boat ride and a tour of various African post offices. I shared it with a few hundred ants, Slade, Tombstone, and big brother. That's right. Garl! He joined us with the new batch of recruits. Did you know he'd signed up? More news. He's an officer. You should be proud. We watched a film on the troop-ship that brought us to this new place. It's called "Desert Victory." If you get a chance, go see it, it will give you an idea of what we've been up to. Although, it was a fair bit more confusing in real life than in the film.

I mentioned Anna's situation in the letter postmarked September 29th. I hope you got that one. Garl says the baby is not his, but I don't believe him. It's not like Anna Tucker is

*out gallivanting. I must sign off now, there's a game of 120s
shaping up and I don't want anyone peeking over my shoulder.*

Love, Arch

———

Cosimo counts his steps to the apples when he sees Abbott and
Costello's heads bobbing along the opposite roof. He doesn't know
their real names, but they're the only boys his age he's seen in
Bologna. At night, they sometimes track each other through the
alleys and streets. It's like a big game of hide-and-seek. Abbott
and Costello know the city and how to get around the Fascist
roadblocks better than he does, but they don't have his spells. He
recites, "*Cuddiwch fi. Helpa fi i ddod o hyd i fwyd.*" Conceal me
and help me find food. A large family rounds the corner of Via
de Marchi. He pounds down the back stairs and steps out of a
doorway, falling in with them. He's licking his lips in anticipation
of the apple's grassy tang. The family is worried about the Allies'
advance and how it will increase milk prices. Cosimo wishes
someone would say where the Allies are, but not wanting to break
his spell, he keeps quiet. When they arrive at the strega, the two
eldest sisters lock arms and start haggling. They offer her a price
that even Cosimo knows is too low and when the strega closes her
eyes to refuse, his hand darts through the women's hips and locks
onto an orb.

———

Caroline eyes her untouched scoops of purple, yellow, and white
potato salad. Reverend Oake says some stories are best untold. She
doesn't want him to see how much she disagrees. She's never heard
of Monte Sole. Nor is there any mention of it in the books she's read.
After lunch, as they're leaving the Legion, she gives Oake her card

and asks if she can write him a letter or two about the routes and locations of the 166th.

—————

Abbott yells, "Occhio!" and all eyes focus in on the lump in Cosi's shirt. How can they see him? He tears down a side street with his prize until he can no longer hear the screams of "Ladro!" If Abbott and Costello are worth their salt, they're filling their arms with apples while everyone is distracted by his thieving. He ducks into an alley to destroy the evidence. The first bite tastes like tin, but he doesn't care. He chews and pretends he has pecorino and honey, just like the stuff Umberto shared with him on the train.

The chatter from the border was about passes, papers, gas shortages, school closures, and rationing. Not one person said the words Cosi was longing to hear: *resistenza, partigiani,* or *Stella Rossa.* He scuffed up his shiny leather shoes and rolled up the sleeves of his school blazer to make it look less foreign. Through scratches in the blackout paint he got his first glimpses of war in Italy. Soldiers digging ditches and sleeping in wheat fields. Germans lounging on train platforms. A passive column of tanks waiting at a crossroads. It looked nothing like the pictures he'd seen in his mother's newspapers. Umberto was good company, but he had trouble understanding Cosi's accent. Every time Cosimo spoke, the old man squinted his eyes and said, "Dirlo de nuovo." Now, he understood how Mama felt when the English asked her to repeat herself. A stupid girl, three seats up, told her mother in a loud voice that she couldn't understand Cosi. That made other passengers turn around in their seats to study his clothes and face. He wanted to punch the girl's lights out even after her mother told her he must be Swiss.

—————

When a manila envelope arrives in her mailbox a few weeks later, Caroline is thrilled. Rev. Oake has answered some of her questions about the whereabouts of the Newfoundlanders, what they were doing on Monte Sole, and he's enclosed two photos. One is of Pop on newsprint. He's leaning against a truck, and the caption says, *Garland Fisher of the 166th waiting for his brother's return from an OP mission at the Sangro.* Her mother always said Pop was a hero for disobeying orders and staying behind to look for Arch. He even lost his pension in the process. But why would he come home and burn Arch's letters? Survivor's guilt? PTSD? Or something else?

The other photo is Wes Oake as a young soldier standing with two Italian girls holding bicycle wheels. They're framed by the roof lines of the Uffizi. Her and Leo had their picture taken in that exact spot when they were art students. On the back, in shaky ballpoint, Oake has written, *my wife always asks which one was my girlfriend, but the truth is, I just helped them with their tires.* She pins Pop, Wes, and the two girls with their impossibly skinny legs and Mona Lisa grins above her desk. The images speed up time in reverse.

———

Taranto Harbour smells of diesel and death. Not even Slade says a word as they pass by a wrecked British minelayer that was offloading troops and ammo when the Luftwaffe bombed. Charred bodies drape the deck. Tombstone whispers that they will be setting a speed record for getting their crap offloaded, but unfortunately the Italian dockworkers do not share their urgency. If they're not drinking coffee at the canteen, they're smoking in the shade and regard the Newfoundlanders as more of a nuisance than valiant liberators.

Arch claims his Chev, ecstatic to drive the truck off the ship and out of town. On the road north they pass a freshly carved road sign that reads *London 1367 ½ miles*, as well as burned-out tanks, bombed and pillaged lorries, and tractor wrecks. The hum of raw sewage forces them to roll up their windows in some places. Civilians emerge from the rubble of flattened buildings and wave. Children hang onto their back bumper for rides. Some chant, "Americani! Americani!" They don't have the heart, or the Italian, to tell them otherwise. Slade flashes V for victory with his left hand while keeping his right hand on his gun. "I don't trust these friggers!"

A green sphere is lobbed into their cab. Tombstone squawks and tries to bat it away, Arch hits the brakes, and Slade launches himself sideways out of the door and into a ditch. They wait for the explosion, but there isn't one.

Tombstone says, "At ease. It's just a pear!"

"A pear?" says Slade. "Why would someone throw a pear?"

Arch bites into it. "Mmmmm!" Before this, he thought all pears tasted like the mealy canned ones they had at home. Gritty cubes swimming in syrup. This pear is crisp and bright.

More fruit is thrown into their truck and they alternate between stuffing their faces and worrying that the next green thing will be a grenade. To the left of the coastal plain they're driving on there's an imposing, mauve range of mountains crowned in clouds. It's an impressive and continuous barrier between them and Rome. Tombstone looks up from the map spread across the dash and says it doesn't look like they'll be liberating the Pope. To their right, the Adriatic is as smooth as a tile, the turquoise water so still it feels like a trap.

———————

Near Parma station, Cosimo's train slowed to a stop in a field. Urgent whispers of "Tedeschi" filled the car. Umberto pointed to the luggage rack and helped him climb up. His new friend moved the packages to hide Cosi's feet and shoulders. It was bloody hot in the ceiling of the train. The stale air reeked of tobacco, sweat, and barnyard. One of the parcels near his face trembled with the faint peeps of chicks. When the Germans climbed into the carriage, the peeps grew louder like an alarm. No one spoke and Cosi dared not breathe. Over the low rumble of the soldiers' questions about papers and destinations, Cosi could hear a whine. Was the stupid girl crying? Then the whine lifted into a higher and more urgent pitch and someone yelled, "Attaco aereo!" The Germans screamed, "Alle Raus!" and everyone piled out through the squeaky train doors. That's how Cosi became the only passenger on the Ventimiglia Express to Parma and Bologna. He grabbed on tight to a slat of the luggage rack, closed his eyes, and repeated, "*Cudd fi o'u llygaid. Gwneud i mi arnofio yn anweledig.*" Conceal me and help me float. The whine deepened into the unmistakable rumble of an approaching bomber. Conceal me and help me float. At Mulleystone, the British soldiers taught him the difference between the sounds of Allied and German engines. There, he ran for cover when he heard an incoming Me-262 or a Messerschmitt. Here, his leg twitches at the approach of his favourite, a Spitfire. He imagined the British pilot in the cockpit following the snaking train track with his thumb on the trigger. He twisted and fretted about the thinness of the metal above his head, but if he jumped down and ran into the field now, the Germans might shoot him, and he could draw fire from the pilot. He peeked out from behind the chicks and wriggled free so he could hang upside down in the empty railcar. Through the scratches in the blacked-out windows, he watched German soldiers throw branches and straw over their lorries. The passengers were crouched in a wheat field with machine guns pointed at them. When the bomber opened fire, Cosimo fell off the rack in fright and crawled under Umberto's seat as glass shards exploded all around him. Spells for floating, flying, and shrinking crowded his mind. Which one? The train rocked with the shock of a nearby bomb and the blood left his limbs. Pee! He desperately needed to pee. Machine gun fire. Not now. Another hit. Farther away? He knelt up. A German lorry was on fire and bloodied soldiers lay on the ground. Others fired their guns after the plane. The Spitfire flew on and Cosi ducked down under the seat counting the seconds, worrying it would turn and come back. His legs stopped shaking at two hundred. When the passengers got back on board some talked a little too loud and some were even laughing, trying to shake off their nerves. Cosimo didn't hear any German spoken, but he stayed under the seat until the train was back at speed. Umberto knew he was there and dropped a blanket over him when he sat down.

When it was safe to sit up, Umberto had sliced a green apple and unfolded a handkerchief that held crumbled pecorino dotted with honey. He shared his treats and suggested that Cosi get off two stops before Bologna Centrale and wait in an alley or ditch until after dark. He warned Cosimo to avoid the Fascist squadri that controlled the city. "Mangiano i bambini," he whispered. Cosimo traded his blazer with Umberto for an old cardigan that smelled like manure. It reminded him of Mulleystone's stables. By the time he walked into the city of his birth, moonlight illuminated bombed-out blocks and rubble. Heeding Umberto's advice about the squadri, he avoided streets with sandbagged checkpoints. A hand-painted sign on a collapsed wall read, *Destroyed by our liberators!* Cosimo smiled. The war would definitely be more exciting here.

———————

Caroline searches for info on the CP photographer, Baldwin Kerr, who took the photo of Pop leaning against his truck. She finds another Kerr shot of Montgomery. He's standing on a bridge with soldiers arrayed like a choir behind him. There's mud, body bags, and the carnage of a battlefield around them. Every other Montgomery photo she's seen must've been shot from below, making him seem taller and more heroic. Why did Kerr choose to reveal the General's short stature? There are also Kerr shots online of Italian resistance fighters, babies sleeping in London bomb shelters, and a group of Brazilian nurses draped over a jeep.

———————

Heavy rain sluices over the windshield. It's been a year or more since they've seen rain. On the other side of Termoli, they rumble across a bridge, as a soldier emerges from the ditch. Arch jams on the brakes again, this time almost catapulting Slade through the windshield. "Jaysus, Arch!"

"Sorry, Slade. Buddy scared me."

Tombstone opens his door and paws at the loose fruit, dropping tomatoes and pears into their helmets to make room as a Canadian lifts himself into the cab. "Thanks, guys. Ron McMahon, Canadian Film Unit, Quebec City. Where you coming from?"

"We just got here from Algeria via Malta. Newfoundlanders 8th Army. What have we missed?"

"Biggest battle so far was back there in Termoli. British commandos came in ahead to capture it, but the Germans managed to blow up the bridge in retreat."

"We got commandos here?" asks Tombstone.

"Monty is not messing around. He's got everyone and everything here. Canucks, Poles, French, Kiwis, Aussies, Scots, Irish, Indians, and Yanks."

Arch swerves around a crater. "Where's your detachment?"

"Down the road a bit. I'm looking for bombed-out camera stores."

Slade asks, "Did you take photos in Termoli?"

"I couldn't. No film. I was too far away anyway and wouldn't have gotten a good shot. Lucky I was watching, though. I was able to warn the CO about the German counterattack."

"We heard the Ted-ashies are long gone," says Slade.

"I wish! They could be anywhere, and they've mined this whole coast. You better get some sandbags down around your feet."

Arch swerves around an ox team pulling a cart of furniture. Ron points to their left. "I was up there, on that ridge, next to a Vickers. I woke up early to piss and saw the counterattack start. It looked like the whole mountain was moving. 16th Panzer, hundreds of tanks."

The mountains are practically vertical. How in the name of God, wonders Arch, will they get ammo and guns up there? Ron digs his thumbnail into the flesh of a pear as Tombstone unfolds the map and asks, "Where was that?"

They follow Ron's finger down the Adriatic coast. "Oh God, this is an Italian map. Is this what the Brits issued?"

"Yeah, they superimposed a British grid over the Italian," says Tombstone.

"Don't trust this. It's completely fucked. The Italian grid underneath is no good. It's the wrong scale to register your guns. Kill a German for his map. They have the best ones. Anyway, I got on the horn and tried to convince the COs in Termoli to cut bait and run. They hadn't even considered the possibility of a counterattack! They thought the Argylls could hold off hundreds of tanks. I stayed at that bridge back there with the sappers. They're the real heroes."

"Who gets your film?" asks Slade.

"Most of it makes it to London where it goes on newsreels so people at home can see that we're winning."

Slade laughs and hands Ron a Maltese cigarette. They're all quiet as Ron lights it and takes his first draw. "Seriously," he says. "When I was watching those sappers, I thought we might just win. The Germans aimed everything they had at that bridge. There were bullets pinging off their bulldozers and a shell came down and blew up five guys right in front of me."

Arch thinks about the bridge dances in Turk's Cove. He slows to avoid a broken-down Fiat. "They pushed the bodies to the side and kept working. They basically built the bridge with their bare hands. No welding. No cranes. The whole thing fit together."

Slade asks, "Like Meccano?"

"Yeah. They made it on one side of the river and pushed it over with a bulldozer. They got it across with about twenty minutes to spare. The Yeomanry and the Irish Brigade had one helluva fight, but they won. Every river along this coast is going to go like that. You guys will probably get it at the Sangro."

Tombstone runs his finger up the map until he finds the tiny blue vein of the Sangro River.

chapter 10

CRACK

A meandering stream when they arrived, the Sangro is now a turbulent, bone-coloured torrent. Water slams down the mountains and bubbles up through the earth, sucking at Arch's shins. The tall willows along the banks have all drowned. He's breathing rainwater and blinking rainwater; his mouth and eyes open and close like a flatfish plucked from the bottom. Every day it's harder to know if they're in the Sangro or if the Adriatic is backing up and engulfing them. The rising, rushing, seeping, and falling water sluices away any awareness of time, but Arch is pretty sure they've been here for a month, drowning in slow-motion while German snipers take pot shots at them.

Tombstone tries to light a rollie, but the paper dissolves on contact with his fingertips and the tobacco ends up all over the front of his poncho.

Slade calls their gun pit Random Island for good luck and to razz Rawlins for making them dig it so far out in the river. Tombstone has been obsessing about Beaumont-Hamel. He is walking up and down the line sizing up everyone's pits and fretting that once again the Brits are pushing the Newfs out front. Arch's biggest concern is that this is so unlike the fighting in North Africa. Here, they're facing off across a raging river with an enemy that has been dug in for months. They don't even know if or how the guns will work in this rain and they're stuck with the shagged-up Italian maps and old ammo from Algeria. The battle has been scheduled, rescheduled, and called off several times. Arch wants to get it over with and get out of this muddy hell. He slaps down another sandbag next to Tombstone who is kneeling in muck up to his hips while Slade gets saucy with Rawlins. "Captain, sir, we've dropped anchor, but we won't be able to hold her much longer, we'll be headed out the Adriatic da once."

"Shut up, Slade. You need to be able to reach the enemy," says Rawlins.

"All due respect, sir, Mozzarella is six miles, our range is seven. We don't need to be this close."

"Want to measure precisely how far *Mozzagrogna* is, Slade? You volunteering for OP duty?"

Slade shakes his head and shuts his mouth. No one wants to be the first to cross the Sangro into German territory. They've been here long enough to hear all the rumours of underground German cities, secret weapons, poison gas, and thousands of reinforcements. Rawlins moves on and Slade floats a new rumour. "I heard the 17th. The Gurkhas. The same fellas that cut off the German's ear and put it in Garl's smokes."

Tombstone rolls his eyes. "That was the Goums, you gom."

Bickering is a comfort. It cuts through their fears of whether their ammo and gas will hold out, how bad the air fight will be overhead. What if the Germans try, like in Termoli, to cross the river in hundreds of tanks and roll right over their gun pits? Arch calls bullshit on that. "Their tanks are just as fucked as ours in this."

Tombstone squints. "No Luftwaffe either. They can't fly in cats and dogs unless they got some newfangled planes we don't know about."

What no one can deny is the deafening magnitude of German firepower already coming down on them from the Fossacesia Ridge. A maniacal roar that never dims. A minute-by-minute reminder that the Krauts have been here longer and can probably keep shooting until well past Christmas.

Slade elbows Arch in the ribs. "How can Monty not know our tanks won't make it across for backup?"

"He's got us all here, Slade, and now he's got to do something big, and he's obviously less concerned with the gory details than we are."

Rawlins all but confirms Arch's theory later in the mess. The only one in a dry uniform, he pulls a piece of paper out of his chest pocket. "I'd like to remind you about our purpose. I'm going to re-read General Montgomery's message from the second of November," he says.

Slade grumbles quietly, "A whole friggin' month ago, before the rain and mud changed everything."

Rawlins reads. "*The Allies have conquered about one-third of Italy since we invaded on the eighth of September. But the Germans still hold the approach to Rome, and that city itself. The time has now come to drive the Germans north of Rome.*" The paper quivers in Rawlins's hands. "*The 8th Army is not advancing on the direct Rome axis; it is the 5th American Army which is on that line. But our help is vital if the 5th is to secure Rome.*" Arch studies the mud caked around his laces and the pool of water under his heels. He just wants to get this over with. They all do. The hum of satched wool uniforms roils his stomach. "*And we will do our part in a manner worthy of the best traditions of the 8th Army and the Desert Air Force. The enemy has been outfought by better troops ever since we first landed in Sicily, and his men don't like what they are getting. The Germans are, in fact, in the very condition in which we want them. We will now hit the Germans a colossal crack! Good luck to you all. And good hunting as we go forward.*"

Splat. A spoonful of Slade's cold stew falls back in his bowl. "This ain't going to be no friggin' fox hunt."

———————

The groan of the wooden bench reverberates through San Paolo di Ravone. Cosimo likes this quiet place with his father's name over the door, but today there are too many people here. He ducks into a closet with a comfy chair and a cross-shaped window. The priest comes out on the stage, stands back on to the audience and talks out loud in an old kind of Italian. Sometimes the audience talks back and sometimes little bells ring. He nods off thinking church is strange.

The priest stops talking mid-word. The silence grows louder and Cosimo's eyes fly open. German soldiers! Two old women sitting near his closet tent their hands, bow their heads, and mumble some sort of spell over and over at top speed. He flicks his wrist and whispers his invisibility spell as his cross-shaped window darkens. Light slices across the floor, illuminating his toe. He stops breathing. The soldier's head is turned watching the priest, but his body fills the doorway of the closet. Cosi could touch the black-gloved hand resting on a submachine gun. A woman near the stage cries out and the soldier turns and runs to help his friends pull a man from one of the seats. The woman screams at them as they drag the man out of the church. People hold her back from running after them.

When the big front doors slam shut, everyone exhales. Is it wrong to be relieved? The priest comes down off the stage and tries to comfort the woman. He tells the audience to follow him. Cosimo slips out of the closet and walks behind the two lady mumblers. He hears them say they've never been on the altar before and whisper to each other about holy ghosts. Cosimo is excited. But there's nothing behind the spooky purple curtain, just a boring office with a desk, a dried-out fern, and a closet filled with empty hangers and priest costumes. They wait as the priest unlocks a tall wooden door that opens onto a green garden.

Cosimo squints as they walk across the sunny softness, past a wooden potting shed and down an alleyway that runs alongside a tennis court. There's tomato and zucchini plants, bean vines, and even caged chickens on some of the nearby balconies. He counts the windows looking onto the grass and decides to come back at night. They pass a locked shed stuffed with bicycles, and the crowd tut-tuts.

The priest leads everyone up a set of stone stairs at the back of an apartment building and unlocks a door. He must have keys to the whole city. Everyone squeezes into a long hallway. The priest waits by the frosted front doors for the whole group to press in. If someone comes down the curving staircase to check their mail, they'll be shocked to see so many people in their lobby. Cosimo catches his reflection in a mirror above the mailboxes and registers that he's visible. He wishes he knew how long the spells last. The priest wears tortoiseshell glasses and has a thick head of black hair and a scar through one eyebrow. He puts his finger to his lips and when they're all quiet, he steps out the front door with his head high, as if he's going to buy a newspaper. Has he forgotten he's wearing a dress? The door closes, and for three, four, five, six, seven seconds they all hold their breath again. The door opens; the priest smiles and says it's safe. They surge forward, but the priest clamps his hand onto Cosimo's shoulder to hold him in place while the others leave left and right, whispering about soldiers, lunch, and afternoon plans.

"Young man, were you sleeping in my confessional?"

"I was just resting."

"Where do you live?"

Cosi knows you're not supposed to lie to a priest. "I'm Cosimo and I live at uh, Via Malcontenti, above the enoteca."

"What brings you to my church, Cosimo?"

"I came in to get out of the heat."

The priest warns him that the Germans are rounding up boys of all ages for labour camps. He asks Cosi why his parents let him roam around the city. Mama had warned him not to trust anyone, but Cosimo is too hungry to think straight. "Mama and I came from Switzerland. We crossed at Ventimiglia." He says, "They kept her there. She told me to get on the train and now I'm here alone."

The priest replies, "I don't have much, but I'd be happy to share my lunch with you, Cosimo, and you can call me Lino."

Mama would never accept such an invitation. She hates the hold that priests have on people, but Cosimo is not about to turn down food. On the way back to the church, he asks about the bicycle shed. Lino says, "The Germans outlawed cycling after two men on bikes rode up to a restaurant and threw in grenades, injuring some German officers."

Cosimo feels like Lino is watching his reaction to the next part of the story. "The men on the bicycles were partisans." Hearing the word *partigiani* is like a jolt of electricity through Cosi's limbs. "There are partisans in the city? I thought they were only in the mountains."

Lino continues. "The cyclists didn't know the Germans had been moved to the back of the restaurant, to make room for a wedding party in the front. Tragically, the grenades killed members of the bride's family."

Back at the church, Lino opens a locked cupboard and takes out half a loaf of bread and a small block of cheese. He lays it on the table in front of Cosimo and says, "I need to find a bread knife. Excuse me."

Beads of moisture glisten on the rind. This is more food than Cosimo has seen in weeks. He watches Lino disappear down the hallway. He touches the crust. The cheese smell is making him dizzy. The back door is open onto the garden and he could easily outrun the priest, but something stops him. He takes his hand off the crust and waits. He hears the swish of Lino's robes. The priest is back without a knife. He seems surprised that Cosi is still at the table with the untouched bread and cheese. "I hope you don't mind, we're going to have to tear the bread with our hands," he says.

If he knew how hungry Cosimo was, he wouldn't ask.

Between chews, the crumbs of Cosimo's story trickle out. He tells the priest how his mother smuggled a note out of the Ventimiglia jail instructing him to get on the next train, how Umberto saved him from the soldiers, that Tia's apartment at Via Malcontenti is empty. He doesn't mention that he hides on rooftops during the day, sleeps in the cemetery at night, and steals food. Not knowing if priests believe in magic, he also says nothing about his spells. Nor does he say Papa is a partisan because Mama told him church people are Fascisti. When Cosimo is finished, Lino takes a long drink of water and looks past him into the sunny garden.

"I'll write to the priest in Ventimiglia and ask him to visit your mother. He'll tell her you're safe. The potting shed in the back is unlocked and a good place to sleep at night, but don't go there during the day. The neighbours might think you're a thief and call the police. If I have any extra food, I will leave it in there on the bench. Stay out of sight during the days. And please don't hide in the confessional again. The Germans no longer respect the sanctity of my church."

Cosimo doesn't know what sanctity means, but he's too afraid to go back to the church anyway. Lino says he'll tell the enoteca owner to keep an eye open for Lucia. Cosimo is so relieved to have help his eyes cloud with tears and then he feels stupid. Lino waits while he wipes his eyes with his sleeve. He takes a letter out of a hidden pocket and lays it on the table between them. "After dark, could you deliver this to the university for me? The office number is here on a separate piece of paper." He pushes a separate scrap of paper towards Cosimo. "Find the door with this number and put the letter under it, but don't be seen doing it. I'll let you know about your mother in a few days."

Cosi asks, "Can't you just use the phone?"

"The Germans control the exchange. I'll draw you a map of the university, to show you which building, but you must memorize it. You can get arrested for having a map in your pocket."

Cosi doesn't tell Lino about the silk map sewn into the lining of his rucksack. Lino tells Cosi it's best to go two hours after curfew when the streets are sure to be empty.

#970408
Gnr. A. Fisher
166th (Newfoundland) Field Regiment RA
Same place, November 27, 1943

Dear Min,

    I got your letter dated October 28th and your package with the razors finally found me. Thanks very much. I was getting pretty scruffy. It's been raining here without a pause for a solid 28 days! We're joking that we'll soon be getting pay from the Navy as well as the Army. Today the Kiwis got a ▬▬▬▬ ▬▬▬▬ *established. If the* ▬▬▬▬▬▬▬ *holds,* ▬▬▬▬▬▬ *will be tonight. Over the pounding rain, I can hear Vera Lynn singing "We'll Meet Again." It's on the Beeb and everyone has their radios turned up on bust. Men are singing along from their tents across the river plain. The Germans could hear it too if they'd only let up on their shelling.*

Before I walk into this, I want to tell you that another regret I've had about leaving St. Bon's. If I'd gotten the collar, I could've heard your confession and freed you from the guilt I suspect you still carry from that time you took me to town and left Garl behind. Where would we be now if the bishop had simply shown you grace? I wish I could've forgiven you, but I'm telling you now from this place, this precipice, which somehow also feels holy, that you should've been forgiven. The sins weren't yours.

If you're reading this, after the fact, and I didn't make it, my final wish is that you take my savings and pension and move to town without Skipper. I want you to know peace. You've always said, "for better or for worse," but he broke his vows to you the first time he raised his hand.

If I make it through, I plan to buy a little rowhouse over-looking the harbour with my pension. Something with a little garden. We'll live there together. Maybe over on the south side and you can watch the boats coming and going from the front window.

PS. Have you been able to check in on Anna? I'm still working on Garl. Thank you for writing every few days, it helps mark the time.

Some Sunny Day, Archibald

————————

A nearby blast sends a fountain of muck up over their pit. Arch is wiping grit off his binoculars when Rawlins hands him a reconnaissance panoramic of the German side. Several photos, stitched together, show major German gun emplacements. The names of villages, paths, and geographic features are handwritten on the emulsion. Rawlins points to a spot where two frames overlap and says that's where the bridgehead will be. He asks Arch if he can count on him and Garl to take the radio across and establish the forward operating post. Arch's face feels numb. He almost says he's not ready, but they've been here a month. If he's not ready now, he'll never be. At least it's him and Garl. He won't have to put up with Slade's shenanigans and they're both used to finding the path in the dark. Rawlins says they'll have two mules to haul the radio and the wires through the mud. He's got to be kidding. The only four-legged creatures Arch has any experience with are dogs and the wild bay ponies that spend their summers biting, fucking, and breaking down fences to eat cabbages and carrots. Look out if you're the first one to tether them after their lusty holidays. He can only hope the mules are less feisty. Studying the photo, he can see that they'll need to make it as far as the hamlet of Santa Maria to find some cover for the antenna. From the water's shifting edge up to there looks to be about three thousand steps. Twenty minutes at a run? Probably more like thirty-five or forty with the mud.

———

By now, Cosi knows which peak is Sole and which Bologna alleyway opens onto which side street and who leaves their courtyard unlocked. He's also keenly aware of where the German barracks are and which cafés they frequent. He's learned a lot from Lino's errands. It's not real partisan stuff, mainly just silly letters and small packages, but in exchange the priest leaves food in the shed and Cosimo is feeling stronger. His clothes, however, are filthy, and his scalp has started to itch. He asked Lino for soap, but the priest said there's not a scrap left in the city. He's heard Mama's stories about Spa Moo. If it wasn't for the German encampments in the city's south, he would walk to Sole, locate Nonno's, have a bath, find Papa, and together break his mother out of jail.

On one of Lino's missions, he spots something ahead in the gutter and his mouth waters. Cheese? How could Abbott and Costello have missed this? He pauses under a doorway to check the rooflines. No sign of his trackers. His stomach grumbles. It must've fallen out of a shopping basket or off a balcony. He darts forward and grabs it, but as soon as his fingertips make contact, he knows it's not cheese. Just a stupid bar of soap. He throws it back down in the gutter and walks on but changes his mind and doubles back. At least he can clean his hair.

Up to now, he's avoided Nettuno, but the fountain will be a great place for a quick bath. He takes off his shoes and tiptoes toward the piazza's mouth, straining to hear the sound of water. The fountain is silent and boxed in. There's a giant white butterfly painted on one side. Strange. He steps forward to size it up. What he thought was a butterfly is a detergent ad with three dancing women in white dresses mocking the soap-starved city. Mama would find this funny too. He hears a vehicle approaching from Rizzoli. He drops to the pavement and rolls under the nearest parked car, flattening himself onto the cobbles. Headlights sweep the base of the tower right where he was standing. Brakes squeal. Cosi feels lightheaded. With the motor still running, two soldiers get out, go around the back, and flip up the canvas. There are grunts, curse words, and a loud thud. The soldiers are only a few inches from Cosimo; their cigarette smoke excites the wrigglers at the nape of his neck. Cosi wants to scratch so badly, but he doesn't dare. He wishes he knew what the Germans were saying. One soldier laughs and coughs, while the other drops his butt and uses his heel to grind it into the cobbles. Boots disappear, lorry doors slam, and the vehicle reverses. Cosimo closes his eyes tight and scrunches up his mouth, hoping his invisibility spell is still working. The lights fade as the lorry drives back the way it came.

He crawls forward in the darkness to see what the Germans dropped and freezes. A man. Uniform? He waits for his eyes to adjust to the darkness. No. No uniform. Cosimo whispers, "They're gone, mister, you can get up." The man is still. Too still. His face has given up holding itself together. A red handkerchief is knotted too tightly around his neck. Stella Rossa? Papa? He studies the man's nose and hair. It's hard to tell. He stands and walks around him. This man is short and stocky, not tall like the picture Mama keeps in her wallet. The sky is brightening. He doesn't want to leave the man here, but he doesn't remember the spell for making someone else invisible and he's got to get back to the potting shed.

A couple of blocks from Lino's church, there's a trough with a horse-shaped water pump. Cosimo hesitates because the sky is already mauve, but he might just have enough time to wash his hair and top half. The bottom half will have to wait. When the water hits the marble trough, it's going to be loud. All the shutters above him are still closed. He calculates the risk. Only two pumps. One to wet his hair and one to rinse. He drops his cardigan and shirt and sticks his head underneath the horse's mouth. He pumps. The cold water sends shivers down his neck and back. He hopes the lice are as shocked as he is. He attacks the crawlies with the soap and his fingers. His scalp burns. It must be lye. Good! That should kill the buggers. He keeps his eyes jammed shut and stops scrubbing now and then to listen for vehicles. Hearing nothing, he pumps again to rinse. Not quite. He pumps the third time letting the water cascade over his head and shoulders before flicking it out of his hair. His eyes clenched shut he reaches out for his shirt. His hand pats bare sidewalk and his eyes fly open. His rucksack! He hears the sound of feet slapping cobblestones and turns in time to see Abbott and Costello disappear down an alley with his bag. Cosimo grabs his sweater and runs hard after them. This is no stupid game. One of Lino's packages and his silk map are in that sack. He can't yell out to them because the curfew is still on, and he doesn't know their real names anyway. His chest burns and he's gasping for air when a sharp pain stabs his foot. The street and buildings tilt.

"Boy! Are you alive?" An old woman pokes at Cosimo with a broom. He curls into a ball, his ankle and the foot Buley ran over throbbing.

She hisses, "The Germans use this street, get up."

People walking to work are giving him funny looks. He's shirtless and filthy and lying in the middle of the road. There are open windows and shutters all around. He doesn't know where he is.

"I'm so hungry."

"We're all hungry. Get up and go."

He breaks Lino's rule and goes to the shed even though it is mid-morning. When he opens the door, he jumps back. His missing rucksack is there on the dirt floor with a note pinned to the top asking him to come to confession. Pencils, marbles, shirt, and his bread crust stash are still there, but the stitching holding the silk lining in place has been loosened and the map is gone. He dumps everything out. The map and Lino's package are missing. His heart sinks. When he enters the confessional, Lino slides open the little window in the wall. "Cosimo, I am relieved you're safe. What happened?"

"I'm sorry. I found some soap and stopped to wash. When my eyes were closed some boys stole my stuff."

Lino's chair creaks. "Luckily, I know those boys. Their families. I don't want to scare you, but had my package fallen into German hands, it would've meant my imprisonment or maybe even execution. The Germans are threatening to kill ten civilians for every partisan action."

Cosimo whispers, "Are we partisans?"

Lino clears his throat. "We're just helping my parishioners."

"Last night, two Germans left a man in Nettuno, I think he was a partisan," says Cosimo.

Lino blesses himself through the screen. "I've heard. He was a young father, with three children. Stella Rossa."

Stella Rossa! Finally! Cosimo says, "My father is also Stella Rossa. His name is Paulo Capponi."

There's a long silence on the other side of the confessional. Lino asks, "Is the map for him? For Volpe?"

"My mother helped make those maps. In England."

A longer pause. "Does she work for the British?"

"She says she works for the worms," Cosimo says. "The woman who owned the silk farm, Lady Zoe, she got us papers. I don't know why Mama's didn't work at the border. That's why she's in jail."

"I have the map in safe keeping. You could be shot for having that," says Lino.

Panic grips Cosi's chest. "Mama has maps in the heels of her shoes."

chapter 11

SANGRO

Tombstone doesn't look up when I say the rain has stopped. He's too wet to know the difference. Thousands of Allied faces squint up at the parting clouds, their hearts thumping, their fingers on triggers, waiting for the agreed-upon signal. The German friggers must also know what's coming. They're sending up barrage balloons. Tombstone shakes his head.

"No wait. Listen," I say.

The cheering starts somewhere down the line as four B-24s slice through the dome of grey. It's on. It's frigging on. Like dropping lit matchbooks on an anthill, the Fossacesia Ridge ignites. Five hundred and ninety-eight Allied gun pits jump to life and with an ungodly whoosh the valley quakes. Gunpowder stings my sinuses and the back of my throat. Blast waves rumble my sternum. They told us poison gas smells like geraniums and garlic, but all I smell is gasoline. Screams and flames. Gun pits along the line are taking direct hits and men run in all directions. Tombstone bellows down the line for more shells. I turn my head to find Garl. My eyes take a second to focus. The racket is impenetrable. Rolling overlapping claps of thunder, waves spitting up beach rocks as storm surges remake the shore, the thuds of thousands of axes falling, windows blowing out, doors hitting walls, church bells falling from spires. Is it the wall of noise that weighs down my legs and slows my progress away from the pit? My brain is trying to make sense of the rhythm in the explosions, only then can I lift my hand to give Garl the signal. We move together, but out of step, towards the bridgehead. He slaps his mule's arse, gets kicked, and shrieks, "Jesus, you saucy cretin!"

"Garl, they're not used to all this r-ra-racket," I say.

"You want me to be gentle with all of Germany firing at us?"

I tug on the radio's webbing. "Come on now, Missy, stay calm."

Garl yells, "You haven't seen its dong?"

"Okay then, B-Buddy. C'mon, B-B-Buddy." The mule can't hear me anyway.

We edge towards the bridgehead with a unit of Gurkhas. Buddy's wobbling with the weight of the radio. German flares light the stage for murder. Garl's leg is jumping. Both of us miss the relative safety of Random Island. He lurches ahead and I grab the back of his uniform. "Hold up! Only mo-move between f-fla-flares." He shakes me off. When the light fades, the Gurkhas sprint forward, and Garl and his mule run alongside. I give Buddy a decisive yank, but he refuses to step onto the swaying decking. I pull again and the animal pulls back. More flares and the din is even more terrific. I put my forehead on Buddy's and inhale through my nose, but this seems to frighten him more and he skitters sideways. "C'mon, Buddy. If we stay here, we're gonna get shot."

The twack twack of Spandaus and the German anti-aircraft barrage rumble against the cloud cover and echo off the mountains. I try pushing the mule's rump, but he sits. Now we're holding up traffic. When the flares open up the sky, the bridge is still. Fade to black, hundreds surge forward. Screams of pain, and sniper bullets pinging metal mix with COs bawling out orders. No one can make any sense of what they're supposed to be at. Kiwis, Indians, Scots, and Brits on the move. It's a flickering film projector of madness.

I lead Buddy down to the riverbank hoping he will be keener to cross the bridge once his hooves feel the frigid water. Steel splinters from the anti-aircraft shells pepper the surface. The river smells like blood, but the animal drinks anyway. I lead him back up to the bridge, peer into his woeful eyes and gently tug the reins. No. Go. Garl is long gone. If I don't get the radio across, there'll be no communication with the guns to cover the Gurkhas. I start unpacking the waterproofed radio. An Indian soldier runs up. "Hello, sir. What are you doing?"

"He won't cross. I'm going to carry the radio," I say as bullets whizz over our heads. He introduces himself as Bishnu. I continue loosening the gritty strap.

"Stop sir," he yells. "I'll take the ass across. Meet us on the other side."

Buddy acquiesces to Bishnu immediately. I wait for the light to fade and copy from one heaving pontoon to another as if crossing Winterton harbour on the ice. On their side, I grab a tree root for balance and flatten against enemy earth. Cold metal. Finger. Tip. Breath catches. Blood pumping ceases. Eyes close. Slow. Slow. I lift my hand away. Time ticks. Spared? Bishnu and Buddy emerge from the river and I trip forward to warn Bishnu about mines. We walk the ribboned tightrope of a trail. The sappers have cleared the way, piling unexploded mines and shells in little pyramids. We've all been warned not to touch anything, not even bodies. The Germans mine the dead, even their own. Bishnu nods goodbye and sprints up the middle of the Mozzagrogna road. Straight into the firefight. I want to yell out, "Take care!" but that would tip off snipers. We continue on, picking our way to Santa Maria. Buddy and I are ducking our heads to avoid shells and tracers crackling in the air above us. I step only on ground that is undisturbed and hope the mule is doing the same or it's curtains for us both. Somehow, we make it to the meeting place. Garl is crouched with his back against a tin shed. "Where the fuck were you?"

"Buddy wouldn't c-c-cross."

"You were hoping I'd go ahead and get shot."

"Why would you sssay that? The ma-mu-mule wouldn't go. A Gurkha got it across." I recognize his skittishness. He wants to get the hell out of here.

Garl stands. "I got the lines strung up. Let's hook up the radio."

I point at a nearby farmhouse, but he shakes his head. "That's out. An Eye-tie told me there's Tedeschi."

"If that's the case, we can't stay here. We gotta m-mo-move!"

Garl steps on my heels as we lead the mules into a separate walled yard well above the farmhouse. I ask him to tie the animals off far away while I connect the radio. He grumbles about chain of command but does what he's told. I carry the radio into a large, smelly henhouse. Shells aimed at Mozzagrogna rip through the clouds. I rig up the antenna on a nearby cactus and am plucking needles out of my sleeve when Garl returns and says, "Alright, let's get going."

"Why? Wh-what did you see?"

"Nothing. We got the goddamned radio over. Let's go."

"We've got to c-contact HQ and then we should probably sussss out the f-f-farmhouse. It might be our first target."

"Why ask for trouble?"

"If they're in there, they're damn well shooting at our g-g-guys crossing the b-bridge."

Garl is thrumming with nerves as I make contact with Rawlins and tell him that we may have found a nest of Germans. When I take off the earpiece, he's spitting mad. "Arch, you're a gunner. I'm an officer, and I'm not having anything to do with that farmhouse."

I've seen soldiers do strange things when they're afraid. I saw it in Algeria and even in training, but you never deny a fellow soldier backup. "G-Garl, I need your help. Just come with m-m-me."

He shakes his head. "What difference will it make to this shit show?"

"I marvel at your ability to wa-ah-w-walk away from responsibility."

I know I shouldn't get into it here, but the tension of waiting for the battle and trying to get the mule across the bridge has burst something open. He stares me down.

"Fuck off. I'm not the father. I told you. She's lying."

As calmly as I can, I say, "Anna T-Tucker is not the lying type. You've been ignoring her le-letters."

The earth shakes. "I'm the commanding officer here. We've done what we came to do. Let's go," he hisses.

"I don't care if you're the P-P-Pope, I'm going to check out the farmhouse. If you're too scared to come with me, stay here and ca-ca-call in this coop, so we don't get ssshelled."

I duck out between flares, scrambling on elbows and my belly across the yard. My tongue tastes of copper. What's the point of forcing him to acknowledge he's the father? He'd only make her miserable anyway. I listen for changes in the rhythm of the shelling. Close to the farmhouse, I roll across the bumpy earth. Thank God the shutters are closed. My left shoulder and hip are pressed to the wall just under a windowsill. I calm my nerves by thinking of the ocean lapping against the wharf. Lying on my belly on the sun-warmed wood, peeking out over the edge with fishing line knotted onto an alder branch. Staying still until the tomcods swim out of the shadows and nibble my bait. An ammo belt clatters to the floor. "Scheisse!"

Germans! It is considerably harder to roll away from the house. The gravel irritates the cactus punctures in my upper arm. When I'm far enough away, I run at a crouch, pausing for darkness before re-entering the henhouse.

"Germans. C-Call it in," I say.

"No need. They called a retreat," says Garl.

"Already?" There's no change in the cadence of the battle. "Did they say that clearly? Use the words f-f-full retreat?" I ask.

Garl doesn't answer. He hands me the receiver and steps outside. I know he's running back to Random Island. I call in the farmhouse and in case Garl was spotted flying the coop, I lug the heavy radio out into a field of thick sugarcane and set it up again behind a hip-high stone wall. I lie in the cane with the receiver pressed to my ear. Some of the Gurkhas made it as far as Mozzagrogna, but the mud is preventing tanks from reaching them for backup. A shell explodes near the farmhouse. A miss. Shit. I release the safety on my pistol in case the Germans start running my way. Two full minutes pass before the second shell makes contact. Rubble, stone, flames, and dust shoot every which way as the second floor collapses inward, flattening the first. I sit up and adjust my binocs. Haloed in fire and smoke, one German drags another out of the burning debris and collapses. No movement. Their bodies are soon consumed by the flames.

A few hours later, I'm relieved and pick my way back to the bridge with Garl's mule and Buddy. I'm surprised to see Bishnu with a dagger in his mouth, flattened against the wall of a mill. I bazz some stones his way to warn him that shells are radioed in, but he doesn't budge. Then I wave my arms and run towards him, tapping my watch to indicate there's a shell coming. He puts the blade back in his sheath, takes Buddy's reins, and together we take cover in a rickety arbour dug into the hillside. The arbour is like a movie set. Four chairs and a table with a checkered tablecloth. Two bread slices soak in olive oil. Empty birdcages hang from the grape vines above our heads. Bishnu grabs one slice and I eat the other. It tastes like dust and cordite. "How far did you get?"

"Mozzagrogna. For a small village, there are a lot of Germans. I got seven in one place."

"Seven Germans by yourself?" I ask.

"I had help. A comrade shot up a wine vat where an officer was hiding," he says with a grin. "When the wine squirted out of the holes, it was like a Donald Duck cartoon."

A shell hits the mill and the explosion lights up a concrete pillbox. An anti-tank gun is firing on the Mozzagrogna road from the keyhole. Between us and three, maybe four Germans, there's only the delicate vines of the arbour and a floppy, ancient cactus. When one of the Krauts comes out for a piss, we'll be shot. I tie the mules on as far away as I can. When I come back, Bishnu is already crawling on his belly. I follow. When we're sitting with our backs against the pillbox outer wall, I hold up two fingers. Bishnu holds up three. He places his dagger between his teeth and motions that he's going to cut the Germans' throats. The racket from the armour-piercing shells rocketing out of the keyhole just above our heads makes it impossible to argue. He directs me to crawl back to the arbour and create a distraction. His plan is madness, but there's no way to tell him I'd rather wait for another option. Bishnu holds up ten fingers and then nine, eight. I scurry back to the arbour with his countdown in my head. At one, I muster my best St. Bon's choir voice. "*There was . . . birch rinds, tar twines, cherry wine, and turpentine . . . Jowls and cavalances.*"

The Germans stop shooting. "*Ginger beer and*"—a cat or a rat jumps on my back—"*TEA!*" My heart stutters and skips as claws sink through the wool of my overcoat and pierce the skin of my shoulder blades. The hag? I must be dead. I try to shake the thing off. A bat? Fear roars in my skull. If I get through this day, I'll marry Anna. No one need know the truth. Min can care for the baby and, as a married woman, Anna will be able to teach. I cock my pistol and run to the pillbox, flattening myself under the keyhole. The German gun is dead quiet. Do I wait for a sign? What was the sign? The weight of my coat lifts off my back and I look up. Bishnu has one arm out of the keyhole, and has a monkey wrapped around his hand. "Gentle Jesus! Where did that come from?"

"That, sir, is the proverbial monkey on your back!"

The pillbox walls and floor are sprayed with blood. He was right. Three. Two are splayed on their backs, their blueing necks slit like cod bellies. The third, a young officer, is slumped between his two dead friends. Is he knocked out? The monkey looks at the scene, at Bishnu, and reaches out to me like a baby. It leaps over the gore and runs down my arm to hide in my hip pocket.

"Is the third guy alive?" I ask.

Bishnu shrugs. "When he comes to, he'll look at his two comrades and hopefully, that will frighten him to death."

I'm about to tell him it's not a great plan when an Allied shell slams into the hillside. The pillbox must be registered. "Bishnu, c'mon!"

He hands me a ceremonial Nazi sword. "You do the honours."

Time stops. This simple, brutal thing. Its weight. Silver oak leaves, enamel swastika. I don't want to be Skipper. "I can't," I say.

Bishnu is flabbergasted. "Then you will die here, sir. Isn't it your bible that says kill or be killed?"

"No, no, I think that wassss J-J-Jack Lon-London."

A flash comes in through the keyhole. Closer than the last one. The air is charged with danger. Bishnu vaults through the door and I try to follow, but my foot is caught. I look down. The young officer has come to and he's holding onto my boot with both hands. I shake my leg as hard as I can, but he won't let go. Without a trace of an accent, he recites, "Kill or be killed, eat or be eaten, that was the law; and this mandate, down and out of the depths of time he obeyed." I would've given him an A for that, but don't want to be impressed. The sword handle slips in my sweaty palm. I need him to be a monster. I conjure Tobin. But even that. I can't. All this time, I've been convinced I can outwit death by following orders, calculating trajectories, and inventing. Now when I must, I can't. Even to save myself. I point the blade at his face. The gaff tip pricking Skipper's neck. "Let g-g-go and we'll b-bo-both live," I scream. The shells' rhythm shifts. Silence? She's gonna hit any second. His arms are tight around my thigh. I shudder. A swell of energy. Now? "Don't you w-wa-want to live?" I bellow.

His hand grazes my erection. He recoils. "Faggot!" He releases my leg. Off balance, the sword drops. He grabs it, makes a half-hearted lunge, and suddenly aware of the air crackling with TNT, rockets out the door. I follow, but the opening blows apart and time splinters into grit, shrapnel, gas, and dirt. Then it flames out and there is just dust and darkness. The weight of an ocean crushing my chest. Plummeting. The flash of the humpback's tail. My mouth opens and closes with the gulls. My ears clang. Bishnu? His arm loops into mine. He's pulling. Lifting. Rocks and cactus chunks pelt our backs. He drags me through the arbour, tripping over broken chair legs, but stumbling forward. We fly over the mined paths and cross back over the Kiwi bridge. My eyes burn and oily grit sands my windpipe. Running, tripping, and skidding, we collapse in the grey muck of the river. We're on the Allied side. My ears are shagged, the sky above us is still flashing with explosions and tracer dots and dashes. Bishnu's mouth is moving. A crack from a nearby artillery pit clears one ear. Bishnu is laughing. He rolls onto his side and extracts the still bloody sword from his coat. I would run if I could.

Back in our pit, Tombstone lifts me off his feet in a bear hug and I yell, "Watch out for the monkey!"

"Jesus, Arch, did you get a head wound?" he asks.

I search my coat for the creature. I'm sure I felt its little heart drumming against my side as we ran for the bridge. It grabs tight onto my thumb and when I take it out, its fur is dusted in grit. How the hell did it survive? It closes its eyes as I gently blow off the dust. Then it turns and bares its teeth at Slade.

"Charming! What in the name of God is that?" he asks.

"I'm going to call it Sangro."

Water, mud, and shell splinters slice into the sandbags and ping off the stacked ammo. The monkey puts its hands over its ears and crawls back into my pocket. Our gun is glowing, the chamber so hot paint is flaking off. Slade slams another shell in. "We got that ragged arse Garl on ammo duty for the rest of the night. There'll be no rest for split fish!"

I'm the only one not shocked by Garl's retreat. "It was his first time under fire," I say, hoping they'll forgive him. Keeping to myself the knowledge that running is what he does. How he survives.

Later that night, when the attack is waning and everyone's nerves are more settled, the crew feeds Sangro milk and peanuts and we share a demijohn of local plonk. Raising tin cups they cheer my safe return. The wine tastes like death. Tombstone, Slade, and the rest want to know what I saw. I try to talk but my jaw feels tight. Everything I want to say would sound boastful or melodramatic. So, I say little. I'm disgusted at myself. At what happened in that moment of power over another. The monkey hops across the pit and sits against my chest nibbling peanuts. It somehow keeps me from plunging deeper.

———

#970408
Gnr. A. Fisher
166th (Newfoundland) Field Regiment RA
▇▇▇▇▇▇ *December 2, 1943*

Dear Min,

    It happened. The infernal rain stopped as fast as it started, and we got across. I came through ok. Now the river valley is choking with smoke from Hindu funeral pyres. The Indians burn their dead, which is practical I suppose, but still seems wrong. I spose the censors will let me tell you we're attached to the 8th Indian Infantry. A soldier named Bishnu saved my life, twice. If we were all as brave as him, the war would've been over years ago. He carries a dagger in his teeth, just like the pirates in the Treasure Island book we used to read. This war is no different than the columns in the merchant's book. It's all about numbers. Who has the most shells, the most trucks, petrol, ammo, food, and the most expendable men. Who can keep going, keep dying and keep shelling? Lines on maps can never represent what we've been up against. Especially in these past few days. Why couldn't the politicians have figured this out before it got to this?

Forgive me, I'm tired and a little heartsick. We lost a couple of Newfoundlanders, but by the looks of the bodies being collected, we were damn lucky. Thousands perished in this valley. Say a prayer for the two who died, I doubt they'll get written up anywhere, they're just fishermen's sons, not men set to inherit fish plants or run Water Street stores. It's impossible to say where or even how they died. Sometime in the last few days, somewhere in the mud and noise. Somehow. In the mess this morning, a body, in canvas, was brought in and a soldier sitting next to me said, "There goes one of the lucky ones." When he said those words, he didn't know the body was his brother's and when he was told, he fainted. Garl did fine, you'd be proud of him. I'll finish this after supper.

It's been a few days; I needed the time to get past all my jumbled feelings. I sent a Marconi telegraph to Anna just after the battle asking her to marry me. If she's married, she'll be able to finish her course and teach, and the child will have us as a family. You and me. Her parents will surely agree to it as they know me. Garl is not coming around, and even if he did, what kind of life would she have with someone who is always taking off? You'll soon have a little grandchild to read to. So, we'll be four counting the little one—in our house overlooking the harbour.

Ask Tobin for a marriage licence when he comes for mass. Mail it to me and I'll sign and send it onto Anna for her signature. When I'm home on leave, hopefully in the new year, I'll have him bless the union. If the old coot refuses, tell him we'll go to the Sally Anns.

Love, Arch

chapter 12

BOOTS

Barbara's front wheel catches a tram rut. Her bike wobbles violently as she squeezes the brakes trying to wrestle back control. It's been months since her Sicily scoop and she's seen Doran a few times, but hasn't had the nerve to bring up her dream. Soon, he'll hear that she applied to the Canadian High Commission for a press pass and he won't be happy. Two steps inside the door of the Red Hart pub, Patsy hands her a beer. "Come and meet my pilot buddy, Lindsay." A jolly brunette with her very own Liberator for delivering mail and supplies, Lindsay asks Barbara about the Leitz hanging off her shoulder. "Officially, I'm an archivist but I freelance for magazines and newspapers. Pictures of life here in London, soldiers on leave, nights in the bomb shelters."

"Can you take our photo? My whole crew?"

————

Caroline struggles out of The Doghouse on Duckworth with a huge bag of dog food. She's almost at her car when a book in the window at Elaine's Books catches her eye. *Gunners World War II: 166th*

(Newfoundland) Field Regiment Royal Artillery. There's a twenty-five-pound artillery gun, just like the one Pop and Arch used in the war, on the cover. Six months ago, she wouldn't have been able to name this weapon. She carries the bag of dog food inside and asks to see the book. As soon as she flips it open, she knows she's going to buy it. *Gunners* is chock-a-block with soldiers' snapshots. There are shots from training in England and Scotland, tidy lines of tents in the sands of North Africa, unidentified Italian hamlets, Cassino, and a large section from their winter in the Apennines. Chummy shots building gun pits, eating on the run, makeshift showers in olive groves, uniforms frozen stiff on clotheslines, swimming holes, skiing, pushing quads out of knee-deep muck. Snowball fights. Mule trains in the snow. Paper crowns at Christmas dinner. Kicking back in gondolas and eating in cafés. It hadn't occurred to her until now that many of the men would have had their own cameras. These pictures tell the stories she's been craving. Images of day-to-day life, glimpses of what they did when they weren't shooting, proof they found some joy and friendship even in war. Did they send these snaps home so their families would worry less? Or did they keep rolls of film and bring them home at the end to avoid the censors? There are few cutlines or credits and most images are grainy, but she buys the book anyway and rushes home to search for Pop and Arch.

———————

Lindsay's crew jumbles into position as Barbara frames the shot to include the pub's missing top half. It was recently blown off by a V-1, making the Hart even more popular with regulars, convinced lightning won't strike twice. On their way back inside, some guy pats Lindsay's backside and gets a sharp elbow in the ribs. Barbara offers to buy her a beer. Doran is at the bar with his arm around a young civilian woman.

"I'll have soda water. Flying tomorrow," Lindsay says.

"Are you going to Italy?" Barbara blurts out. "I need to get to Italy."

"Ha! So does everyone."

"Just for a day or two. A few hours really."

"Is this a Canadian Army–approved operation, Barbara, or something more romantic?"

Barbara blushes. "It's official. I'll get approval from my CO right now."

"If you can manage that, I'll make room. We're headed to Foggia at dawn."

Doran is draping a raglan over his date's shoulders when Barbara catches up with him. He won't like to be interrupted, but if she doesn't ask him now, she'll lose her nerve. "Sir, excuse me. I need your permission for something."

He whispers in the young woman's ear, and she walks outside to wait. His smile is tight when he turns to Barbara. "What can I do for you, Sergeant Kerr?"

"Sir, I'd like permission to fly to Italy tomorrow."

"How much have you had to drink?" he asks.

"Just a pint, sir. the guys can't work. The big battle at the Sangro happened and they had no way to document it."

"There'll be other big battles."

"Yes, sir, but they won't have film for those either."

"Okay, that's enough, Kerr, it's getting late. We'll send film the way we've always done."

"About that, sir, in the past three months I've recorded twenty-seven instances where our maple syrup film has gone missing. I suspect British couriers are selling it back to the black market or sending it directly to BBC cameramen."

His face reddens. "They wouldn't dare!"

"Our guys have seen Canadian film passed around by British shooters and they've bought our film from marketeers in Italy."

"How do you know that?" he demands.

"They write me letters with their dope sheets. Sir, I've filled a duffel. If I bring it to them in person, they'll be able to work for the next six months."

"It's always difficult to get supplies to the front, Kerr."

She appeals to his ego. "Yes, you're right, sir. And yet despite that, we're winning . . . the newsreel war. Canada had the Italy scoop, and our footage is preferred by Pathé, News of the World, and Gaumont. The British archivists told me their superiors complain all the time that the Canadians get the most exciting footage. And sir, the Americans sometimes borrow our shots to add more oomph to their own reels."

"Alright, Sergeant, you can stop buttering me up."

She interrupts him. "There's an ATA mail plane leaving tomorrow from Duxford. I've been chatting with the pilot. She . . . they can take me."

He takes a long draw from his cigarillo. She promises to stay at Foggia and have one of their guys come and pick up the duffel. Doran turns and looks out the window. It's drizzling and his friend folds her arms. He turns back to Barbara. "Women are not permitted at the front," he says.

"Yes, sir, I know that."

"The American women face court martial if found at the front."

She nods. "Yes, sir, I've heard that."

Doran's date is tapping her foot. "Okay, okay," he relents. "Do not leave Foggia, Kerr. You hear me? If you're not back in a week, I'll post your job."

———————

Black smoke from Hindu funeral pyres obscures the first sunlight in over a month. Arch rolls up the window, not wanting to breathe in the ash. Sangro sits on Arch's shoulder holding its tail and staring straight ahead. Tombstone grips the steering wheel. Even Slade is quiet. A whistle blows. The infantry in front of their truck all lift their right legs and put them down. Their left. Again. Again. Again. Their steps refill the vacuum of time lost to the battle. Boots hit the earth and become seconds, seconds become minutes, minutes become hours, and hours become days and nights. Their energy is creating the future. The truck in front of them stops on the new bridgehead opposite Paglieta. Sappers have laid logs in the mud to give vehicles enough traction to get up onto the bridge, but the logs are already slimy. A mule has skittered off and is drowning, twisting to keep its head above the mire. The animal is making a pitiful noise. Tombstone is muttering and his leg is bouncing. He asks Arch for his pistol. He wants to put the animal out of its misery.

––––––––––

Barbara meets Lindsay on the tarmac and warns her that her duffel is stuffed with highly flammable film. Lindsay grins and says, "We're carrying petrol, oil, explosives, belted ammo, and oxygen, it will just add to the pyrotechnics if we're shot down." Barbara was so focused on the film; she hadn't thought much about the danger of flying over occupied Europe.

"I've got to complete my checklist. Corporal Schweriner here will give you a parachute lesson," Lindsay says. Schweriner helps Barbara into a Mae West with a parachute already looped over the shoulders. He zips her up and tells her what to pull and what not to pull. And how to fall. She asks him if the parachute will still work if she's holding her heavy duffel. He tells her she won't care about the film if she has to use the chute.

"You're obviously not a photographer," she says.

Barbara has seen so many photos of USO girls looking glamorous in their Mae Wests. Why does she feel like a stuffed sausage with a lambswool collar? She asks for the next size up and offers to take the crew's picture when they land in Foggia. She once considered group shots a waste of film, but now understands them as currency: payback for rides, a bed, a meal, and a Mae West that fits. In the plane, Schweriner shows her where they've removed a couple of bombs to make room for her and all the mailbags.

"My very own metal tube with a trapdoor, you shouldn't have," she says.

Lindsay calls out from the cockpit. "We'll be staying high to avoid enemy fire and if you're lucky, Barbara, you'll see the sunrise over the Alps. Now boys, Sergeant Kerr is our guest, and we're cooped up in this bird for the night; if you could keep the dirty jokes to a minimum, that would be preferable."

Barbara wiggles into place, grateful that Lindsay warned her to ditch her skirt and wear pants. They gain altitude quickly and despite the deafening drone of the engines, she drifts off and misses the channel and most of France. When she wakes up, cold is seeping through the letters underneath her. Her parachute and Mae West have shimmied loose. She struggles to get the straps back in place. Sun rays glint off rocky peaks dusted with mauve and pink snow. She asks Schweriner, "The Alps?"

"Yes, ma'am, that's Italy's border with Switzerland."

She desperately wants to pee but there's no way she's squatting on the shared Elsen bucket in front of the crew. "How far to Foggia?"

Lindsay says, "About an hour. We're going to fly a little lower as we cross the German line in the Apennines. We've got orders to take some photos of our own, Barbara." The Lancaster pierces a towering cloud and the fuselage shudders and creaks. Barbara closes her eyes and tries to calm her bladder.

———

The Canadians are pushing north for Ortona and then onto Pescara. What's left of the Kiwis are heading west to Orsogna. The 166th is following the Indians northwest to Lanciano, but for now they're stalled. Eventually the reason for the delay comes into view. A mule train is coming across the bridge towards them loaded with the dead. Tombstone looks the other way. "Imagine digging them out, finding their parts, sorting, wrapping, tagging, and planting them until a proper cemetery can be sorted out."

Garl jumps out of the lorry ahead of them and runs past the dead to the other side of the bridge. He picks his way down to the valley floor where sappers are bulldozing debris. The valley has gone from battle to mass funerals and is now a construction site. Tombstone rolls down his window to get a better look at what Garl is up to. "If he's not careful, he's going to get bulldozed."

Garl sticks his hands into the slime up to his elbows to work at something under the surface. He extracts it and shakes the muck off. A boot. He reaches back in and repeats the movements until he has a pair. He knocks the soles together, ties the laces, and slings them over his shoulder. Tombstone rolls up the window. "Your brother just took the boots off a body."

Slade is incredulous. "G'won! He did not!"

Vehicles rumble to life and Garl's ride leaves the bridge. He steps onto the decking as their lorry crosses and he jogs alongside, knocking on the passenger window. Arch knows Tombstone and Slade are still poisoned with Garl's dereliction of duties, but says, "We're going to have to let him in, there's room." Tombstone curses as the convoy pauses long enough to give Garl a chance to open the door and lift himself into the cab. He shuffles them all over with his hip, oblivious to everyone's sour mood. He points at the monkey dozing on Arch's shoulder. "I got lice from that thing."

"Its name is Sangro, and it does not have lice," says Arch.

"Well, I didn't get lice from Slade," says Garl. "Then again, maybe I did."

Tombstone scratches. "We all got lice. It comes with the territory."

Arch doesn't tell them that the monkey picks his hair and collar clean and provides a lot of relief.

Slade clears his throat. "A little shoe shopping there, Garl?"

"Spruce owed me from cards and he can hardly pay up now."

Arch says, "That was Spruce?"

"His shoulder patch was sticking out of the mud. I was lucky to get to him before the bulldozer. We should tell Rawlins, I s'pose. He'll want to know where he ended up."

Tombstone's face is as red as the hair sticking out of his collar. "You stole boots off one of ours?"

Garl brushes the caked mud off his pant legs. "Jeez, he's not going to need them." They sit in silence. Garl reveals that he'd left his jacket on Rawlins's bed so that he'd also get infested. He figures if the CO is scratching, he'll send them all to get de-loused.

At Lanciano, when Garl lopes off to join his own crew, Tombstone turns to Arch. "That is the last time we give your brother a lift."

———

Barbara has been sitting in the Foggia mess for three days listening in on conversations in hopes someone mentions a Canadian unit. A Scottish soldier tells her the awful coffee is made from ground lupin seeds. Everyone here is talking about the big battle at the Sangro and how the fighting is headed north. Somehow, she's got to get the film to the Canadians before Lindsay's return flight in two days. A group of Kiwi drivers are complaining over their powdered eggs, about an upcoming Monty photo op. "He's no better than a small-town mayor cutting a ribbon to get his maw in the newspapers."

This is her chance. Barbara slides down the bench and chats up a Kiwi private named Vince who offers her a lift. He's delivering the ribbon and some other supplies to Montgomery's caravans at Paglieta and doesn't ask to see her non-existent press pass. He says, "It's a wicked road. You might have to help me push." The men watch her reaction. She says, "I grew up pushing our logging sled out of snowbanks. I can certainly push your lorry out of a little mud."

————————

Lino has left a note under a tomato summoning Cosimo. When Cosi closes the door and kneels, the window slides open and the priest whispers, "We were able to get your mother moved here. She's in the prison near Piazza San Giovanni in Monte."

Cosi's heart leaps. "Can I see her?"

"It's not safe for you, but priests can visit. There's paper on your kneeler. Write her a note—write something so she'll know it's you."

Tears blister the paper and Cosimo's hand trembles. What should he say? That he's hungry? She's probably hungrier. He asks, "Can you bring her some cheese, Lino?"

"I'll try. Don't say anything about the shed, or me, in case the letter is confiscated."

He writes, *Mama, I am dreaming of Spa Moo. Tia is not here, but the spells are keeping me safe. Amore, Cosi*

"Father, please ask her if I should wait or go to Sole alone."

"I'm afraid I have some news about that," says Lino.

Cosimo's holds his breath.

"I don't know how to tell you this. So, I'm just going to say it. Your father. Paolo. He's dead."

The stone floor of the confessional falls away. "How? How do you know?"

Cosi hates the sound of his squeaky little boy voice.

Lino says, "I sent a message to ask for your safe passage to Sole and word came back that your father died about a year ago in an ambush. He died defending our freedom. If you wish, we can pray for him."

Cosimo doesn't want to tell the priest that he and his mother never pray. He nods and Lino launches into it. The first words are

"Our father." Nothing after that makes any sense, but the rhythm helps Cosi feel a little calmer. He doesn't believe his father is dead. Wouldn't he know? Wouldn't he feel it? When Lino is finished, he waits for Cosi to stop sniffling and whispers there'll be something soon. A mission he can help with.

———

Arch, Tombstone, and Slade catch up with their Indian unit at Lanciano's main square. Soldiers ring a sunken fountain of stone faces. Water pours out of pursed lips. The mayor unfurls Italian and Indian flags and thanks them. Someone in the crowd steps forward and, shouting over the mayor, says they should be recognizing the bravery of the locals who attacked the Germans on their own. Before he is hustled away, he says Montgomery's delays meant the Germans had time to find the resisters and execute them. Arch watches several women scrubbing laundry in the fountain. They keep their backs to the soldiers and their heads bent to the mossy Roman faces.

After the ceremony they drive northwest. Sunrays pierce through clouds making the sky look like an altar painting. Arch swallows surges of emotion. What an idiot he has been, thinking that he could become a soldier. The hair on the back of his neck has been standing on end since the battle. He feels out of step and is glad to be driving. It gives him something to do with his hands. Would Garl be that quick to take his, Tombstone's, or Slade's boots? Tombstone fidgets next to him. Arch knows if he cries, it will be a huge relief, but it might break the big man. Out loud, Tombstone calculates the time difference and says he'd be coming in from work about now and his missus would be cutting up onions or peeling carrots for a bit of stew while the older girls help the younger kids with their lessons. Arch has no idea what Anna might be doing or where she is. He wonders if Garl has written her.

———

Cosimo goes to an outdoor market a few nights after the confessional to wait for a delivery. He slinks into the shadows, annoyed with Lino because he doesn't know who he's meeting or why he's here in this unfamiliar neighbourhood. Two cats fight nearby. His lids are heavy. He sits behind a cart, dropping into a fitful sleep and dreams about his mother serving him and Papa lasagna Bolognese. His bad foot cramps. Ow! He wakes to a German officer and two Fascist policemen standing over him. The officer nudges his bad foot again and Cosimo closes his eyes tight against the painful nightmare. One of the policemen hauls him up to standing. Cosimo flicks his wrist and mumbles the first spell that comes to mind, but nothing happens. His legs are jelly. He will never see his mother again. The German throws down his cigarette. "Andiamo."

The German officer tells the policemen they've got to get to the main gate before the morning shift change. His Italian is good. They march him a couple of blocks east. Cosi's bad foot slows him down and they're annoyed with him. They stop at a tall metal gate in front of a dark guardhouse. The glowing red eyes of two cigarettes smoulder inside. Nothing is said and the silence is heavy. One red eye blinks and a guard with jangling keys steps out and walks slowly towards them. Like the soldier in the church, he's got a submachine gun slung across his chest. There's a clang and a creak as he unlocks the gate. Cosimo is dragged forward. He just might piss himself in front of all these men. Spittle and hard-edged words slice through the night air. A cloud sweeps over the moon and fingers touch triggers. Brakes squeal. Cosi's head swivels and his eyes ping off a lorry, brick walls, shuttered piazza windows, and someone busting through a boarded-up alley. The other guard is yelling and pointing his pistol. One policeman pushes Cosimo down and the other opens fire. The second guard falls to the stones with a slap. The first guard tries to ram the gate closed, but the German officer puts his arm through the rungs and shoots him in the head. The metal moans as the dead guards' bodies are kicked into place to hold the gates open. Boots and shoes pound past Cosi's face. The German officer shakes him hard and shouts, "Thanks, kid! Now run! Get the hell out of here now!"

At first, he is only able to run at a crouch, too terrified to straighten up and take a lungful of air. His foot throbs as he scrabbles into the busted-open alley passing waiters, farmers, and students of all sizes and ages with guns, bats, pitchforks, and axes running in the opposite direction. Lino didn't tell him it would be this dangerous. Pops like corn on the stove puncture the stillness. Then the dull thud of a massive explosion propels Cosi at full speed back to the potting shed where he opens the door and falls onto the dirt. His lungs and thighs burn and muscles jump all over. He kicks off his shoes. Tomorrow, he will go to Sole. Enough of Lino's crazy errands.

———

Hello, Newfoundland! This is Penelope Moore, signing off for this broadcast. I bring you greetings from the 166th Newfoundland Regiment who are currently attached to the 8th Indian Infantry in eastern Italy.

Disgusted, Tombstone switches off the radio. "Well, it might be two months late, but at least the missus knows which friggin' continent I'm on."

"Please God Min's cakes will find us now," says Slade.

Arch shakes his head. "Not likely. I was gabbing with a driver who came up from Bari. He says the port was bombed. Destroyed. Ammo, supplies, a shit ton of fuel, the mail. All our Christmas parcels."

"You're bullshitting, Fisher."

"Full-on Luftwaffe attack. Getting back at us I s'pose for driving them out of the Sangro. There's tons of casualties. The driver said he only got out alive because he was already at the edge of the town when the place went up."

"Why wasn't that on the radio?" asks Tombstone.

"Bad for morale, I s'pose. I don't know how they'll crack through Ortona and Pescara with no fuel and no ammo."

"And no smokes," says Slade. "Hey, did ya see Rawlins scratching this morning? I think Garl's ploy worked."

The next day, they are sent to Bari on "lice leave." There they can see the effect of the surprise attack for themselves. The old city has been flattened about seven streets back from the harbour and the hospital is packed with civilian and army victims. The overworked nursing sister is not too impressed with their request for relief and is about to send them packing when they all start scratching their heads and necks. She sighs and points to the DDT ward.

———

Cosimo is startled awake by a sharp rap on the shed door. Lino never comes to the shed and his legs re-flood with fear. He grabs a rake and stands. His legs are still burning.

"Cosi?"

A dream?

"Cosi, it's me. Unlatch the door."

He swings the door wide and his mother falls into the gloom. He holds her and kicks the door closed as they sink to their knees on the earth. He touches her face. One of her front teeth is chipped and she smells like sour lemons. She's wearing a nun's robe and between sobs, says she was in San Giovanni prison until partisans dressed as German and Fascist soldiers broke in and released everyone. Cosi feels a flutter of pride but knows he can never tell her that he was there. If she knew he'd been that close to real guns and real German soldiers, she'd march right back to that cell and lock herself in out of spite. He holds her shaking hands and whispers, "Ma, Papa is dead."

chapter 13

THE CHOIR

As soon as she sits in his lorry, Vince squeezes Barbara's thigh and thanks her for coming along to keep him company on the long drive. So much for thinking her sergeant stripes and camera would offer protection. She puts her duffel bag of film on the seat between them. He was right about the Via Adriatico. Deeply rutted, overflowing with mud and shell holes, collapsing shoulders, blown-up bridges, and burned-out vehicles. How did the Allies move so many soldiers, tanks, quads, lorries, tractors, and guns on this? Barbara keeps the conversation on Vince's wife, their kids, and life in New Zealand. About an hour from the Sangro, they get properly bogged down in the muck. Vince steps out of the cab and his legs are instantly swallowed in grey mire. "You stay here, Babs. I'm going to clear the rear wheels. When I give you the signal, hit the accelerator with everything you've got."

She scootches over to the driver's side and grips the steering wheel. On his signal, she slams on the accelerator. Grey slime fans up over Vince's chest and face, over and over again. Each time it happens she laughs and apologizes. When the wheels finally find purchase and the lorry lurches ahead, she drives a few feet onto higher ground and waits for him to catch up. When Vince opens the driver's door, only his teeth and eyes are clean. She lifts her camera and takes a snap. "You've just had an Italian beauty treatment!" she says.

"Babs," he says, "you're the only beauty I've seen in Italy."

Barbara is acutely aware she hasn't told anyone where she is. Vince asks her to retrieve a towel from behind the seat. She kneels up and reaches behind for something that feels like a towel. But before she can hand it over, he is on top of her. "Hey!" she yells. She tries to squirm away, but he's fast. The weight of her camera pulls the strap tight around her neck. "You're quite something, aren't you?" he says. "Coming here all by yourself to take photos." Barbara pushes against his chest but her hands slide on the muddy wool.

"Get off me. Vince, get off!"

"I can't be the only one that gets dirty," he says.

He's heavy, and his grip is strong. He kisses her lips and she twists her head away. "I'm a sergeant," she says. "Let me go!" Mud drips down the neck of her blouse.

"You're not really, though, are you?" he says nuzzling her neck. "You're just a beautiful woman."

One hand free, she grabs the camera and smacks him hard in the side of the head. He howls and sits up, banging his head on the lorry's ceiling. She pulls one leg out from under him, puts her foot against his chest, and pushes him out the door. He lands back in the mud with a splat. "Quite the little spitfire, aren't you?" he says, as blood drips from the side of his head. Hands shaking, she locks the lorry door and starts the engine. Vince is up and banging on the window. Though his words are contrite, his face is tense. "I'm sorry. It was just a little fun. It's been a long time."

"I don't care how long it's been," she says. "I could have you court-martialled."

"C'mon now, Babs, you wouldn't really," he pleads while rattling the handle with all his strength.

She'd rather walk the rest of the way to the Sangro. "Maybe I should write your wife," she says. "You don't think I can find Susan's address?" Bingo. His New Zealand driver's licence is clipped on the sun visor.

He watches her take a picture of it. His jaw is clenched. "Okay, look, I'm sorry, Babs. Okay."

A Nepali jeep drives up and the young driver asks if they've broken down. Barbara cracks open the lorry window and asks him for a lift. He agrees and she jumps out of Vince's lorry with her duffel and doesn't look back.

As they get closer to the river, the fields on either side of the road turn grey, most of the trees, crops, and vines are flattened, and the sky is clouded with smoke. It feels like they're driving into a newsreel. Prasad tells her the smoke is from the funeral pyres. Fields are soon pockmarked with gun pits. Pyramids of mines and shells are stacked next to rows of bodies wrapped in muddy canvas. Barbara scans vehicles for maple leaf insignias. All she has to do is find a Canadian regiment that knows the whereabouts of the unit photographers. Prasad slows to drive around a crater. "Before I deliver the birdseed, let me take you up to Torino di Sangro," he says.

"Birdseed?"

"Yeah, Montgomery has a couple of parrots or something. Here! Can you believe it? I've got three sacks. Flown here from London."

Did she sleep on Monty's birdseed in the plane?

They mount a narrow stone road. "There's a great view of the battlefield and the new bridge up here," Prasad says. Once they're above the mud line, they're back in the world of colour. Pink and yellow houses. Grey-green olive groves, and a roadside niche with a blue and white ceramic Madonna and child. At the top, Prasad points to the spot in the valley where Monty's photo op is planned.

Barbara takes a series of shots. From this height, the bridge looks like a bar magnet laid in iron filings, with trucks, jeeps, bulldozers, and soldiers blooming out of both blunt ends.

Back on the floor of the valley, they stop at two bloated canvas tubs filled with chalky water. She's quite thirsty, but she's seen too many body bags to drink this. Prasad reads her mind. "It's okay, the water comes from the mountains, they truck it down and filter it three or four times. It's just the limestone that makes it milky."

He ladles up a cup and hands it to her. She tips it back and drinks, flicking her tongue across her front teeth to get rid of the grit. She thanks him, hands the cup back, and gasps, "Thanks so much for the ride. There's Ron!"

She steps right off the boardwalk into the muck which forces her to take exaggerated, mud-sucking strides to the bridgehead where Ron is setting up his camera. She walks into his frame, stamping the mud off her boots.

"Excuse me, sir, uh lady, Sergeant, I'm trying to set up a shot here."

She takes off her tin hat and lets her hair fall around her shoulders. "That's no way to speak to Aunty Babs."

He almost drops his camera. "Barbara?" He leans the camera against the railing and lifts her off the decking in a hug that goes on several seconds too long. "What the hell are you doing here?" he asks.

She hands him the duffel, relieved her mission has not been in vain. When he feels its weight, his face brightens. "Film!" His voice drops to a whisper. "You brought film!"

"I suspected my care packages weren't getting through."

"And we lost some in the Bari bombing," he says.

"Bari?"

"It doesn't matter. You're here now, and you brought film. I was faking it just now. Pretending I had film to take Monty's picture because I'm the only one here. All the others have gone ahead to Ortona."

Soldiers are being arranged in rows. Ron whispers, "Monty's PR department. Hold this while I load up."

He hands her the Bren gun he's been using as a monopod, drapes a blanket over his head, and loads his camera. With her free hand, Barbara pokes her hair back up into her helmet. The soldiers are arrayed to block the gore and destruction leading up to the bridge. Monty strolls towards them with an intense scowl. Barbara puts her Ray-Bans on. The General's bony hips are swaddled in thick, wool trousers and an oversized Mae West gives his upper body bulk. Ron emerges from his blanket and drops to one knee. His shot will make the Allied leader look taller. What he lacks in height, he certainly makes up for in confidence, strolling onto the bridge with clean boots as if he's accepting an award. His chin juts forward as he opens the scissor's mouth to receive the ribbon. Just as Ron is about to snap the picture, he elbows Barbara. "You take it, Babs. My thanks for the film and your first picture in the newspapers back home."

How could Ron know that this is what she craves? She stands and can't help but grin as she lifts her Speed Graphic. She captures a flicker of irritation on Monty's face. Perhaps he's thinking, a woman? Here? He doesn't know she's using a wide-angle lens that will capture much of the destruction his PR department is attempting to camouflage. Before the general can voice his displeasure, she snaps the shutter, then boldly steps forward and presses the shutter two more times. In her photos, he will not appear heroic, but will be a small, frail man, towered over by a choir of soldiers who gave so much here.

Back at Foggia, she calls London hoping to catch Patsy. As the ring buzzes in her ear, she surveys her mud-caked boots, rucksack, and her own case of maple syrup film. She has a Thermos, notebook, two pencils, gloves, a comb, cardigan, rain poncho, bra, wool socks, soap, four pairs of clean undies, and her camera. It's all she needs. By the time Patsy picks up, Barbara has made her decision. She announces to her friend that for once she was the official photographer, not just someone lurking around the edges for a stolen image or a side story. She got to take the only official shot of Monty on the longest Bailey in Italy. Patsy squeals. It feels good to share the excitement of the day with someone.

"Did you see Ron?" Patsy asks with a flirtatious lilt.

Barbara watches the female operator to see if she is listening. "Yes, I gave him the film on the bridge. He's taking it north to the others at Ortona. For God's sake, Pats, don't tell Doran I was at the Sangro. I had to hand over the stuff in person, otherwise it would've been stolen."

"My lips are sealed," says Patsy. "Who will get the Monty photo? CP or *Maclean's*?"

"I wasn't supposed to be there. I can hardly put my name on it. And besides, they won't publish a photo from an unknown woman."

"What's your middle name?" Patsy asks.

"Baldwin. It's my mother's maiden name."

"Perfect!" says Patsy. "Baldwin Kerr. Canada's newest freelance war photographer. They'll never know the difference."

The nearby operator nods in agreement.

"Okay, and one more thing, I'm going to stay. If I don't do it now, I'll miss my chance," says Barbara. "It's my dream and I might screw it up. I mean, I've never worked in the field before, but I've got to try."

"I am so proud of you," says Patsy. "And don't worry about Doran. I'll cover for you for a few weeks in case you change your mind. You can do this as well as any of the men. Get off this call and send me the shots. I'll contact CP."

Barbara says goodbye and hangs up. Her father always reads the photographer's credit. If the *Evening Telegram* or *The Daily News* picks up Baldwin Kerr's photo of Monty, he'll know right away it's her.

chapter 14

THE WATERFORD

Caroline turns the page and a bolt of recognition travels from the grainy black and white dots to her chest. It's Pop! Well, the face is his, but the long, lean body is foreign. Teeth clamped on a toothpick, he sits on the ground with four other men, in what looks like a trench. Maybe a gun pit? He's Walker's age and looks incredibly pleased with himself. Is that a piano behind them? Can't be. She turns the next few pages until she recognizes Arch's smile from Min's sitting-room portrait. It's dated November 1943 at the Sangro. A giant soldier has his arm draped around Arch's shoulders and a smirking, younger soldier with a turned eye hangs from a branch above them. Weirdly, there's a doll or monkey toy on Arch's shoulder.

#970408
Gnr. A. Fisher
166th (Newfoundland) Field Regiment RA
Cassino, February 21, 1944

Dear Min,

We've been on the move, getting bags of shooting in, and the mail has had trouble catching up with us. The last batch—they sometimes arrive in batches—had a package from Aunt Theresa with cigarettes, please thank her. There were two letters from you with the Evening Telegrams—wildly popular, almost as good (not really!) as a trip home. It was great to read about the 75th and what they're up to in France. I must keep this letter short. I heard from Garl that Anna's parents sent her to the Waterford a few weeks after the baby was born. He said a police car came right up to their front gate and took her out of the house and drove her all the way to town. I'm sure the gossips up and down Trinity Bay are chattering on bust. Is it true? Did her parents have her committed because she had a child? Or is there something else? Garl says she's working there in the laundry and they're holding back her pay? Why? Are her parents putting her pay in the bank for the child? Are they trying to pass off the baby as their own? If you have any reason to visit Winterton, with your cakes, try to find out will you? In the last letter from her, she said she wanted to call the child Bridget, but her father was against it—too Pope-ish. She also said he refused to sign the marriage licence. Too bad they're teetotallers, your shine might be just the thing for this problem. Seriously though, they know me and trust me. Can you tell them my plans are to work in a garage, buy a house, look after the child and allow her to teach. I certainly won't force Anna to go to the Catholic church. Tell Captain Tucker we'll get married in the citadel if that makes him feel better. There's talk of leave soon—so we can make it official. Most soldiers have leave at least once a year and it's been almost four years for us without it. I'm *trying to look on the bright side by hoping that means it could happen any time.*

Much love to you, Arch

PS. *I haven't told Garl about marrying Anna. He's made it clear that he has no intention, but I haven't brought it up.*

———

Caroline sees that the ingenuity of Newfoundlanders is on full display in *Gunners*: stoves and walkways made of used shell casings; dugouts with names, windows, and doors—one even has a covered porch. There are also Italian women and children cooking and doing laundry. Unfortunately there are few locations and dates. These aren't flash points or liberation celebrations, nor do they depict the horror of the Nazi death machine. There's little suffering or fear, instead the book shows how they managed to find a little peace.

———

Arch leaps from one glistening orb to another. Myrrh tickles his nostrils and water rushes around mossy green rocks to meet the sea. A ladder of bombs clatters from a Liberator. Pink dust blooms where marble stood. He sits up. It's pointless to try to sleep while the Americans bomb Christ off Cassino's cross. Through the tent flaps, he counts hundreds of aircraft. The monks are probably a bunch of guys who, like him, joined up to impress their mothers, or avoid a life of farming, an unwanted baby, or their father's fists, and now they're in the crosshairs of ten Allied armies. He hopes their cellars are deep.

They're with the Kiwis here and firing day and night. They've already lost A Troop's No. 1 crew and two gunners from No. 4. The New Zealand Padre served them green beer last night, so it must be mid-March. As if the battle isn't enough, the brass has asked them to experiment with their twenty-five-pound guns to try to reach the Germans on the top of Cassino. Chuffed that the 166th has been tapped, Rawlins tells Arch he's got two days to come up with a plan. Having to perfect a new way to use the guns in the middle of the firestorm fries Arch's already frazzled nerves. They're already pointing up as far as they can go now. Slade lays down an ammo case. "What if we dig the guns down into the ground?"

"Yeah, that will keep them from tipping over alright, but the shells will come back down on top of us," says Tombstone.

Arch says he's thinking about timers. "We'll shoot straight up. If it's timed exactly right, the bombs will explode over their heads."

"Unless there's a dud," says Tombstone.

"Or a shagged timer," says Slade.

Arch says, "And we'll have to take into account the earth's rotation."

"I was thinkin' that too," says Slade.

Tombstone rolls his eyes.

———

Caroline finds the family of the large man who is usually standing next to Arch in the book's photos. The Regimental Museum in Pleasantville tells her his name was Tom Walsh, and he lived on Livingstone. After a cold call, she makes a coffee date with Tom's great nephew TJ. When he walks into Jumping Bean, it's as if the *Gunners* photo has come to life. Like his uncle, TJ is a tall, burly redhead with a broad forehead and an easy smile. He's carrying a hard-shelled Samsonite briefcase and hugs her with his huge arms like they're long-lost comrades. When she comes back to the table with their coffees, he's trying to pry open the briefcase with a butter knife. "This hasn't been opened in decades," he says.

He eventually is able to jimmy it open and extracts a postcard of a bridge with a caption that reads, *At 1,000 feet, the Sangro's Bailey is the longest Allied bridge in Italy.* Scribbled on the back in fading pencil: *Deadliest too—three dead soldiers for every foot.*

"That's Uncle Tom's writing," TJ says. He lays the postcard on the table between them and flips through a pile of papers. "I was born after the war, but Mom and her ten siblings all have fun memories of him from before. But when he came home from Italy and found out his wife had died, he went straight to the mental. Sorry. The Waterford Hospital. And he never came out."

"I didn't know. I'm so sorry."

"You know how people talk about triggers now? Well, Uncle Tom had a lot of triggers. Loud noises, bright lights, heavy rain, even pasta. He never got over what he saw in Italy." Caroline recalls Reverend Oake's tears.

"Once, when my mother was visiting, he asked her to open his cigarettes and take one out. He was always warning her not to smoke and here he was handing her the pack. He told her your Pop handed him a pack once that had an ear in it, a trophy from a dead German, but you probably know that story."

Mortified, Caroline shakes her head and says, "Pop never talked about the war."

"Funny. Mom says Uncle Tom couldn't stop talking about it. You must've heard the story of Spruce's boots. He told that one over and over. It was just after the Sangro. He said the valley was filled with thousands of dead bodies. Your Pop jumped off the road and got down in the mud and hauled the boots off a dead Newfoundlander. A man they called Spruce."

Her cheeks redden. Maybe this meeting was a mistake.

TJ reads her distress. "I'm sorry, Caroline. I thought you knew this stuff. On the brighter side, Mom says your Great-uncle Arch was a hero. He fed Uncle Tom, covered for him, and kept him out of harm's way. Slade too, they both kept him going, and even helped him write letters home."

"Do you have any of those letters?" asks Caroline.

"Nah. There was a flood in the basement on Livingstone. They lost everything."

———————

"Fisher! We'll call it starlight firing."

I don't look up from my notes. He can come up with all the fancy names he wants. It's not ready.

"Sir, I'm going to need more time to figure this out."

"The brass wants us up there yesterday, Fisher. You know what this'll mean for us."

"Yes, sir, there's a lot riding on it, which is why it needs to work."

"Enough tinkering. I need volunteers to go up and test it out."

I'm not surprised when Rawlins's request for chumps is met with silence. He says to the group, "I know what I'm asking is possibly more dangerous than any other forward operating mission we've undertaken. That's why I'm going along as well."

When Garl steps forward, I exchange glances with Tombstone.

Since the Sangro, Garl has been feeling the chill. Men pick up their tin cups and move when he sits down next to them. No one laughs at his jokes. I feel bad about the shunning, but if he'd abandon me and steal the boots off one of ours, he wouldn't think twice about putting any of us in danger. All I see, though, are the flat, terrified eyes of twelve-year-old Garl peeking through the stair spindles. Going up on Cassino is a suicide mission, and Garl is willing, just to be forgiven. I grab Tombstone's arm and whisper, "He won't be able to sit it out up there. He can't sit still. He'll run, he'll be killed."

Tombstone bites his lip and says, "I should go. I'm Number One." Jesus, no. Tombstone isn't fit either. He's been a mess of nerves since we got here. Before Tombstone can put up his hand, I step forward.

"Look here, Rawlins, sir, it's my invention and it still needs fine-tuning, so I'll go."

Tombstone looks relieved, but Garl is frowning when Rawlins slaps my back and says, "The 166th will go down in history when we root out those Huns."

———————

TJ hands Caroline a sketch, hand drawn, from the point of view of the Newfoundland gun pits at Cassino. She's read history books and looked at official battle maps, but only now, looking at this freehand drawing, can she see how close the men were to the monastery. "Did your Uncle Tom draw this?"

TJ says, "Probably. He was a great draftsman. Before the war, he carved lettering into headstones."

"Oh. That explains the nickname."

TJ unfolds a mimeographed map on two pages. The tape has disintegrated into a brown smudge across the kneecap of the boot, but Caroline's heart leaps. The blue map shows in fine detail the exact route of the 166th through Italy. The locations of their camps are marked with Xs. There are even dates and notes about which army they were with, in each place.

"Oh my God, TJ, I've been trying to figure this out for months!"

"They had a mimeograph machine at the hospital and the doctors were always encouraging Uncle Tom to talk about the war."

He loans Caroline the map, then lifts a package out of the case. "When we were kids, we were never allowed to touch this."

He peels back clouded cellophane revealing a tarnished silver dress sword with a black and white enamel swastika and a silver eagle on the hilt. Oak leaves criss-cross the sheath. Caroline glances around the café to make sure no one else has seen it.

———————

Tombstone's breath catches, followed by a long stretch of silence. Arch is awake now and so is Tombstone. "Arch, tell me about Rawlins again."

It's no good telling him to forget it, so Arch launches into his week up on Cassino. He says, "During daylight we had to lay still as corpses behind piles of rocks. There was no getting up for nothing. More than once, I had to let piss run down my leg. The snipers knew exactly where we were, one twitch could bring down fire." Tombstone sits up and drinks melted snow from his tin cup. "That was the game," says Arch. "Then at night, the tables would turn. We could get up in the dark and have a wash and shave, eat, and as long as you didn't use any lights, shoot up at the buggers. It was completely arsed up."

"Was it a whole week?" asks Tombstone.

"Six days," says Arch. "After the fifth, Rawlins decided we could go back to our post. I was so fucking relieved I gave him my bunk in the farmhouse. We weren't asleep an hour when the mortar hit. I ran into the rubble and tried to wake him. I got to slap him pretty hard a few times. Let me tell you, that gave me a certain amount of satisfaction, but he was gone. All we had to show for that week was some sooty German collars, a few notebook scribbles, and a dead CO."

Tombstone says, "It was his stupid idea."

Arch nods. "I wanted to bring him down right away, but there was too much going on with the mortar hit, so I had to wait for the next night. That last day, the sixth, was the longest. Once it got dark enough, I stuffed Rawlins down behind the seat of the jeep and wrote on the cover of my notebook: *If found, please return these men to the 166th Newfoundland Regiment HQ.* I buttoned it into my chest pocket for the descent."

Arch is soaping up his face for a shave. Tombstone asks, "Did you radio to let us know you were coming?"

"Nah. That could've tipped off Jerry. Now, naturally, I wanted to take off like a shot, but that would've been deadly. Couldn't go fast anyway near the top, I had to pick my way through hundreds of bodies. I figured Jerry would use the first crossroads for aim, and that the gunner would calculate based on the jeep's top speed. So, I went slower and stopped well short of the intersection. And by Jesus it worked! The shell fell and exploded twenty feet in front of me. All I had to do was register my location in the German gunner's mind as I was driving. Stop short or zoom past that point, wait for the bomb to fall, then do it all over again."

Tombstone swings his feet out of his bunk on the other side of the dugout. "Genius, Arch."

"Nah, I'm just lucky the German gunner was a stickler. In some ways the drive down was easier than the strength it took not to strangle that Pommy Major back at HQ. When I handed over the notebook, he had the nerve to ask me if that was all there was to the upper register shooting experiment. Imagine? A man who's never squeezed off a round of artillery in his life. I saluted and told him the result of his experiment was wedged in behind the back seat of the jeep."

———

TJ jams the sword back into its wrapper as if it's burning his hand. He hesitates but says, "Your Pop brought it to the hospital and gave it to Uncle Tom. He said it was cursed and he didn't want it anymore."

"When was that?" Caroline asks.

"Sometime after they came back. I don't know exactly when."

Why would Pop have a Nazi sword? She picks up a scrap of fabric that had been wrapped around the blade. "Don't forget this. Oh, it's silk."

"Yeah, check it out." TJ smooths out the wrinkles revealing topographic lines and place names. "The British made silk maps and smuggled them into Italy. There were POWs hiding with partisans in the mountains and these were made to help them escape into Switzerland. This one is for the area south of Bologna where the 166th spent the winter of '44 and the spring of '45. Just before they came home. Mom says the sword was wrapped in it when your Pop gave it to Uncle Tom."

Caroline traces the Reno River with her finger. "It's really detailed. Can I take a picture of it? If this is their last post, that's where Arch went missing."

TJ holds the edges of the fabric so she can get a shot. "Uncle Tom always said Arch wasn't AWOL. He was injured just before they got leave and sent to a hospital, then the whole hospital moved north and somehow, Arch got lost. He never made it back to camp. Uncle Tom was convinced Garl knew a lot more than he let on."

Caroline doesn't want to believe her Pop had anything to do with Arch's death, although it would explain why he burned the letters. "Did your uncle have any evidence of that?" she asks.

"No, and after Spruce's boots and the ear in the cigarettes, he didn't have a lot of time for Garl."

She taps notes into her phone. "Did your uncle ever say anything about Bologna? Being there for the liberation?"

"Weren't they home by then?" He flips through some papers held together with a brass clip. "Yeah, says here they left Monte Sole in late March 1945. When was Bologna liberated?"

"Mid-April. After a few rum and cokes, Pop once said he rode into Bologna on a tank with the partisans, that women and children threw yellow flowers at them. It was a lot of detail from a man who rarely talked about the war. But I guess he could've seen it on a newsreel and made up the story."

"I do remember Uncle Tom saying Garl got court-martialled or he lost his pension or something. Maybe for staying to look for Arch?"

TJ asks about Slade, and she tells him that she tracked down his daughter, and he has already passed away.

chapter 15

THE ARNO

I try to push away thoughts of German snipers and Skipper's gaff as the current slides around my ribs. This is not the ocean. It's a river. Not just any river now, mind you. It's da Vinci's Arno. Now there's an inventor. The wire spool creaks. Is Tombstone telling me to stop? I wait. Dead quiet. No rustling reeds, no radio static. Anna shivers under a thin hospital blanket. Her beautiful hair is matted to her scalp. I take another step. Have I passed the deepest point? Fuck, if Tobin was handy, I'd choke him. I know damn well he's tangled up in Bridget's adoption. Don't let the teeth float away. Fuck! I'm going to have to swim. Or pretend to. I lift both arms and try to soar like a gull. Okay. Not swimming exactly, but the river holds me up and moves me forward. Wary of splashing, I conjure oar tips circling on the surface of the cove. I do that for a few yards, and it works better than pretending to be a bird. The toe of my right boot strikes something. Mine? I sink. Nothing happens. I push up from the bottom. Spared again. Tombstone tugs on the wire, and I trip forward into shallower water until I'm kneeling on enemy ground. The moon slides behind a cloud and critters flutter through the grasses. If there were Germans waiting, the animals wouldn't be on the move. Pushing up through the water's weight, I plunge into the reeds and sit with my back against the riverbank. I tug hard on the wire three times to signal that I'm across, pleased for almost swimming and only once thinking of Skipper trying to drown me.

Walking north up into the Apennine foothills, in the hottest kind of weather, is exhausting. When we stop, we just crash on the ground and let sleep take over. One day, I was the first awake and when I sat up, it looked like I was the only survivor in a field of dead soldiers. At Castiglione, Slade found a cemetery and we shimmied into empty niches. Tombstone was appalled by the death drawers and refused. "C'mon, b'y Tombstone, it's dry and the neighbours are real quiet." He stood swaying with exhaustion for a long while before blessing himself and crawling into the drawer next to mine.

While the mucky-mucks plot their next move, we commandeered an abandoned four-storey mill near Porretta Terme. The top two storeys are gone, but the second-floor living quarters are more or less solid, with a kitchen, six bedrooms, a massive fireplace, and a fountain. It's a good place to dry off and for Tombstone to get some solid sleep. Slade and I have been bringing him extra rum rations and doing his chores since Cassino when he got a letter that one of his daughters is engaged to an American serviceman. From now on we'll be intercepting his mail, and only passing on happy ones.

Even though it's hotter than Hades, Slade is stoking a roaring fire in the fireplace to dry out blankets, sleeping bags, and clothes. I'm working at getting the water running in the fountain when Garl shows up bragging that he traded a pair of ladies' shoes for a sack of spuds. Garl is a master scavenger who never gets caught. He strips off his coat and poncho, drapes them over a clothesline, and announces, "Fries for supper," before loping off to the kitchen. He emerges a few minutes later with a crock. "Lard! Oh Lard!"

"Like fuck you found lard!" says Slade.

"Way in under the sink. Here, smell."

Slade leans over the crock. "Jesus Mary, he's right."

As Garl slices the potatoes into thin disks. Tombstone sits near the fire warming his hands, saying nothing. "Little brother, make yourself useful and go find us a pot and maybe some salt while you're at it."

Slade pipes up, "Vinegar too. Malt!"

There's a spirited discussion about whether fries are better with the skin or without, but Garl refuses to peel them, so that settles that. Even without salt or vinegar, the taste of those chips reminds us all of home. We compare fries from the St. Bon's canteen, and the Regatta. Whose mother made the best and for a while, we forget where we are. When the lard is getting low, Garl tips the crock over the fire causing a *schlump*, splatter, and hiss. Tombstone springs to his feet. "What the fuck was that?" Sizzling on top of the log is a perfectly preserved rat, its tail coiled in the shape of the crock. The flames jump with grease from the animal's fur. Slade bolts away to vomit, and Tombstone stares with disbelief. Garl flicks the sizzling corpse into the cinders with his boot. "Ah, don't mind that, b'ys. Extra vitamins!"

––––––––

#970408
Gnr. A. Fisher
166th (Newfoundland) Field Regiment RA
█████████████ *September 29, 1944*

Dear Min,

We've just crossed the river that outsmarted da Vinci, so we're feeling pretty chuffed. We're with a ███████████████
███████ *outfit who promised the first unit across, a weekly*

case of brandy until war's end. No matter what you hear in the news, we are now drinking that sweet (maybe too sweet) plum brandy. There are rumours that some ████████████ *might have crossed a couple of hours before us, but we still got the brandy. Tombstone is hoping that for coming 'first', the 166th will finally get a write up in the dispatches or the newspapers instead of getting lumped in with whatever crowd we're attached to. He wants his kids at home to hear that their father helped drive the Germans away from* ████████████ ████████ *. I can't tell you where we're headed next, but every Italian we meet warns us, "Neve, neve!" (Snow). What a laugh. It's so hot here the stone walls and roads radiate heat back at you all night long.*

The giant leaf I've folded in here is from a fig. You can certainly see why Adam and Eve would've chosen it. Fig fruits are falling out the trees and laying all over the roads, they taste like honey, but you gotta be careful. Some of them are full of hornets. Slade popped one in his gob yesterday and got his tongue stung. He hasn't been able to talk for a day which Tombstone says is a gift from God. We're hoping all this foolishness will be over before Christmas. We got Jerry on the run now. We walked through one camp where they didn't even have time to take down their tents or grab their clothes off the line. I ate a cold (but tasty) breakfast of German eggs and sausages that I found cooling in a frying pan. Tombstone got some fine wool socks, shirts, and sweaters, which will no doubt come in handy where we're going. Despite those souvenirs, they haven't left us much in the way of roads, or bridges, and we haven't seen many locals.

Hi Mrs. Fisher, Slade here. Your Arch is some boy, he's managed to get the fountain working here in the Casa Neufo. We've all had a bath and washed out our clothes and at night we has a grand fire in the fireplace. My blanket is dry for the first time since we landed in Italy. Quite the digs. Bye for now!

Me again. Before we got here, I got a letter from Anna, she says she sent one every week or so and when I didn't reply she gave up and thought I'd changed my mind about the marriage. Someone at the hospital must be holding her letters back or giving them to her parents? The only reason I got that one is because her friend Elayne mailed it. She is getting desperate to know where Bridget is.

Before the weather turns, do you think you could go to town and visit her? Take money out of my account for the train fare. Assure her that as soon as I'm home, I'll help her find Bridget and find a way to marry her without her parents' signatures. Don't mention our leave—it's getting ridiculous, I got a mind to write Anthony Eden and complain. I'm not kidding. The 75th have already had two home leaves.

Amore, Arch

PS. I wrote her back and told her to walk right out of the Waterford to get a job at Fort Pepperrell. The Americans don't care if she's had a child out of wedlock and they certainly won't hold back her pay.

Children are playing in and around overturned railcars outside the mill. Tombstone is best kind when he's around kids, so they climb down onto the tracks. The kids scatter except for one skinny boy, about twelve, in filthy shorts and a sweater vest. He stands in the doorway of a railcar and gives them a Fascist salute, puffing his chest out like a dictator. "Buongiorno, Americani. Io sono Il Duce!"

"Buon Giorno, Benito," Arch responds. "Non siamo Americani. Noi siamo di Terra Nova."

The boy exhales and is twelve years old again. "Io sono Enrico. Non lo so Terra Nova."

Slade smiles. "No, b'y Enrico, no one knows where it is."

"Coca-Cola?"

"No, sorry."

Arch asks Enrico if they can see his railcar. "Posso entrare?"

The boy makes a sweeping gesture with his arm. "Si, si. Benvenuto."

They're gobsmacked at the railcar's luxe interior. Their young guide announces that it was Mussolini's. Whether or not that is true, it is certainly more opulent than the usual red and chrome Fiat commuter trains. This interior is black and brown leather with bronze dials and shiny satin curtains on the windows. There's a large table area in the middle with banquettes on either side.

"A map table. He had his war meetings here!" says Slade who sticks his pocketknife into the leather banquettes and starts ripping.

"I can use this to patch up my boots."

Tombstone announces he's going to stink up Musso's can. Enrico watches Arch dig around in the motor. There's a couple of wet cell batteries that he can use. Slade comes to help him and that's when they hear the shootout. Enrico jumps out of the train, and Arch and Slade run to the privy. Slade kicks in the door. Arch expects to see Tombstone bloodied by a sniper's bullet. Instead, he's standing with his pants around his ankles. The reek of shit and gunpowder is overpowering.

"What the fuck just happened?" asks Arch.

"I shot him." Tombstone says proudly.

"Who?"

"Mussolini."

Slade says, "He ain't here, b'y."

"He was. He was just behind the mirror. I got him, the bastard."

Arch traces a ding in the polished chrome mirror. Slade points to where the bullet ricocheted around the tiny loo before embedding itself into a wall just behind Tombstone's head. Slade exhales. "Jesus, Tombstone, you're one lucky bastard."

Tombstone says, "I don't think so."

chapter 16

DIAVOLETTO

Lucia doesn't trust Lino. He looked after Cosi and may have gotten her sprung from prison, but the resistance has been double-crossed many times by Catholic priests. Paolo called them cowards for not protesting the Vatican's collusion with Mussolini. At Madonna di San Luca, Lino introduces Lucia to a young nun named Caterina. She was born in Marzabotto near Lucia's hometown and is the youngest of fourteen. Caterina chatters away in Lucia's dialect, asking her questions about her family, the location of their farm, and her father's name. Lucia nods politely and pretends she doesn't understand. She's been gone too long to know who she can trust.

They are led to a room with vaulted ceilings, stained glass, and two steaming copper bathtubs. Lucia almost falls on her knees in gratitude. At the border, she'd been given salt water to bathe with and it had dried her hair into a bird's nest. The convent's soap is scented with lavender and when she slips under the warm scented surface to scrub the tangles out. Even though she's an atheist, it feels like a religious experience.

After their baths, Caterina gives Lucia a clean nun's habit and presents Cosimo with a Fascist scout get-up. Lucia recoils, but Caterina explains that the Balilla uniform signals Cosi is only fourteen. Any older, and the Germans will pick him up for labour camp. In a room off the kitchen, Caterina serves them large bowls of bean soup, the same kind Lucia's mother makes. The herbs and broth fill her nostrils and she aches for her parents. She is so close to home now, but they've got to get across the German lines first.

After their soup supper, Caterina drapes a tablecloth around Cosimo's shoulders and shaves his head. She is gentle and playful with him and Lucia wishes she wasn't suspicious. When they're ready, Lino leads them through miles of tunnels underneath the shrine to a long-forgotten exit well outside the city's walls. Cosimo hugs Lino and the priest thanks him for his help. Suspecting he may have put her only child in danger, Lucia thanks Lino tersely.

It's a moonless night and they stumble south for hours along unfamiliar paths, through trees and undergrowth, avoiding roads, stopping and crouching in ditches when they hear noises. Most of the sounds are from hunting owls or frisky *cinghiali*. Even though he's dead, Lucia can't help but be annoyed with Paolo. All those years living apart from her family and risking her life and there's not one Stella Rossa member here to guide them to safety. If they're caught, they will surely be used to force the resistance to give up infor-mation or exchange prisoners. When the sun comes up, she leaves Cosimo napping on boughs in a small cave while she backtracks to ensure no one has been following them. If she had allowed Caterina to come with them, she wouldn't have to leave Cosi alone. Lucia's forgotten how exhausting it is to always question people's motives. She misses the anonymity she had in England.

———

With Tombstone in the gun pit, disputes are handled with a razz, and they all work seamlessly as if they're protecting their own homes. Without him, there's sniping, backbiting, and stupid accidents. They're backing up the Scots Guards and some South African tank units on a mountain called Stanco, and everything is going smoothly until one of their gunners, a few pits down, is decapitated by faulty ammo, right in front of his crew. They're all upset. The gunner has a family at home and was well liked. They can't even stop to grieve or comfort each other or check for more faulty shells. They have orders to keep shooting. Tombstone steps away from their gun. Arch steps in to take his place, looking over his shoulder at the big guy watching the medics bag up the body and the head. When they leave, Tombstone walks off alone into the trees.

The accident proves what they've all suspected about the three-year-old ammo from North Africa. They've warned their new CO Knox that the stuff is unstable and if a gun gets too hot, shells will explode in the chamber and more of them could die. Slade says, "Jesus Murphy, it's one thing to get blown to bits by the enemy but killed by your own shitty equipment. That will be hard to get over."

When there's finally a lull in the fighting, Arch goes to look for Tombstone. After an hour of walking, he finds him crouched between two boulders studying a map like a confused tourist.

"When I looks at this," he says, tracing his finger across the Arno up to their present position in the Apennines, "I gets the sense we're up here for the winter and really what the fuck for? We're just a distraction. The main event is in France."

"Nah, b'y," says Arch, "we're going to liberate Bologna. Slade is already planning his dates with the city's horny maidens."

"He's going to be sadly disappointed."

Arch asks, "You coming back?"

Tombstone shakes his head. "It's too much. I'm addled, Arch. I'm gonna fuck something up and someone's going to get killed. And what for? I don't really care if there are Germans in Italy."

"They're bastards," says Arch. "Killers."

"We're killers too, Arch b'y. It's all numbers on maps, but we're killing people too, families, soldiers, we don't know. And what for? They've lost Rome, what the hell are they hanging on here for?"

"Maybe they just like tormenting us."

"Yeah, well, it's working," says Tombstone.

Arch touches Tombstone's shoulder. "I know you're missing your kids and your missus. We're done firing now, on the way back to the post we'll pick some flowers to press into a letter. Min loves that. She says it makes Italy seem more real."

"Do you miss home?" asks Tombstone.

Arch certainly doesn't miss Turk's Cove and Skipper. He says he misses his mother and he's trying to miss Anna, but he can only picture her as his student, leaning over her sums with a furrowed brow. He admits to Tombstone he sometimes worries his marriage plan will never pan out and other times worries that it will.

Tombstone says, "Once we gets leave and you can talk to her, it'll all work out."

"That just might happen sooner than you think," Arch says. "I wrote a letter to Anthony Eden."

"Jesus, Arch, that was a waste of your precious paper. Eden's got better things to be at."

"Nah, b'y, they owes us four leaves by now. They obviously can't run the war without us."

Tombstone grins. He stands slowly and walks back to the post with Arch. They arrive back during a German counterattack and Tombstone carries out his role like an automaton. Afterwards, there are harrowing stories of roads collapsing, a Bofors gun and its crew going straight through a booby-trapped bridge, and hand-to-hand combat after some of the South African tanks get bellied in the mud. There's also talk that the Germans have a new type of rocket.

The nun's habit and Cosi's Balilla uniform get them through a couple of checkpoints with a nod. Once they cross the Reno and start climbing the familiar paths on Sole, Lucia can't stop grinning. But after an hour or so, her smile fades. There are no farmers in the fields, no families on the usually busy paths. The mountain is deathly quiet, and her anticipation is replaced by dread.

To lighten the mood in the mess after the German counterattack, Slade starts a singalong. "*Ye ladies and ye gentlemen . . .*"

The mess is quiet. The men are tired but relieved to be alive and eating. Tombstone is sipping his pea soup and humming along.

"*I pray you lend an ear,*" sings Slade.

Garl responds. "What he really means is, shut up, will ya?"

"*While I locate the residence of a lovely charmer fair.*"

Another crack from Garl: "Oh yeah? Hunting for a bit of tail!"

Arch steps out of the mess for a piss. He listens to the laughter as he unzips.

"*The curling of her yellow locks.*"

Something moves in the brambles. "*First stole my heart away.*"

Another counterattack! Fuck! He zips up and goes for his pistol. Shit! Shit! Shit! It's inside on the bench. "*And her place of habitation was down in Logy Bay.*"

He screams out to be heard over the singalong, "HALT!"

The men hit the ground on the other side of the canvas. A figure in white stumbles out of the bushes and collapses on the ground. Arch rushes forward. "It's alright, b'ys, it's . . . a woman. Just a woman."

Bloodstained nightgown. Her hair a mess of curls and leaves. Arch helps her up. She's trembling. "Signora, va bene? Vieni, vieni."

He leads her into the mess and the men fall silent. A tiny newborn mewls in her arms. Arch says, "Slade, go get a blanket and the medic. Jackie, you got milk?"

The medic checks the woman's wounds and translates. Her name is Pia and the four-day-old is Eleanora. Pia says the mountains are being *rastrellato*. The medic says the word has something to do with a hoe or a rake. He guesses it's something about the harvest. She goes on to say she was crammed in a storeroom along with family members and neighbours. She pauses for a breath and her mouth contorts. German and Fascist soldiers locked the doors and threw grenades into the room. Those who didn't die from the concussions and shrapnel burned to death. She survived because she was trapped under the bloodied and burned bodies of her family. Her mouth opens, but no sound comes out. The medic takes a break from cleaning her wounds and holds her hand. He asks her gently if that's what she means by *rastrellato*. She nods. Tombstone is mesmerized by the newborn in Pia's arms. Jackie shows him how to drop the goat's milk around the infant's lips with the tip of a pease pudding bag.

Eleanora cries out and Pia caresses her cheek. She says when she heard the little dove whimpering, she was terrified the soldiers would come back, so she pried her from her dead mother's arms and carried her through a window that had been blown apart by the explosion.

She lays her hand gently on Eleanora's bird-like chest and says before they threw in the grenades, the soldiers said it was punishment for feeding Stella Rossa.

Garl is livid. "Red Stars! What are they, commies?"

Pia blinks in shock and explains that Stella Rossa are family, their brothers and fathers, uncles. Of course they're feeding them, and they've also shared their food with the Germans, for years. And now, she says, there are dead families in fields and burning homes all over Stanco and Sole. Arch asks the medic to ask her if the Germans they fed are the same soldiers doing the raking. She shakes her head and explains that the killers are new Germans, older ones, with skulls and thunderbolts on their shoulders. Arch, Slade, and Tombstone lock eyes. Tombstone gets up and Arch follows. They find Knox in the privy and repeat what Pia told them through the door.

"Walsh and Fisher, so nice of you to respect my privacy."

Notching his belt as he exits, he says, "Look, our orders from South African command is to throw everything we have at Stanco."

When Tombstone says villages minutes away are being attacked and burned, that it's SS, Knox shakes his head. "That can't be true. Why would German command waste resources on villagers?"

"She said they had thunderbolts on their arms. They're SS. She says they're being punished for helping the partisans," says Tombstone.

Knox nods. "And there you have it, boys. What did they expect would happen if they helped the rebels?"

"But, sir," Arch says, "they're family and mostly unarmed civilians."

"The British Army has been told not to get involved with local politics especially when it comes to partisans and their vendettas. The Witwatersrand Rifles and the Cape Town Highlanders are on their way, and we have orders to help them break through the German line."

The colour is rising in Tombstone's face. "It seems like you don't care, sir."

"That's exactly right, Walsh. I don't care about local farmers settling scores."

Before Arch can stop him, Tombstone is up in Knox's face and gesturing wildly. "Settling scores? It's a massacre! Who cares about

Stanco? Who cares about Mussolini and fucking Churchill? No one really cares, sir. But a few miles from here there are babies, children, and women being slaughtered in their night clothes and we can stop it!"

Arch slides in between Knox and Tombstone to cool things down. "What Sergeant Walsh is suggesting, sir, is that we could mount a couple of patrols between now and the next barrage, to ensure the safety of the nearby villagers."

Knox is too pissed to reason with. He points his finger at Tombstone. "Walsh, you've been slacking off for weeks. If you don't carry your weight and lead your crew in taking back Stanco, you'll be heading home to see your youngsters all right. With a dishonourable discharge. Your orders are to start slamming the mountain at 4:45 a.m., keep firing until 10:10 a.m., then turn the guns and fire on a sham target."

Tombstone pushes Arch aside and growls, "An uncle? That is as stupid as the starlight firing idea. The Germans aren't just killing villagers so the partisans will starve. It means we'll starve too."

"Let's go, big fella," Arch says as he grabs Tombstone around the waist. He needs to get him out of there before he gets court-martialled, but Tombstone is as immovable as a tree. As he struggles to pull him away from Knox, Arch hears a squelch. A shell? "Incoming!"

———

At the farm, Lucia wants to run into the kitchen and wrap her arms around her mother and luxuriate in her father's laughter over her nun get-up. Cosimo is mostly focused on food. "So there probably won't be any meat because of the shortages, but there will be bread and pasta. Right?"

Lucia nods. "And sugo, bruschetta, soup, frittatas . . ." Her words trail off. Her mother's clothesline is taut. There is always laundry pulling it into a wide curve across the yard. She pulls Cosi back and they crouch behind a hedge. She says they'll wait until they see a relative. Even as she's saying this, she knows the farmhouse is empty. It's far too quiet; her father's radio is always on bust in the barn. He believes the horses, chickens, and pigs love arias as much as he does. Her grandmother, aunts, and mother are always bickering and slamming pans around in the kitchen, cousins should be yelling to one another from the hayloft or splashing around in the water tank. Today, not even the crows are cawing.

Eventually, one of her father's hunting dogs comes into view, nosing the ground near the back door. Lucia makes a kissing sound, and its head snaps up. The animal approaches warily with its tail low but is soon licking her hands and pushing its snout into her armpit. Its tail thumping the ground. "Ah, Dido, you remember me?"

She tells Cosi that as a puppy Dido loved to rip sheets off the clothesline. Her father joked that he should've been named Il Duce for taking what wasn't rightfully his, but her mother forbade him from repeating the joke. She was worried neighbours might overhear and turn them into the police. Dido puts his paws on Lucia's legs and the extra weight forces her to stand. Wearing a brave face for Cosimo, she strides towards the house. "C'mon, let's go see who's home."

The dog's snout bumps off the back of her calf in a wet Morse code. What is he trying to tell her? The dog stops when they cross the threshold.

———

Tombstone and Knox run in opposite directions as the squelch lifts into a squeal. I jump behind the privy and cover my head. Count to ten, eleven, no one moves or speaks. Just silence. A dud? Timer? How long should I wait? I peek around the privy corner and see Tombstone flat out in the mud with a shell across the back of his calves. Christ. He's cut in half? I'm next to him without knowing how I got here. He's whole. One. He was sliding on his belly, stealing

home, but only made it halfway into the trench. Breathe. The big
guy is in one piece. He's whole. For the most part.

Kneeling, I push his shoulders up to angle his death mask of
muck away from the throbbing metal. Christ, he weighs a ton, but
if I let go, he'll sink back into the mire and might detonate the shell.
I lean in to suck the mud out of his mouth and nostrils. Spit out
warm grit. The shell's no dud. I gag on the disgusting mixture of fuel
and rot. His ear is caked too, but I say, "There's a shell. You're under
a shell. If you can hear me, Tombstone, don't make any sudden
moves."

The medic arrives at a run but brings up short.

"Fuck! That's a Moaning Minnie, Fisher. It'll blow us to
smithereens."

He steps forward cautiously to put two fingers on Tombstone's
neck. "He's just knocked out. You keep holding him and I'm going
to take off his boots and dig at the earth under his knees. Then we'll
try sliding him out."

Lucia picks up a crumpled rag splayed on the seat of the hallway
chair. It smells musty. She wants to call out but has lost her voice.
For years, in dreams, she's walked through these doors into the joyful
embrace of her family, but today the house feels ripped open. The
stillness is violent and Cosi is devastated. All of his knowledge of
Italy is based on her stories about people in this room. Because she
and Paolo were blacklisted, she could never visit when Cosi was
growing up. No one is here to welcome her son home. Her mother
and father smile down at them from their wedding portrait as she
takes the pulse of the place. The water barrel is dry and the pots in
the fireplace are cold. There's no bread, farro, or even beans in the
larder. There's no yeast stuck to the sides of the dough bowl. She
breaks off a brittle leaf of dried sage hanging from a rafter and

savours the medicinal smell on her fingertips. In the coffee grinder, she finds a dusting of grounds in the back of the drawer, just enough she thinks for a cup, and ties it into a handkerchief for later.

They could be with neighbours or maybe they went south to Florence. Smoke drifts in through the open windows. It's not the right time of the year for burning the mosta. Something is off on the mountain.

The family bible leans against the Virgin's hip in the prayer niche. If Lucia's family was planning to go anywhere for a long time, her father would've taken it. It has the farm's history, crop yields, deeds, baptism, wedding, and communion announcements, old ID cards, photos, and the family tree. It's been rebound several times and is held together with one of Lucia's childhood belts. Once when her parents had to leave suddenly to take Nonna to hospital in Bologna, her mother left a note inside the front cover. Lucia flips it open but there's nothing. Cosi is looking over her shoulder as she caresses the endpapers. She tells him that when she was four or five, her mother took a rare moment away from chores to swirl beet juice and olive oil together with a paintbrush so she could create the pink marbled patterns. She closes the bible and puts it in her bag. Cosi asks about the cloven hoof sticking up in the back of the niche. Ah! Lucia reaches in and extracts her grandmother's lucky charm. Her diavoletto. She kisses its red velvet buttocks, still prickled with Nonna's faux pearl–topped pins. She puts the pincushion in her bag, leaving Mary alone to continue her godly eye roll.

Tombstone is released from the medic tent at dawn and joins them in the pit in time for the dummy barrage. Although they're happy to use up most of the dodgy North African ammo, shooting wildly off to the side during a battle feels ridiculous. When they're down to their last shells, they get news that the Germans are in retreat. Arch sits where he was standing and nods off at the base of the gun and Tombstone leans back and closes his eyes, while Slade counts empty ammo boxes. "Over ten thousand shells on a mountain no one even heard of before yesterday."

German POWs later confirm that they were tricked by the uncle, that it broke the back of another counterattack. They don't tell Knox, knowing it will encourage him to come up with more crazy ideas. Across the valley, white sheets hang out of windows. It's a signal from the women of Grizzana that the Germans have left. Arch has never been so happy to see laundry in all his life.

———

Desperate to rid himself of the silly Fascist uniform, Cosimo undoes his chin strap and rips off his hat. Lucia goes upstairs to find clothes. In her parents' bedroom, the sheets are aswirl and pillows are on the floor. She picks them up and breathes in the scent of her parents. Her tears stain the linen. There's no night clothes on the back of the chair. They must've left in a hurry. The scent of the room and the sight of familiar patterned fabrics in their wardrobe makes her throat ache. She can't cry in front of Cosi, so she sits on the bed and steadies herself before going downstairs. She tries hard to picture her family safe in a refugee camp or staying in her uncle's cramped farmhouse in Le Pizze, well behind Allied lines. She changes into one of her mother's dresses and a blazer, adds a pair of her father's trousers, and slips her feet into her mother's favourite red party shoes. She keeps the dull habit, though, folding it into her bag. Cosi's slight frame will be swimming in her father's clothes, but at least he'll have the comfort of Nonno's scent. When she comes downstairs, Cosi is waiting in the front hall in his boxers and undershirt. The Balilla uniform is balled up under the hall chair and Dido sits in the doorway with the musketeer hat perched between his ears. "Dido dislikes that hat as much as you did," she says. "Get dressed. I'm going to look in the barn for rope to hold up your pants until I can take them in."

Dido follows her to the barn, but when she detours to the chicken coop, he sits on his haunches and waits, watching her lift the wooden hatch and step in. No chickens. No eggs. Someone or something has pawed through the straw disturbing the roosting spots. The barn too is empty. Maybe they rode off on the horses? In their pyjamas? As she's closing the barn doors, she notices a trail of blood droplets in the earth leading to the water tank's ladder. She feels sick to her stomach but follows it. Her hands shake as she climbs. When she looks over the edge, she gasps. Two bloated corpses, her aunt and uncle from the city, float in the still water. She scrambles down the ladder and runs to the house for Cosi. Dido chases them through the yard but skitters to a stop at the trees.

––––––––––

Pia spends the night next to the stove, rocking Eleanora and trying to get her to suckle at the corner of the pease pudding bag. Tombstone changes the teat when the milk sours and keeps the fire going. The next morning, Arch comes in to relieve him and they've nodded off. He's as quiet as he can be, but the stove door creaks and Pia wakes with a start. She looks down at Eleanora and stands, tearing at the blanket and her clothing, putting her ear on the infant's chest. She cries out, "È morta!" Tombstone stares. Unmoving.

Padre leads the funeral service. Arch reads Mark 10:13–16, and Pia manages to say, through the medic, that Eleanora was the last survivor of a family from Caprara di Sopra that had been farming Monte Sole since the Etruscans. Slade sings "The Maid on the Shore" at the graveside. After the service, Tombstone takes to his bunk, refusing food or company.

––––––––––

Like me, he's haunted by what ifs. What if we'd tried harder to convince Knox to help the villagers. What if we'd walked farther, faster, slept less, dug deeper, had fewer breaks, carried more ammo, or bombed more roads? Any one of those things might've prevented Eleanora's death. What if we'd simply refused to follow Knox's orders? We might be bunking with Eleanora's family tonight, eating pasta and telling stories about what we'll all do when the war is over.

chapter 17

SOLE

Monte Sole is a rocky fortress infested with the enemy and connected by a ridge to Monte Caprara. Garl, Arch, and Tombstone are sent into the funnel-shaped valley between the two to bring supplies to one of the forward observation posts. Not yet used to the altitude, they're breathing hard. Garl stops to catch his breath and whispers, "Arch, all those goddamned NAAFI biscuits are backed up."

"Just let it slide down your leg."

"Keep watch while I takes a dump."

Garl steps off the path and Tombstone grabs his shoulder. "Don't be so stunned. Pick a random spot."

Garl beats his way through a bramble. As he's cursing the thorns, Tombstone leans against a tree for a smoke. Arch releases the safety on his rifle. They've all heard of soldiers shot while shitting, their glowing arses providing an irresistible target for snipers. Arch scans the trees beyond Garl for movement and Tombstone turns his face towards the moon. Dropping to one knee, Arch sees movement in a nearby orchard and takes aim. Clouds cloak the moon, and his mouth goes dry. His sternum is pressed into the prow of Skipper's dory. His grandfather's heavy musket strains his wrists. He wills the seal to resurface while slob ice grates the dory's ribs. Skipper complains he can smell seal gravy and dumplings, and he's tired of eating gull. If Arch misses, the old man will be livid. He squints. Pushes doubts down. Locks onto the hand moving on the tree's trunk. Squeezes. The seal screams and falls backwards. There's a thud before the shot echoes off the surrounding hills. The moon reveals itself. Red shoes. Slender feet. Christ! He's shot a woman. Arch sprints to the tree. Alive? A nun. Oh shit. She sits up and cradles her hand. Blood.

"Sister, are you okay, sister? Sorry. Bene? Stai bene?"

———————

Dark brown eyes, a single frown line etched in her forehead. Red suede shoes and a veil in the dirt of the tree's roots. The scent of lavender. With her unbloodied hand she brushes clay off her arms and face. I want to reach out and pluck the dried olive leaves from her hair, but her eyes stop me. Trousers under her skirt? She struggles to stand.

"Sister, I'm so sorry" is all I can muster. My ears are still ringing from the shot. She holds her clenched bloody fist to her chest and pants with shock. Thank God, like with the seal, I missed. I want to look away from her gaze and scan the horizon for Germans, for snipers, but know that if I look away, she'll be gone, sprinting through the trees, maybe getting herself blown to bits. Tombstone is whispering loudly, second guessing mines as he creeps towards us. Just a few more minutes alone with her. I ask to see her hand to clean it. What's that word? "Purifico?"

Her shoulders relax and she grins as she offers me her partially opened palm. "Are you trying to tell me you'd like to clean it?"

"You speak English?"

"Yes. You do know *purifico* is Latin?"

"Yes. I sang it in a hymn once. It's all I could come up with. I'm very sorry about your hand. I thought you were a German sniper."

Tombstone waves an iodine wand, and she tells us she came down from Bologna. Her family's farm is on Sole in a place called Casaglia, but no one's there. Do I tell her about the raking? She gasps when Tombstone applies the tincture. The red shoes aren't right and her English is almost perfect. Could she be a spy? Tombstone asks why she was climbing the tree.

"I was looking for food and I heard you coming. I climbed up in the olive to hide."

"There are German snipers and mines everywhere."

"The Germans didn't shoot me, you did."

"I'm Arch, Arch Fisher, and I'm sorry, I really am, but it's not safe here."

"This is my home," she says.

Tombstone rolls up the gauze. "Arch b'y, we better get moving. The Germans no doubt heard that shot."

I release her hand. "The Germans are burning villages. It's not safe. Allied HQ in Pian di Setta can get you to Florence where the Red Cross can help you find your family." I hand over her red shoes.

"Thank you, Private. I'm not leaving," she says. "It's taken me a decade to get back here."

Furious whispers from the bushes. Garl says, "Thanks for the shootout, Archie. You scared the shit back into me!"

When I turn back to ask the nun her name, she's gone. Garl smacks his lips together. "Snazzy sister!"

It's not even lunchtime and Jackie is already beside himself, asking Knox for extra guards on their supplies saying they'll run out in a couple of days with the number of Italians accumulating at their post. At last count, thirty-six, but every hour a few more trickle in. They're all starving and sharing photos of missing loved ones with anyone who'll pause long enough to look. Garl accuses them of stealing tea bags, potatoes, flour, even their road salt. Arch has seen kids eating potato peels and the women are squabbling over who will wash the dishes so they can scrape their fingers through the scraps left on the plates and pots. When the men are in the mess, the Italians sit on the ground outside and watch them eat. Arch can only manage a few bites before he passes his plate to the smallest child.

The padre sends Arch out to ask if anyone speaks English. A woman speaks up and Arch recognizes her voice. His nun! She's not wearing a habit today but is sporting her red shoes. "Sister, I didn't get your name."

She grins. "Hello, Private Fisher. I'm Lucia and this is my son Cosimo."

A gangly blond teenager nods at Arch.

"So, not a nun?" he says.

With a twinkle in her eye, she says, "The habit gives a widow some protection."

Arch asks her to relay the padre's message that a Red Cross truck is on the way to take everyone to Florence where they'll be much safer. She stands on a chair to address the group and an older gentleman shakes his cane, motioning for her to sit. Lucia folds her arms across her chest and tells Arch she's been demoted.

Arch directs information to the man, but he stares back without comprehension. Lucia whispers to Arch, "He's a man. He doesn't need to know English to tell everyone what to do." A couple of nearby women giggle. Without speaking directly to the group, Lucia conveys Arch's information to the women in furious whispers and they pass it on. The spokesman remains standing like a conductor without an orchestra. Lucia soon reports back that people don't want to go to Firenze, where they'll be refugees in overcrowded camps. Arch and the padre tell her there'll be shelling on the mountain every day, and the post can't feed everyone. Lucia says that most are waiting a day or so until they're sure the Germans are gone. That everyone has crops in the fields they need to harvest, and they want to go home. She adds, "Although some say they're waiting for the Allies."

Garl overhears this, and in a loud voice says, "We are the Allies!"

"I know," she says quietly. "I guess they mean the Americans."

Garl puts his hands on his hips. "Listen here, missy, tell 'em if they wants Yanks, Florence is full of 'em. Up here it's Brits, Poles, South Africans, and Brazilians and we've all been ordered to stay put until spring. So, you'd better get used to us."

Lucia glares at Garl. Before Arch can break the tension, the padre asks her to invite the mountain people to join him for prayers. She does what she's told, and relays the information to the group, but doesn't follow them into the mess to join in. Instead, she and Cosimo lean against a tree and turn their faces to the sun. Arch offers her a cigarette. She accepts and he asks when she last heard from her family. She looks from Cosimo to Arch.

"About three years ago . . . we were in England and . . ." She stops and swallows hard. Arch is overwhelmed by the desire to reach out and comfort her. The boy's cheeks redden, and he stares at Arch as if he knows what he's thinking. As he's searching for something encouraging to say, a loud crack echoes across the valley. Gunners scatter to pits and trenches, steel splinters crackle, and red-hot shell casings roll on the ground. Many of the praying Italians are under the mess tables, while others have run back into the trees. The 166th guns leap. Arch fires off a round and looks back to make sure Lucia and Cosimo are out of harm's way.

———

Garl opens the driver's door and falls face-first into a snowbank. Arch and Slade drop what they're doing and run. When Arch turns him over and pulls up his balaclava, his brother's face is contorted in pain. "My toes are as cold as a walrus tusk," he says.

They carry him into the warmth of the mess where Lucia is mending by the wood stove. They lay him on a table and his teeth are chattering. Slade unties his boots, and Arch carefully rolls off his socks exposing red feet with white splotches. One big toe has a blue tinge. Arch gently holds his brother's freezing feet in his hands to warm them. Garl grimaces. "It feels like needles!"

Lucia pours warm water from the kettle onto a tea towel and brings it to Arch. She says, "When this has cooled down a bit, wrap his feet up, it should help with the blood flow."

Garl squirms. "Lucy, will you rub me down, darling? That'll get the blood flowing."

Arch is tempted to give Garl's feet a painful squeeze. Instead, he asks, "How in the fuck did you get frostbite in sunny Italy?"

"I was doing recce for HQ. The floor of your GD truck is rusted out, the frigging wind blows right in around your ankles, and I got a little side-tracked. I found a gift for the lovely Lucy here and I didn't notice my feet getting numb." Even though his teeth are chattering, Garl turns on the charm. "Lucy, sweetheart, I brought you a piano so we can sing duets!"

Slade is ecstatic. "A piano!"

Arch's heart sinks. Grand gestures like this means Garl is smitten. When he had the hots for Anna, he flew her father's aeroplane around Winterton's harbour, before clipping a tree and crashing it in the woods. Lucia thanks Garl, but says she has no need for someone else's piano. She gathers her mending and leaves without saying goodbye.

Garl sneers, "Jeez, I knows she's not stuck up."

————

#970408
Gnr. A. Fisher
166th (Newfoundland) Field Regiment RA
The sun, October 30, 1944

Dear Min,

I read your last letter a couple of times. What did you say to Mrs. Tucker when she claimed I was fickle? What did she mean? Because I left the priesthood? Or simply because I'm Catholic? How can she not see that I am trying to do the right thing and save her daughter from the gossip? Does she think Anna will be better off with Garl? Does she want her to stay in the mental for the rest of her days? Is she feeling guilty for sending her only grandchild out for adoption?

I know you don't have the answers. It just feels good to write them out. We're keeping in shape here by walking, rabbit snaring, and building dugouts into hillsides and underground. Safer that way if there's shelling. One of the townies has called his dugout the Caribou Club 2 (the first one collapsed). There's also a Casa Apennino, and a Wabana Shack. Tombstone scrounged the back of a caboose for ours. The metal is painted green, and it holds up the front nicely. Gives us a little veranda. We've called it 'Casa Grasshopper.' That's a little joke that I'll tell you about when I'm home. We've got a nice table for cards. The CO's has a picture window and Garl's has a piano! He burned his feet with frostbite to get the damn thing, but he's the life of the party now and could care less about his toes.

There's an Italian boy named Cosimo living at the post with us. He's keeping Tombstone's mind off his own youngsters, somewhat. Would you knit him a pair of vamps for Christmas?

It's getting cold up here now, and he has nothing. He's a tall fella, about 14-years-old. I've traced his shoes on the back of the letter. He could use a sweater too if you've got the wool and the time. I'm making him a radio for his dugout. His mother helps in the mess and with our laundry.

Slade here! Hello Mrs. Fisher! Cosi's mother—we call him Cosi for short—is Lucy. She's not hard on the eyes and she's been hired to wash and mend our clothes for a few bob. She's mending my back passage now. That's the last place you wants a draft blowing through. She's also a fine scrounger. Good thing because the brass has forgotten about us up here. Don't spose you've got any spare fruit cake laying about that you can send our way? Arch wants the letter back now. Nice chatting with ya! XO Slade.

Me again. It's no secret that we're here for the winter, Alexander told everyone, on the BBC. I don't understand why he let the enemy know we're not going any further. It leaves us open to ▮▮▮▮▮▮▮▮ *and knowing what we do about their death camps, it is inhuman to leave us here when we could be saving lives. We're still attached to the South* ▮▮▮▮▮▮ ▮▮▮▮. *You should've seen them at the first snowfall, sticking out their tongues to catch the flakes like youngsters.*

Mountains of love, Arch

PS. I sent a letter to Tobin and told him my plans to come home, marry Anna, and find Bridget. If you happen to get to town to do a little Christmas shopping please take enough money out of my account to buy a simple ring, a gold band and get it to Anna. In a year, she'll be old enough to walk right out of the hospital and we won't need her parents' signatures for the licence.

———

Tombstone has become obsessed with the depth of his cellar on Livingstone. He's convinced the Germans are planning to bomb St. John's and frets about his family's proximity to the harbour. U-boats have sunk two iron ore carriers off Bell Island, and they all know someone who died in the fire at the Knights of Columbus. They help him write a letter home asking his family to go to their cabin in Salmonier, assuring them it can't go on for much longer.

He's not the only one feeling unmoored. When we first got up here, Knox warned us that the air is thinner and it might make us moody. Jesus, I can laugh, be pissed off, and feel like crying all in the same day. But I'm starting to think it may have more to do with Lucia and less to do with the altitude. She is something else. After being transported to Pian di Setta with the others, she somehow talked her way out of the transport to Florence and walked back up here, marched into Knox's tent, and convinced him to pay her as the post's laundress and cook's assistant. She said it was her work at Hartnell's that cinched it.

———

Garl tells Arch he plans to bring her every piece of clothing he owns, one piece every few days, so he can spend as much time as possible with her. Arch doesn't let on that he's bothered by that. They all like having her around. She's fun and she knows the mountains better than any of them. She taught Jackie how to make pasta from chestnuts and she's a great hand for scavenging, which is tricky business with the mines, but she's assured Arch she won't take any unnecessary risks. To keep Tombstone away from Knox and his threat of a dishonourable discharge, they've got him working on Lucia and Cosi's dugout. Arch overheard the young fella telling Tombstone they won't need it for long because his papa is a partisan leader and he'll soon come for them. How many Italian boys harbour similar fantasies?

The next morning in the mess, Lucia is telling me about their life in London when she absentmindedly pulls a gold band on a necklace from the neck of her blouse. Without thinking, I blurt out, "You're married?"

She drops the ring back in her neckline and says she is. Was. She picks up her sewing but can't thread the needle because her hands are shaking.

"Well, not really. I was. I'm a widow. But don't mention that to Knox. He was concerned about fraternization, so I assured him I was married."

"Okay, I get it."

"But when we were in Bologna, a priest, Father Lino, told us Cosi's father, Paolo, my husband, is dead. One of the reasons I came back up in the mountains was to make sure. And I am sure, Arch. The Paolo I married would've moved Sole to see his son."

Slade skids down over a muddy embankment. There's a distinct metallic clank in the brambles and Arch braces for an explosion. The rabbit on his back slides off and hits the ground with a thud. He leaves it where it landed and backs away, fumbling to release the safety on his pistol, and bawling, "Fuori!" The branches shiver and to his surprise, three grown men emerge from a bush. A father and two sons? Partisans? Fascists? Either way, this is no doubt the crowd who've been raiding his rabbit slips. One young fella is wearing a beret and a grey jacket, the other is in a holey sweater and overalls, and the father wears a balaclava and a deep green leather coat. They all raise their hands.

"Pistole! Hand over your pistole," Arch demands.

Slade grabs the leader's gun and sticks it in his belt. The sons turn around slowly to show they're unarmed. Moving carefully, one picks up Arch's rabbit and offers it back to him. "Buono!"

Arch is glad he thinks so. Jackie complains that he needs over a dozen to make a pot of soup. The leader asks if they'd like a coffee. Arch can't imagine anything better but is not sure he wants to accept hospitality from these men. He asks the leader to remove his balaclava. He pulls it halfway up, revealing his nose and mouth, then sweeps back the branches to reveal a cave opening. Slade balks. "We're not going in there for coffee, Fisher! There might be more of them."

The leader steps back into the void. Arch and Slade cock their guns and point at the sons, who put their hands up again. The youngest one attempts to explain. "Papa. Sta prendendo un caffè per voi."

"Si," Slade says. "He's getting a coffee for us. But are there more people in there?"

"No, no. Solo Papà, Armando, e io."

When Papa returns, Arch and Slade step back in case he comes out shooting. Instead, he emerges at a crouch, with two steaming tin mugs.

"You go first, Fisher, and I'll keep an eye," says Slade.

Arch drinks. The sludgy coffee is the exact same chicory shit they have, probably stolen from their mess.

"Ti piace?" Papa asks.

"Si, si. Grazie," says Arch. "Go ahead, Slade."

Slade sips and watches the men over the rim of his cup. Arch keeps his gun cocked but lowers it to let the boys drop their hands. Papa asks about the wire slips on his belt. Arch hands him one and tells him to keep it. This pleases Papa. Wire is impossible to find. The Germans confiscate everything that could be used as a weapon. Slade shakes his head, but Arch would rather they set their own slips and stop robbing his. Papa opens a handkerchief and shows them some shrivelled-looking things. Slade leans in. "What in the name of Christ are they?"

"Some kind of mushroom, I think," says Arch.

Papa wraps them back up. "Si, porcini. Good with . . . grasshoppers." He makes a leaping motion with his hand.

Slade smirks. "Grasshoppers?"

"Si! Armando hunt grasshopper. Mangia fragole tutte estate."

Slade turns to Arch. "What the frig is a fragole?"

"Strawberries. I think he's saying the grasshoppers eat strawberries all summer."

"L'intero villaggio l'ha mangiato."

"The whole village ate some," says Arch.

"I can't imagine there's much meat on those things," says Slade. "But let's not get into a big gab here. They might be pissed about our stay-put orders."

Arch wants to find out if they're partisans and ask them if they know a Paolo Capponi, so he keeps the conversation going. He waves his hands around to mime a grasshopper. "Do you mean a green grasshopper, verde?"

Papa shows his teeth in a tight smile. "Si, green . . . è un miracolo."

Slade nods. "I'd say it was a miracle."

Papa wraps the mushrooms up and says, "Signore, why Alexander says Allies stop here? We need Germans out now."

Slade stiffens. "Told ya this would come up. Let's go, Fisher."

Arch says, "Yes, we want the Germans out too."

"Pericoloso now. Very bad for mountain people."

"It is dangerous, you're right. But we're here to help."

Papa motions upward. "Help? Abbiamo bisogno di pistole e cibo."

Arch has heard on Cosimo's Radio London program that the partisans have requested airdrops of arms and food. Requests British HQ have refused.

"Do you know anyone named Paolo? Paolo Capponi?" asks Arch.

The men exchange glances and shake their heads. No one says anything. Arch asks again about the grasshopper to break the awkward silence. "How much did the grasshopper weigh?"

"Due kili."

Playing up his astonishment to change the subject from HQ's refusal of aid, Slade says, "Two kilos? Holy shit!"

Papa says, "Si, si, salta." He makes the leaping motions with his hands again and goes on to say it jumped through the erba, that they roasted it on a spit, and someone took a picture that ended up in the local giornale.

Arch thanks the men for the coffee and says they have to go. Papa asks for his gun. "Slade, give the man back his gun."

"You cracked, Fisher?"

Arch says, "Okay. Take the bullets out."

Slade takes the bullets out of the magazine and reluctantly gives Papa back his weapon. In exchange, he offers the mushrooms to Arch.

"No, grazie, you keep them."

Slade keeps his hand on his gun as they walk off. Once the men are out of sight, Arch and Slade check the cave. Its narrow passage opens into a large room with a roof supported by giant boulders and tree roots. Bigger than some of their dugouts, half a dozen people could stand in the cave's main room where there's a battered table, three small barrels for chairs, and a fire pit with a coffee pot on a metal grill.

Slade whistles and drops the bullets into a tin mug. "We could have a fine game of crib in here."

Arch notices a gap between the rocks that gives a clear view of the cave's approach. If the men had wanted to, they could've easily shot him and Slade.

After supper, Arch and Slade bring Tombstone a bowl of rabbit soup.

"Met the friggers who are robbing my slips," says Arch as he lays the soup on the table.

"Partisans?" asks Tombstone from his bunk.

"Probably. They're pissed that the Allies aren't going on to Bologna. Said they need guns and food."

"Where was that?" asks Tombstone.

"Up in that gully, where I've been setting snares."

Slade tells him the grasshopper story and Tombstone's blanket shifts. He turns over and says, "A grasshopper?"

"Yeah, two kilos. Gorged on strawberries all summer and the whole village ate some. It made the newspaper."

"What was the word he used?"

"Miracolo!"

"Don't be so stunned, Slade. What was the word buddy used for the grasshopper?"

"I don't know, con-lee-something."

It's the longest conversation the three of them have had since Eleanora's funeral. Tombstone's face lifts into a silly grin. "Slade, you fool. You speak just enough Italian to get yourself in trouble. It wasn't a grasshopper, cone-eel-ee-oh is rabbit. Even I know that."

"No. He called it a grasshopper. He said it hopped through the grass."

Tombstone sits up. "What else hops through the grass?"

"Rabbits, yes, I s'pose. But he said it was green."

"The strawberries were green, b'ys. That's what he was saying. The rabbit was snarfing green strawberries."

They all laugh. Arch is pleased the big man is sitting up and tasting his soup. "Jesus, I'm relieved to know there's no five-pound insects up here," Tombstone says between spoonfuls.

———

I don't mention my plans to bring Lucia to the cave. It's a good place for her and Cosi to hide if there's an attack and a quiet spot for us to talk away from prying eyes and ears. Tombstone keeps warning me not to fall under Lucia's spell. That's what he calls it, as if she was a magician. He doesn't approve because she's Italian, has a child, and was married. Every other day he reminds me about the plan to marry Anna. Assuring me that romantic feelings will develop nicely once we're sharing a bed.

chapter 18
MALCONTENTI

"Turn left at the station . . . in, wait . . . five hundred metres."

Caroline is annoyed with the Irish GPS lady. "What are you going on about?" There is no station, just a fenced-in cement staircase in the middle of a field. Even though it's early spring, the Sangro Valley is an intense green quilt and some plants, maybe tobacco, are already three feet high. At home, her beet and kale seeds are struggling to germinate under grow lights.

She wants to see where the Sangro empties into the sea, but the GPS is sending her in circles. "You'd better not send me back up onto the highway," Caroline says.

She tries again, following the voice's counterintuitive but lilting instructions and is pleasantly surprised when she drives under an industrial overpass, around a corner, and finds herself in a sunny vacation neighbourhood of yellow stucco, geraniums, and striped awnings. The Adriatic is only a few hundred feet away. She parks her rental between two garbage bins and walks onto the unfenced beach. It's mid-week in off-season and the mini-mart and pizza parlour are both shuttered. She wishes she'd brought a granola bar. A man and woman stroll out of a walled compound called Sun Camping. He's sporting a down vest and his missus is wearing a fur coat. They assess Caroline's jean jacket, flip-flops, and summer skirt with raised eyebrows. She says, "Bella giornata," wishing her Italian was good enough to explain how fifteen degrees and sunny is a fine summer day at home.

At the mouth of the Sangro, milky water has turned the Adriatic opaque green. Caroline slips off her flip-flops and wades in. Did Pop and Arch notice that the river is not much wider than the stream at Turk's Cove? The beach rocks are smooth and warm on the soles of her feet as she threads the seashore looking for treasures. Somewhere behind her a bulldozer pushes gravel into a trench. The map on her phone tells her she's only a mile or so from the battle site. They must've been able to smell the sea from their gun pits.

Before coming to Italy, she read an unpublished memoir from TJ's briefcase. It wasn't his Uncle Tom's, but another soldier's collection of somewhat scattered scenes, typed on legal paper and held together by brass paper fasteners. Stories about the "extra messing" they had to do to keep themselves fed. Nothing at all about his fears, how the Sangro or any other battles went, or how he felt about killing. Probably written for his family, he held back. She still mourns the loss of Arch's letters, but maybe he held back in them too. Maybe he only told Min what he wanted her to know. Maybe he painted a rosy picture not wanting to frighten her. What she would give to know how Arch and Pop felt about this place, the people, the war, and their role in it. Why they signed up. What they feared. Dying, yes, but what else? So much is left out of all the accounts she's read. Maybe they didn't have time to keep journals or write letters, but it's more likely they didn't think what they were living through was extraordinary in any way.

She wraps her jean jacket around her hips and wades in up to her knees. The water is pleasant. What did they do between battles? She read that the weather here that month was brutal. Twenty-eight days straight of heavy rain and even snow, which is difficult to imagine as she stands in the warm sea. In the car, she'd been listening to a podcast about the build-up of carbon in the atmosphere. How the rise in greenhouse gases started during the war and kept climbing throughout the post-war boom. That most of that excess carbon comes from the last thirty years. During her lifetime. She has benefited from that planetary destruction. Somehow, she wants to connect that in her artwork to what the men in the *Gunners* photographs thought they were fighting for. She's not sure how she'll tie it all together, but she's learned to trust her imagination, not to force or dismiss the connections that surface. She sits on a concrete pier looking out over the water and enjoying the sun's warmth on her bare shoulders.

Two cops get out of a police car parked on the next pier over. They look out to sea through binoculars at an approaching fishing boat. The boat makes a wide arc and turns. The wind has come up and the waves are white capped. The boat zigs and zags and keeps turning in circles. Have they lost control? Then it heads straight for the shore at full speed. Can they see the breakwater? Caroline stands. The police jump back in their car, turn on their siren, and reverse off the pier. Just as they stop on the beach, the boat hits the breakwater with a terrible crack and flips up and sideways. Wave after wave grinds the overturned hull against the rocks and concrete. Two men emerge from the wreckage and belly into a small dinghy. They motor out to sea. None of this makes any sense. Blaze-orange life jackets bloom in the waves. Caroline and the cops are the only witnesses. It's siesta time and all the metal shutters up and down the beach are closed. No one is coming to help. The boat has almost completely disappeared below the waves as arms reach above the surface. A woman screams. A child's head? Flailing? Caroline runs into the water towards the breakwater. She hears a siren. Hands and arms attempt to put a lifejacket on a child in the water. Caroline is up to her hips. The channel on her side of the breakwater is too deep. The water too rough to swim in. People are climbing up gasping on the jumbled concrete. A baby wails. The cops are on their cellphones. An ambulance pulls up and two medics slog into the water and throw a lifebuoy. A man and woman grab it and tumble in. Caroline helps the medics pull them in while counting heads. She can't take her eyes off the children bobbing in the waves. Sinking. Coughing. Did they have swimming lessons? The lifebuoy goes out again. She pulls the rope with all her might to drag in a man holding a child. He hands her a young child reeking of diesel and swims back to the breakwater as the medics throw the ring out again. She finds someone on the beach and leaves the shivering child, a boy, with them. The medics say something in Italian that she doesn't understand. The swimmer lowers a woman and two children into the water in front of them. Caroline and the medics pull with everything they've got.

Hours later, wrapped in a foil blanket, she hands out Red Cross cookies and water bottles. More cops arrive in a van. Someone speaks into a walkie-talkie. Caroline finds the little boy, who she guesses is two or maybe three years old. He clings to her neck. His shirt still smells of gas. She manages to take it off him and wrap him in her dry jean jacket, rocking him gently and making soothing sounds in his ear. He is still shivering. She searches the faces of the people sitting on the sand for his mother, but no one makes eye contact. There are six women, eight men, a baby, and six children, including the boy in her arms. On the beach behind them, there are six bodies wrapped in canvas body bags. One of the survivors collects the cookie wrappers and empty plastic bottles. He passes them to the Red Cross volunteer and bows. No one can answer the police questions; they speak even less Italian than Caroline. They are led to the police van and Caroline hands the boy to a woman sitting nearest to the door. The boy reaches for Caroline and wails as the doors are closed.

The fuselage shudders and Caroline jolts awake on the flight from Pescara. She's still numb from the rescue. The medics shrugged when she asked where the people were from and where they were going. Her arm and back muscles ache. The pilot announces their descent to Guglielmo Marconi Airport. She thinks about Marconi's theory that sound waves never die. One of his last inventions was an antenna that he said could pick up voices from the past still shimmering in the atmosphere. It's a completely romantic notion, but not far off what she's doing in Italy. The plane passes over deep green mountains peppered with white limestone ridges and granite summits. When she lived here, she didn't give a hoot about the war. It was ancient history and no one in her family talked about Arch and Pop being here in the war. Arch still being here. Now, it's twenty-five years later, and she feels like she can reach out and touch that past. How does that work? That thinning of the veil between the past and the present as you age. In the Sangro River War Cemetery, at Spruce Osmond's grave, she felt the shameful memory of her grandfather's fingers in the mud loosening laces and gripping the heel of each boot, the slurp when it was freed from the dead man's muddy foot. To apologize for Pop's insensitivity, she placed a pebble on Spruce's headstone, a stone from his childhood beach at Broad Cove.

The plane touches down roughly and when the pilot hits the brakes it lifts her out of her seat. For a split second she is flying. The GPS lady was useless for finding the graveyard, but Caroline had jotted down some instructions from the Commonwealth War Graves website before she left the hotel. Those scribbles led her to a hand-carved, wooden sign for *Cimitero Inglesi*. On the winding uphill track, she passed a prayer niche with a blue and white Madonna and child, a farmyard running with chickens and geese, and tilled fields erupting in clumps of heavy grey soil. High up on the Torino del

Sangro ridge, next to the cemetery gates, she stepped out of her car and there was the image from Tom Walsh's postcard. It was as if she was standing next to Baldwin Kerr when he took his shot of the war's longest Bailey. A shot she'd assumed was an aerial.

A twisted, ancient olive pointed the way to the book of remembrance at the cemetery entrance. Caroline read the names of visitors from all over the world and wanted to do more than just add her own. She wanted to write a whole story about how sixteen Newfoundlanders ended up buried here so very far from home. When she walked onto the grounds, her steps faltered at the sight of 2,600 marble headstones in curving rows. Even though the graves were elegantly staged with luxurious grass, marble stones, pruned hedges, and small rose bushes to soften the shock of the scale of death, her throat ached. She was the only visitor that afternoon and wanted to pay respects to every soldier, by reading names, ages, and country of origin. But after a while, it all blurred into a fog of crushing loss. Near the Gurkha memorial honouring five hundred men who'd been cremated in the valley below, she found the Newfoundlanders. Her tears came hard and fast reading the familiar surnames buried next to each other.

At BLQ arrivals, she takes a selfie with a shiny red Ferrari and texts Leo and the kids claiming it's her rental. They don't buy it. They know her too well. She takes a bus to her hotel, drops her bags, and heads out for a walk, stepping into the current of people trudging home from work under Bologna's loggias. There are makeshift market stands selling food, books, jewellery, and antiques. She takes a few snaps of shop windows for her kids. Over-the-top Prada and Gucci sneakers with fur and metallic leather. The opulence is ridiculous and she thinks of the canvas sneakers of the boy on the beach. Faded and soiled stars and worn rubber soles. She hopes someone thinks to wash the diesel off him before he goes to sleep.

Disoriented in the winding alleyways near Piazza del Nettuno, she pauses and a man hands her a tumbler of wine from the top of a barrel. She thanks him, sips it, and gazes through lace curtains into a cozy enoteca where the tables are mostly full. The walls are lined from floor to ceiling with wine bottles. It doesn't look like a total tourist trap and the free sample is delicious, so she enters, sits, and orders something to eat. The waiter brings her a crisp, metallic wine from the volcanic soil of Mount Etna and a sliced green pear that prickles her tongue. Hearing Italians speaking at other tables reminds her of that magical university year of painting, art history, and falling in love. There's a day-old newspaper on her table and she uses Google Translate to read a story about the Venice Biennale. She attended the massive art fair as a student and the political energy of the contemporary art was like a punch in the gut after a year of studying frescoes, marble sculptures, and altar paintings. The trip inspired her to start using photos and videos in her artwork, recognizing how emulsion, time, and light, could infuse her work with mortality and memory in a way that oil paint could not.

A jewel-like rectangle of paper-thin spinach pasta and béchamel arrives and the waiter explains that the meat is local rabbit roasted with rosemary and honey. Caroline tastes it and swoons. "Ti piace?" he asks.

Her Italian evaporates. "Oh my God, it's delicious!"

Pleased, he bows and goes back behind the bar. While savouring the lasagna, she turns the page on the Biennale article. There's a photograph of two young women taking selfies in front of a sculpture called *Barca Nostra* by Christoph Büchel. The writer is outraged that people would use the sculpture as a backdrop for social media, calling it la sepolcro. A tomb. *Barca Nostra* is made from an actual ship's hull that sank in the Mediterranean drowning a thousand people. A thousand. The hopelessness she felt on the beach floods back again and she hopes the survivors are warm and dry, and eating a good meal tonight. Her thoughts are interrupted by the waiter cursing loudly at the TV suspended above the bar. A breaking news bulletin blares from a screen busy with lottery numbers, soccer scores, and scrolling headlines. A reporter speaks to the camera. Behind her, police pull a woman out of a shack, cuff her wrists with plastic ties, and push an old man wearing a kufi into a police car. Carabinieri climb on top of a flimsy metal shack, grabbing a child. People sitting at the next table join the waiter in angry shouts. The child looks to be about eight. His small fists flail as he fights the policemen passing him down to colleagues. The waiter addresses the whole restaurant. "They had a hot tub. Did you see it? The kid was hiding in a hot tub. Those bloody illegals. You can't even sit outside anymore without one of them trying to pick your pocket."

The lasagna in Caroline's mouth turns to sand. She stands, wishing she hadn't chosen this restaurant. Who cares if they had a hot tub? Maybe they were using it to collect rainwater. Unlikely it was hooked up to electricity and water and so what if it was? She puts just enough money on the table to cover the bill. As she's leaving the waiter is blaming the recession on Syrian refugees and she wishes her Italian was good enough to challenge them all to take a long look at *Barca Nostra*. To imagine their families crammed into a ship with a thousand others. The street sign outside reads *Via Malcontenti*. How fitting.

She walks to Fontana di Nettuno to wash away the enoteca's hatred. When she gets there, half a dozen young people are chasing each other around the base. They're the same age she was the last time she stood here looking up at Neptune's provocative hips. His stance is similar to Firenze's *David*, but the king of the sea has more props: a crown, a trident, and a voluptuous harem of merwomen at each corner of the fountain with water arcing out of their nipples. The streams catch the light from a three-storey, glass fast food restaurant marring the piazza. A young woman who has paused to catch her breath tells Caroline it's a tradition to circle Neptune for good exam marks. Caroline wishes her good luck. The students head to lunch and she walks around Neptune thinking about Pop and Arch. What were they aware of when they were here? Did they know about the concentration camps? Did they get news about other battles or have any sense they were winning? There are steel towers by the train station: memorials to the Jews shipped by train to Nazi concentration camps. The Italian plaque said the work was about time's passage and how it impacts our understanding of war. How we choose to monumentalize it while ignoring the roots of the conflicts. The othering of people. The corrugated metal shacks from the news, the shrugs of the paramedics. The anti-Semitism of the 1930s and '40s is being replaced with anti-Muslim and anti-immigration hatred. She plunges her hands in the fountain and brings the water to her face.

On her way back to the hotel, she passes a wall of unlit black and white portraits. Some smile, some hold bicycles, most gaze into the piazza with a stoicism reserved for identity cards. A marble plaque states these are the faces of the resistance. But these are not rebels, they're just regular people; moms, nonnas, farmers, professors, teenagers, waiters, even nuns and priests. Back at the hotel, she reads that the memorial sprang up organically while the city was still occupied by Germans. People risked their lives to leave flowers, candles, and photos where the Nazis had dumped the body of a murdered partisan. After the war, the memorial grew to include photos from all over the city and countryside, to pay tribute to all the regular people who resisted Fascism.

chapter 19

ATTENDESI

Tombstone opens the Christmas gift his old man mailed and lays out the items for all to inspect. Rat traps, anti-lice pomade, and an army humour magazine. Garl says, "Well, this would be grand if we were fighting in trenches."

"He survived Beaumont-Hamel," says Tombstone. "He's being practical."

"Ah. A sweet, innocent fool of the Great War," Garl announces as he moves the toothpick from one side of his mouth to the other. Tombstone's eyes widen in anger. Arch steps between them to head off a fight. Luckily, Slade arrives and distracts everyone with a two-foot-tall pine tree decorated with tinsel. Padre put Slade's name on a list for lonely soldiers, and ever since, single Anglican women from every bay and tickle have been sending him weekly updates on their chores and dreams. These days, he's far less likely to ask Arch if he can write a few lines to Min. One of the ladies mailed him a package of tinsel and Slade fashioned a star out of sticks and lime wash.

"A gift for you and the German snipers!" says Tombstone.

"Merry friggin' Christmas, Tombstone," Slade says. "Have ye heard? Jackie is finally going to let us at his shine."

For months now Jackie and Lucia have been brewing moonshine with potato and carrot peels, herbs, and sugar rations. Kept under lock and key, its rumoured potency is discussed daily. On Christmas afternoon, they follow Padre to the Oratorio di San Lorenzo, where Catholics sing "O Come All Ye Faithful" along with Sally Anns, Methodists, and Anglicans. The small stone chapel with one blown-out window is double the size of the tiny Catholic church in Turk's Cove where Min will probably sing the same hymn later today. Arch wonders if Anna will be back in Winterton for Christmas, or if she will spend the day in the hospital in town. Even though he is surrounded by his friends, thinking about Anna engulfs him with loneliness. The barrenness of home. Sheets frozen to the clothesline, rotten clapboard, the lonely *put-put* of a motor in the fog, circling, hungry gulls. What will happen to Min, Anna, and Bridget if he doesn't make it home soon?

On the way into the mess for Christmas dinner, Lucia falls in step with Arch and his mood lifts. Everyone's already had a cup or two of Jackie's slush and there's a wonderful racket. The tables are decorated with olive branches in spent artillery shells. Slade's tinsel tree is on the piano illuminated with headlight bulbs. As is the Christmas custom, the officers serve supper to the lower ranks who are all wearing paper crowns. Even though they're sharing the same wooden benches they occupy every day, tonight there are no gripes. Jackie has cooked sheep, hare, and wild turkey with mashed potatoes and cauliflowers. There's a whole side table weighed down with Christmas duff boiled in tobacco tins. The water jugs are filled with slush made from Jackie's shine and snow, in defiance of the no-alcohol rule. Slade is playing the stolen piano and singing "A Fairy on the Christmas Tree."

Arch is grateful that Jerry is quiet. Last Christmas, the bastards never let up for a second and they chewed dry turkey while firing their guns. This is a kind of peace he's never known before. He feels settled. Like himself. Tombstone leans back, belches, and undoes his belt. Spoons hit tin cups to signal the start of gift giving and Slade walks in through the flaps wearing one of Lucia's dresses with socks stuffed into his shirt. He's got a tea towel over his head like a bandana and his lips are stained with jam. He shrieks, "Signore Tombstone? Signore Tombstone? Un regalo por te!"

Garl and others goose "Missus Slade" as she walks between the tables. He bats their hands away dramatically before depositing a handkerchief tied in a bow on Tombstone's lap. Slade stands back with hands on hips while Tombstone unties it, revealing a dozen large ravioli dusted with flour. He's puzzled. Slade says, "Signore Tombstone, you must eat. Mangia, mangia!"

The mess chimes in, "Man-gia! Man-gia!"

Tombstone holds a ravioli up to the light. He can't see through the dough, but he's been the butt of too many of Slade's pranks to go along blindly. He bites down gently on a corner, spits out the pasta, and examines the filling. Sure enough, something inedible protrudes. He breaks the ravioli open and extracts a French letter. Slade snatches it, blows it up like a balloon, and the mess goes nuts. "Basta! Signore Tombstone, basta! Eleven infanti! Enough!"

Tombstone's cheeks redden. "Slade, with the love letters you've been getting, you need this pasta more than I do . . . so here ya go." He stuffs the remaining ravioli into Slade's sock cleavage to roars of approval. Padre cues Garl to lead the men in a round of "Jingle Bells" to settle everyone down. Arch hands Cosimo his gift and like every teen who receives socks for Christmas, he shrugs and mumbles thanks. Lucia admires Min's stitches and asks for her address so she can properly thank her. Tombstone gives the boy three rabbit slips, wrapped in propaganda paper. "In a month or so, when the grasshoppers"—Tombstone winks at Arch—"when the grass-hopping rabbits are getting bigger, I'll take you hunting with these, they'll help us catch the cor-neel-ee-oh."

"Grazie, Tombstone. I'd like that very much," says Cosimo.

Arch lifts a large crate out from under the table. Dishes are cleared and cups moved, as he lays it on the surface. The curious gather. "This is a gift for the whole battery," he says.

"That's getting you off the hook, Fisher," says Tombstone.

Arch says, "I hope it'll help us keep our edge."

Impatient, Slade starts pulling at the strapping. Arch says, "Hands off, Slade. Cosimo, would you like to open it?"

Cosimo opens the box, peers in, and shrugs again. Tombstone lifts out an unwieldy contraption with a heavy wooden base, sandwiched between two layers of metal. An arm with a tuna tin soldered to it sticks out from the side.

"Okay, Fisher, enlighten us," says Tombstone.

"It's a skeet shooter."

Garl drops a NAAFI biscuit into the tuna tin. "Finally, a good use for the biscuits." Slade wants to try it out right away but is overruled. No one wants to trigger a German barrage tonight.

Garl hands Arch a long narrow gift wrapped in newspaper. Arch smiles at his brother. This is the first gift he's ever given him. When he tears open the paper and sees the Nazi sword the mess suddenly feels too crowded. "Where did you get this?" he asks weakly.

"Your little man from India, Biffy, Boffy. He wanted you to have it."

"His name is Bishnu."

Arch wraps the paper back around the sword and stuffs it under the bench before anyone else asks him about it.

————

Monte Sole is just ten miles away, but Caroline's drive through Bologna's southern industrial outskirts is hair-raising. There are baffling tolls, triple roundabouts, kamikaze drivers who drive straight through instead of around the circles, and highways that change numbers for no apparent reason. At one exit, she passes a Fiat 500 squeezed like an accordion, between two transport trucks. All three must've attempted the same exit at the same moment. She says a little prayer for the Fiat driver and is thankful to be going in the opposite direction.

Her destination is the Monte Sole Park. She hopes the people there will be able to direct her to the 166th post. The last place Garl and Arch lived. According to Tombstone's mimeographed map, the Newfoundlanders' winter quarters were on Monte Salvaro straight across the valley from Sole. But as she drives south, the Apennines loom large. It's going to be difficult to find the exact location.

The park's welcome centre echoes with the excited voices of a class outing. A glass cabinet, near the front desk, displays rusting helmets, shell casings, hooks, buttons, and fading war photos, but none of the items connect to the 166th. When the class trickles out with their guide, she asks about British Army posts. The attendee acknowledges they existed, but says they've never been mapped. Caroline is disappointed but accepts a walking map and chooses a quiet route away from the boisterous students. The sun is shining, and the path is wide and even. The gullies on either side of the road are deep and draped with vines, broom trees, oaks, figs, cedars, olives, evergreens, and other trees she doesn't recognize. Broken roof lines and wall remnants peep through brambles in the valleys and on ridges. Magpies swoop over freshly tilled earth picking at forgotten vegetables. She walks to a set of stone ruins at the peak. If there was better cell coverage, she could check her location. Instead, she films the peaceful ruins, hoping to capture the light and the unfamiliar birdsong. A Mercedes rumbles past with a child crying in the back seat. Once she's finished filming, she reads the information plaque and her chest feels heavy. She is standing in Caprara di Sopra, which was a lively hamlet with four families, a store, and an inn until October 1944, when Nazis and local Fascists locked the inhabitants in a barn, threw in grenades, and killed everyone. The murders were part of a raking operation ordered by German command to clear the mountains of partisan support as the Allies approached.

Pop and Arch were here in early October 1944. Were they here when this happened? She's never read about raking operations in any of the Allied history books or memoirs. Why would it be left out of the official stories? The mountain air is cooling and she feels like an intruder, so she gathers her tripod and camera and heads back. On the way down, an elderly nun dressed in a dove-grey habit walks towards her. They are the only two people on the road. The nun is barefoot and picks her steps carefully. When they are close enough, Caroline says, "Buongiorno," and the nun beams at her. Her smile feels like a blessing and the heaviness Caroline carries from the ruins lifts a little.

———

The blood-spattered walls of the pillbox, the slit throats, the young German's grip. His unnecessary death. Why didn't he take the easy way out? Why did I? Garl must know. What did Bishnu tell him? Just the sight of that dreaded thing. Dread for the animal instincts we've given into. Dread for the tainted life stolen from that young man. I don't want that thing near me and I don't want anyone to ask about it. Can't we just have a few hours when we aren't thinking or talking about killing?

Garl leans in and says, "Little brother, I was surprised to hear about your murderous streak. I didn't think you were up to it . . . hand-to-hand and all that."

Lucia sees my rising distress and asks Garl to sing another song.

Happy to oblige, he strides to the head table. When everyone is quiet, he places his hand over his heart.

The 166 boys, the one-sixty-six!

Fierce Newfoundlanders sir, you won't soon trick.

We came from an island to fight on the boot.

All we've done since is shoot, shoot, and shoot.

Lucia gets up and starts collecting the dirty dishes.

We left behind girlfriends and wee babes too.

Garl catches her eye and motions dramatically to Arch.

South African brandy keeps us from getting too blue.

When the snow melts, it's Bologna or bust!

He grabs the corners of the tablecloth, trapping Lucia. "*There we'll give Jerry a one-two-three THRUST!*" He thrusts his hips against her backside. Lucia whips around to face Garl with her fists clenched. I can't see her face, but Garl's smirk stokes the drunken energy in the mess.

I stand, but Tombstone puts his paw on my shoulder and pushes me back down. "She's a big girl," he says. "She can take care of herself."

Garl allows Lucia to escape, licking his lips for effect.

And when it's all over, ragazzi, no more shall we roam,

It's Terra Nova for us! The place we call home.

The men shout, "Hurrah!" and raise their glasses. Garl grabs the four corners of the tablecloth, trapping all the dirty dishes, centrepieces, and empty slush jugs, and hoists the whole works out the tent flaps to screams of laughter.

———

Lucia and Cosimo look up as Arch enters the potato-peeling tent. "It was getting a little too rambunctious in the mess," says Lucia.

"I'm sorry. I don't know what to say . . ."

"It's okay. I know how strong the shine is and how much you men miss your wives and girlfriends."

Before he sits, Arch gives Lucia a cardboard box decorated with an olive sprig. "A little something to thank you for everything you do."

Lucia's cheeks redden. She accepts the box and places the olive sprig behind her ear. She unties the twine, opens the flaps, and gasps. "A Necchi!"

Arch is flustered when she jumps up and wraps her arms around him. He doesn't know what to do with his hands and pats her on the back. When she lets go, he feels bereft. Cosimo frowns.

"These are the absolute best. My mother had one of these sewing machines. Thank you, Archibald. My mending will go so much faster!"

She extracts a fist-sized lump wrapped in a tea towel from her bag and tells Cosimo it's his special gift. He peels back the fabric to reveal a bronze devil with a red velvet rump dotted with pins.

Lucia says, "The diavoletto is your great Nonna's good-luck charm. I took him from our house, to keep us safe, and it worked. It's why we found Arch."

Arch smiles like a fool and Cosimo rolls his eyes. "It's just a pincushion."

"It's something to remind you that you belong here, Cosimo," she says. "And if you get mad, you can stick a pin in its rump, it'll make you feel better."

Cosimo says, "Only when Stella Rossa drive the invaders away will I feel better."

Arch knows that Cosimo considers him and the Newfoundlanders invaders along with the Germans. Cosimo stands. His fists are clenched. "Unlike you, I am not content to be attendesi," he says. The rest of the conversation is a rapid-fire mixture of Italian and dialect that ends with Cosimo grabbing the devil and stalking off. Lucia is fighting back tears. Arch holds her in his arms and she explains that attendesi are those who wait for Allied salvation instead of taking up arms against the Nazis and Fascists.

At Grizzana, Caroline cracks open the patio door. She wants to fall asleep to the same sounds Pop and Arch would've heard in 1944. There are crickets. Cedars creak. The wind sounds different than it does at home. Did they notice that too? Owls call to each other. Something, wild boar maybe, grunt and crash through the undergrowth. Where did Pop get that awful sword? And why would he give it to Tombstone?

Dogs bound along mountain paths. Deep, resonant barks. They gallop, cornering her against a ruined wall. Lips pull back and teeth are bared. Low growls. They flick their heads back and forth in anger. One lunges. She gasps awake. The room is bright, and an emerald grasshopper is perched on her pillow. It's beautiful in an insect-y way. A low horn calls and its eyes swivel. Can grasshoppers hear? It wasn't just a dream. There are dogs. Barks loop up and down the gullies. It's difficult to know how close they are. A dog sprints past her open patio door. She pulls back the sheets to get up and close the door and the grasshopper leaps onto the threshold. Before it can jump back outside, the dog circles back and sticks its snout into her room. It growls at her or the grasshopper. She shakes her sheet to frighten the animal away. "Stella! Vieni! Vieni!" An elderly gentleman peeks his head into the open door. He's breathing hard. He shoos the dog away with his walking stick. "Signora, scusi." He's gone before she can reply.

Arch steadies Cosimo's hand as he solders two ammo crates together. He's teaching the boy how to make a stove. Radio London burbles in the background. When the jingle signals the end of the newscast, Cosimo lays down the welding torch. "Bologna is only twenty miles away. Why won't Alexander let the Allies keep going?"

"We should have kept going, I agree with you. But Cosi, if we didn't follow orders, it would be chaos." Arch says this even though he no longer believes it.

Cosi says, "That's the difference between you and us." Cosimo considers himself one of the rebels. "We will do everything necessary for our freedom, while the British are just waiting for the spoils to be divided."

"Now hold on, that's not fair," says Arch. "We also want Italy to be free."

"If you really did, you wouldn't have let the Germans hunt the resistance all winter." Arch regrets making the radio for Cosi. The Radio London broadcasts are stoking his radicalism. A few days ago, coming back from patrol, Arch ran into Cosi carrying a full knapsack and a bedroll, hours away from their post. He managed to convince the boy to return to his mother and since then he has been working hard to keep him occupied.

Garl finds Cosi welding with Arch and invites the boy for a hot chocolate. He can tell Arch doesn't like the intrusion. He tilts his head and is about to say something about finishing the foolish stove they're making, but before he can speak, Cosimo jumps up. It doesn't take much for Garl to feel that gut burble of judgment from his high and mighty little brother. As they're walking away, he asks the kid, "What are your plans after all this foolishness is over with?" Cosi shrugs. Garl says, "I'm thinking I'll get some work in a fish plant."

"You plant fish?" asks Cosimo.

Garl laughs. "Fish plants are like factories," he says. "They buy the fish from the fishermen, clean them, freeze them, box them, and sell them to stores."

Cosimo says, "I'll be here in the mountains with Mama and Papa."

"That sounds good. You'll be able to go to school, have a girl-friend, all the stuff a young fella like you is supposed to be at."

They drink their hot chocolate in a snowbank next to the South African canteen. Garl feels at ease. Maybe he was too quick to go along with Tobin's plan to adopt out Bridget. He sometimes thinks about being a father, doing the right thing by Anna. If he did, Arch would have nothing to lord over him, but that would also free his little brother up to pursue Lucy, and Garl is not letting that happen.

As if reading Garl's mind, Cosimo asks what Arch will do after the war. Garl shrugs and says, "Before, ya know, he was a priest."

Cosimo is surprised. "Arch was a priest?"

"Yeah," Garl says, "and a teacher, but he quit that and asked a girl to marry him, and she's got a kid, so he'll have to get a job when he gets back home."

Cosimo sips his hot chocolate and is silent for a long time. "Do you think the war will be over soon?"

Garl says, "As soon as the snow melts, the race will be on. Every-one wants to beat the Yanks to Bologna. Especially after they cheated the Canadians out of Rome."

Cosimo almost spits out his hot chocolate in anger. "Stella Rossa will liberate Bologna and I'll be with them!"

Garl is taken aback by Cosi's passion. "Alright, b'y, no need to get excited. Are there that many partisans up here? I certainly haven't seen any."

Garl knows better than to let on that he's selling supplies from Jackie's storeroom as well as stuff he finds in a hollow tree outside the post. He suspects Lucia is the one filling the tree. Who knows how much the lire will be worth after the war, but Garl's hoping to have enough saved up for a nice little place in Windsor or Sudbury. He'd rather work underground or on an assembly line than be trapped in an unwanted marriage, raising a youngster. Let Arch sweep in and play the hero. Cosimo thanks Garl for the cocoa and skulks off. Garl takes his last gulp and hopes Cosi tells Lucia about Arch's prior engagement.

chapter 20

THE CONFESSIONAL

No matter how often Arch bathes here, the heat surprises him, even though the water has been steaming out of the earth well before the Etrusci who claimed the pools for their king. He's so grateful for the warmth and peace away from the post's complaints and idleness. If they don't get leave or orders to march on Bologna soon, they may kill each other. He unbuttons, un-belts, and strips down. Steps out of his boots, peels off his socks, and cocks his pistol before laying it next to his sliver of soap. Overhead, thick, dried grape vines twist around an arbour. Not much protection from a sniper, but they keep the steam and heat in and provide some privacy. He shivers in the pleasant warmth and soaps up his hair. Did the Etruscan king convince his subjects that he heated the water? Arch sinks under, releasing his soapy crown to float free. Eyes squeezed shut, he scrubs his fingertips through his curls loosening more suds before coming up for air. A dark silhouette ripples on the pool's surface. He reaches for his pistol.

Lucia says, "Don't shoot me . . . not again!"

Arch covers his privates and prepares to jump out. "What's happening? Is there something going on back at the post?"

She shakes her head and smiles. "Everyone's fine. I just wanted to see you, Arch."

She steps out of her red shoes. "May I get in?" she asks.

He nods. She's told him what happens to Italian women who take up with Allied soldiers. Her partisan brothers and sisters will accuse her of sleeping with the enemy and her neighbours will call her a whore. She certainly won't get the post-war teaching position she's hoping for. The fading crescent moon is tinted pink as she pulls her sweater over her head and steps out of her skirt and bloomers. His breath catches. He watches her pin her hair up. Her boldness and beauty spark currents through his limbs.

Garl adjusts the focus on his binocs in time to see Lucia drop her clothes and pause at the edge of the spring. Hot damn! He followed her from the camp to see once and for all if she's the one stuffing the empty tree with supplies and undercutting his resale market.

Lucia tells him that the locals call the spring "the confessional." Arch shivers the memory of Tobin away. She draws a circle on the water's surface with her fingers and says, "Is it true you were a priest?"

Arch's face tightens. "Yesss," he says. "That's t-true. I wanted to get an education and it w-was really the only way." Before his shame can burble up and ruin this moment, he tells her why he quit. He's never told anyone about Tobin. The shame curls into the steam rising into the stars above them. She nods and says priests commit the same crimes in Italy and he will feel freer now that he's talked about it. He wants to believe her. She baptizes her shoulders with palmfuls of water and he asks her about Paolo.

"I have not really had a chance to mourn him." They face each other. Arch searches for her hands under the water and holds them.

She tells him Paolo studied law but was impatient with the Fascist system. She studied literature and was assisting a professor until Jews were forbidden to teach, and the professor left for the States. Paolo dropped out of school around the same time and went to Spain to fight Franco. Lucia came home to help build the network in the mountains.

"So, you were both rebels?" he asks with a smirk.

"I wasn't armed, but I planned missions, printed documents, ran errands, and delivered food. The Fascists would always let me cross the checkpoints. Sometimes I carried papers, sometimes guns. They never checked. They think women are only good for cleaning and childbearing."

She says, "When he came back from Spain, there was a clumsy attempt to kidnap me. So, he smuggled us over the Alps to Switzerland and onto England."

She pulls her hands away. He asks, "Any regrets?"

"Only that I have not allowed myself to feel anything for a decade. Even after I knew it was over with Paolo." She holds his gaze and says, "Until now, I closed myself off to love." His cheeks are burning. She glides to his side of the pool and says, "Even when Paolo was still alive, his letters were more often about missions. In the last few years, I was no longer the little sparrow he fell for. I became Cosimo's mama."

They sit shoulder to shoulder watching the dawn streak across the sky. Arch aches to turn and hold her, even though she's remembering her dead husband.

"When Cosi told me his father was gone, I was sad for him, but I didn't mourn Paolo as a lover, it was more like feeling the loss of a comrade."

———

The curve of Lucia's back sinks below the pool's surface, shaking out a memory of Garl's one fumble with Anna. The smell of talcum on her neck. His struggle with the hundreds of buttons on her Sally Ann uniform. Before that walk, they'd only ever kissed on the bridge. Even though she was a goody-two-shoes, it didn't take much to convince her. Too bad she had to go and get pregnant. Arch moves into view and Garl's jaw clenches. That son of a bitch!

———

She wipes soap bubbles from my temple. Her lips are parted. "What are you looking for, Arch? What do you wish for?"

No one has ever asked me that question. Words tumble out. "I want. I want you. Lucia, you're the one. I've never felt like this. I dream of living above a garage in Bologna, fixing cars, helping Cosi with his homework, you and I will share a big creaky brass bed, and I'll watch you stitch love into everything you sew."

I kiss her lips and soar. She breaks away. She's panting. Her hand on my chest. "Wait," she says. "At Christmas, you said Tombstone keeps your secrets. What are they?"

Stay calm. How do I tell her about Anna? Her fingers are tangled through the hair on my chest. "I'd like it if. You." I grasp her hand, turn it over, and kiss her palm. She slides against me, her mouth, her breasts.

We lift off like parachute silk in a gale. Tight leaf fists push along the arbour. Hips coax. The Etruscan King laughs as our pulses race together. Hesitation evaporates and dreams pass back and forth between our mouths. I stroke the curve of her back. Wingbeats flap in overlapping circles above us. The arbour shakes. Water sloshes and spills over the pool's edge. Lucia gasps and I shudder into her neck.

———

Garl cocks his rifle. Bile rising in his throat as he searches for a target close enough to startle them apart. He aims at a nearby scarecrow.

———

Leaves release cool dew onto their shoulders. They shiver and hold onto each other trying to stay in the spring's spell. She says, "Cosimo told me you have a sweetheart and a baby at home. That you're engaged. Please tell me it is just one of Garl's stories."

She must've felt his heart stop because she pulls away. Sulphur clouds his head. He's much too warm and when he brings water to his face, he wishes it was the ice-cold Atlantic.

"So, it's true," she says. "The baby in Garl's Christmas poem?" His heart sinks. If he tells her the child is not his, she will think he's one of those soldiers who lies about the realities at home to get laid. If he doesn't tell her the whole story, God knows what Garl will make up.

"I t-tutored a girl, Anna. I helped her with her sumsss so she could get into teaching college," he says. "She wrote to say she's pregnant and since then she's had a little girl."

Lucia's eyes widen and she says, "Your student? How is that different from the priest?"

Her accusation needles his shame. "I promise you, Lucia, I did not. I have never taken advantage of Anna. It happened after I left."

"How convenient," she says.

"No. It's true. I've only ever been her teacher and her friend, but I offered to marry her and help raise the child. To save her from gossip."

"You're going to marry her for the sake of appearances?" She spits out the words.

"The child is not mine. It's Garl's and he—"

"Oh my God. Is this a game? You and your brother? Both competing for my attention."

———

Garl grabs the binoculars. Fuck! He missed again, but the space between them is widening.

———

A vortex of dried leaves spins counter-clockwise on the water's surface as she gets out of the pool.

"It's not like that at all. I've never loved Anna," Arch says.

She steps into her skirt, pulls on her sweater. The wool sticks to her wet skin. "Is Anna the consolation prize or am I?" she asks.

She yanks the sweater down roughly and stomps off with her shoes in her hand.

How can he convince her he's only trying to right his brother's wrongs? That if Min had a grandchild to love, she might leave Skipper. That married, Anna might find Bridget. He opens his mouth, but nothing comes out.

———

Garl follows the swish of Lucia's hips and spots two partisans in a gully below him with their binocs also trained on the spring.

chapter 21

TORCHES

Cosimo hands the silk scarf to his father. He tells him how they risked their lives to come home with maps hidden in his mama's shoes and in the lining of his rucksack. The silk trembles and Cosi feels taller. He wants Paolo to be proud of his son for his bravery, for bringing such a useful thing to the camp. Paolo holds the map to his nose and blows as hard as he can then he announces, "This war will not be won with silk hankies!" Cosimo pleads. "Papa, it's not just that, it's a map to help British POWs escape over the Alps."

"Kid, I don't want the POWs escaping. I need every one of them with me and listen, here in camp, call me Volpe like every-one else."

He stuffs the map into his chest pocket and walks away leaving Cosimo standing alone. Clumps of men sleep on the ground, three teenagers water mules, and two women stir a giant pot over a fire. Cosimo shifts from one foot to the other weighing up his situation. It's not the reunion he imagined, but he's here and he was right. Lino and his mother were lying about his father.

———

Slade's tongue is dry and sour. His temples throb. He sits up slowly, the room whips into a spin and he almost retches. 120s. Tombstone slamming cards on the table. Their triumph. Baymen beating townies in the final game before leave. Three shells brimming with South African happiness. Too much happiness. He gently manoeuvres his feet to the floor. Wills his gritty eyes to focus and croaks, "Get up, Mr. Walsh, it's time to make your water."

Bed bugs skitter into their daytime hiding places when he throws back Arch's blanket. Since he was sent to the hospital, Slade has been sleeping in his bunk to keep an eye on the big guy. He rubs his eyes and refocuses, but the scene doesn't change. Tombstone's bunk is empty. Arch is going to flatten him. He shoves his hands into his armpits for warmth and thinks about starting a fire. Maybe Tombstone stayed in the mess? No, he remembers leaving arm and arm with him. He opens the dugout door and shivers. Thick ice coats every surface. A glitter storm right here on the boot. A little send-off from the mountain. Yeah. They did leave the mess. They were skating in the drainage ditches. Tombstone leaning on a mop he said he was going to turn into an ugly stick. Not wanting to go home half-cracked and empty-handed.

Slade steps onto the ice and pushes off, gliding through an early morning snowfall. He is picking up speed when his right boot slams into something and he sprawls forward in the darkness. He moans and waits for the wicked stinging in his knees and palms to subside before opening his eyes. Kneeling, he sees it's the Jesus mop and a lump of . . . Tombstone! Shit! Shit! Shit! Laid out like the bog man in the British Museum. Only his forehead, nose, toes, and mop head peek above the surface. Downy snow crystals collect on his brow. Slade smashes at the ice around Tombstone's face. He tries to wrench the mop handle from his hands, but there's no give. He's a solid chunk. He leans over Tombstone's face to listen for breathing. Just a quiet rattle. He slaps the blueing skin on Tombstone's cheeks as hard as he can. "Wake up, shithead!" he yells. "We're going home in a few days, and you'll finally see your youngsters!"

————

Lucia gathers her sewing kit and tiptoes out of the dugout to let Cosi sleep in. She has a few more uniforms to patch before the men go home. When they leave the post, she plans to go to Firenze, like Arch suggested all those months ago. She should be able to find work in one of the ateliers, enrol Cosi in school, and meet face to face with the Red Cross about her family. She's bracing herself for Cosi's arguments about leaving the mountains. His obsession with the partisan cause grows daily. Younger Lucia would've been proud of him, but present-day Lucia is weary.

The spring haunts her. She feels like a foolish schoolgirl for falling for Arch. Since he was sent to the hospital in Pistoia, Garl is proving her theory that she is part of some sibling contest. Every morning, he shows up at the mess to watch her mend, helps himself to her coffee, and sits too close. Today, he asks for thread for ice fishing.

"I can spare some," she says, "but I've got a few more uniforms to mend and thread is hard to come by."

Uninvited, Garl opens her sewing tin and digs around for a spool.

"The way I sees it, Lucy," he says, "the British Army pays for the thread, so I have every right to it."

She keeps stitching and hopes his fingers find the sharp end of a pin. He pockets a full spool of her best heavy black thread and stands. Way too close.

"I caught that trout you ate last night. I noticed you cleaned your plate."

"Yes, it was delicious, Garl. It's been a long time since I've had fish."

He lowers his voice. "How about tasting my fish?"

Before she can react, he unzips and pulls her head towards his fly. She struggles against his hand in her hair, one hand pushes against his thigh, and the other fumbles for her scissors. She jabs hard with the sharp tips. He jumps back. "You bitch!"

She spits out, "I'm no whore!"

"Coulda fooled me. I saw you with Archie at the hot springs. You're as common as bog water."

Lucia's stomach drops. Before she can speak, Slade bursts in through the canvas flaps and she's never been happier to see him. When he catches his breath, he says, "Lucy, help me with Tombstone. He's froze solid."

She pockets her weapon, grabs a handful of fabric and the warm kettle, to run after Slade. Grateful to get away from Garl.

When they climb down into the drainage ditch, a cry gets caught in her throat. They've all tried to protect Tombstone from himself and get him home to his kids without a discharge and now it looks as if it was all for naught. She instructs Slade to pour the water over the fabric and pack the warm material around Tombstone's submerged head and shoulders. She can hear a quiet crinkle of his breath over Slade's cursing. Once the ice is weakened, they bash away at it with their fists and elbows. Lucia straddles Tombstone's chest and warms his face with her hands. She kisses his forehead and makes a wish. A kind of prayer to the mountain that he will revive. Once his upper body is freed, Slade pulls him up into a sitting position and Lucia leans against his back to keep him upright. Slade wallops his chest. "Come on, ya big galoot, breathe!"

Tombstone sputters and gasps. "I can't feel my legs!"

Slade and Lucia exhale.

"I've got the polio! I always knew I'd get the polio!" Tombstone says.

"Don't be so fucking foolish. You don't have polio. You can't feel your legs because they're froze," Slade says. "You passed out in the ditch."

They wiggle him backwards out of his tomb and help him hobble back to the mess. Lucia pours him a cup of coffee and drapes the wet fabric on the line to dry. When she puts her scissors back in her sewing kit, she is startled to see the diavoletto staring up at her. It can only signal one thing. Cosimo is gone.

A jeepful of Brazilian nurses pulls up in a swirl of dust. They're all curly hair, big gestures, Ray-Bans, and effortless glamour. Barbara is keenly aware that she hasn't washed in six days, but as soon as she steps forward and directs them to pose, she's in charge. They scamper into place, draping themselves playfully over the jeep and driver. She loves capturing this. She likes to think she's creating a new future for women out of sunlight and emulsion.

She's earning a fine living as a freelance war photographer. Even managing from time to time to scoop the official government-paid male photographers who have drivers, baths, and hotel rooms. The guys who are paid whether their pictures sell or not. Officially, when asked, she tells the brass she stays well behind the front lines, not telling them she's already been to the battle sites and back and her rolls have already been sent off to newspapers and magazines. She trades photos for food and rides, sleeps in barns and farmhouses, in dugouts, and sometimes under mess tables. She took this hospital assignment because it gets her closer to Bologna. She's determined to get to the liberation before the Americans.

One of the nurses strides over with her hand out. "Bom Dia, I'm Ana Maria Pereira. Welcome to the 36th Evacuation Hospital, Barbara. Let me show you around."

Ana Maria talks Barbara through a series of interconnected tents: administration, labs, severe wounds, maternity, and surgery. The sprawling city of canvas smells of Dettol, sweat, bleach, and iodine. Barbara snaps photos of the nurses and learns that Ana Maria came to Italy as a volunteer medic and learned nursing on the job. Ana Maria says, "I didn't know women were allowed to do what you do."

Barbara winks. "I didn't know either."

Volpe gives Cosimo directions to a nearby village where a farmer has collected some much-needed weapons. He follows a stream down to the village, hiding in the trees around the edges of a farmhouse until he's sure there's no Germans around. He finds the farmer in the barn and announces the password with pride. The man lifts a tarp on a cart of rotten cauliflower. Cosi clamps his hand over his nose. The guns are hidden underneath, but the hum off the vegetables is overwhelming. Demeaning, Cosi thinks, to the seriousness of his mission. The farmer scratches his paunch. "I've disguised the guns, now what about you?"

"What do you mean?" asks Cosimo.

"Going back up the mountain, we've got to take some of the main roads. If we're stopped, you'll be shot or sent to work digging the German line. You need a disguise."

He brings Cosi a frilly, powder-blue dress and kerchief. Cosi is appalled and shakes his head, and the farmer says, "The only other dress I have is pink."

Humiliated in blue frills, Cosimo's mission becomes less about guarding the arms and more about guarding the slimey vegetable cover. All along the roads and paths, people drift out of the woods and crawl out of ditches, begging for a handful of the mouldy stink. One woman cries out that it could keep her babies alive. His cheeks burn when he pushes her hand away. If only he still believed in invisibility spells.

Before they enter the camp, he tears off the dress and hands it back to the farmer. Volpe thanks the farmer for risking his life but says nothing to Cosimo. He wants to yell at Papa that it's not his fault the Allies abandoned the partisans for the winter, that he and his mother also experienced hunger, fear, enemy bombings, and hatred. That they almost drowned in a ship full of deportees! But instead, he gets in line for a bowl of nettle soup and watches Volpe pick through the guns.

———————

Barbara tells Ana Maria she's taking photos for a British publication and the nurse leads her into a humongous, dark ward. The canvas above them is a swooping Milky Way of flak holes. Sun rays piercing the holes and the listing posts holding up the roof makes it feel like she's entering a circus big top.

"Please don't use your flash. The soldiers in here are recovering from head trauma," says Ana Maria.

Barbara adjusts her f-stop and takes several shots of a doctor with his hands on his hips in the background shadows. Two nurses in the foreground lean over a patient's bed. She may not be able to sell these shots to a newspaper, but she's pleased to have captured the grace of this strange scene. Ana Maria tilts her head, perhaps trying to imagine the photo, but gives up and points to a nearby bed. "Barbara, this is Archibald Fisher. He's a British private with the . . ." She flips through the clipboard at the end of his bed. "Newfoundland Regiment."

Barbara's heart jumps. This is the first time she's met someone from home.

"Are you with the 166th?"

He struggles to sit up. "Yes. Who are you?"

"I'm Barbara Kerr. My dad has the camera store on Water Street next to McMurdo's Soda Shop. Are you from town?"

Arch regards the woman through his one good eye.

Should he tell her that it was his own fault? He knew there were snipers always watching and he shouldn't have been outside with a mirror, but Lucia had stopped talking to him and he just didn't care.

He'd better put his dentures in before she takes any more photos with that thing.

"No, I taught for a while in town, but I'm from Trinity Bay."

"Do you mind if I ask what happened?"

"I was getting a shave, and the mirror must've given me away. Luckily the sniper had crap aim. He just skimmed my brow."

So stupid. He thought it was the throaty laugh of a crow posing a high-pitched question until his frigging face started to burn and he was lifted into a twisting tunnel of snow and grit.

"Sorry, I don't know if I'm making sense. I'm still a bit shagged up. You're the photographer who was coming up to take our photos?"

Barbara nods. "Yeah, but I had to change my plans when you guys got leave."

"Leave? We haven't had leave in four years."

"That doesn't sound right. Your CO Knox told me not to come. He said they're packing up the post. Everyone is going home. How long have you been in hospital?"

Arch doesn't know the answer to that question, but his pulse is racing. He has got to get out of here and back up on Salvaro. He needs to tell Lucia he loves her, even though he's got to go home and find Bridget. That he'll be back, that they can still have their dream. He stares at the tubes in his arm and says, "Can you spare a couple of pages of paper and a pencil? I need to write a letter to someone."

Barbara rips two pages from her notebook and hands over her one precious pencil. "I'll take a few more shots and come back for your letter and my pencil. Okay?" She turns back at the doorway to the ward and takes a shot of Private Fisher hunched over in his bed writing.

———

Cosimo descends into a busy village market with the men. They're looking for a notary who Volpe says is a sympathizer. Some of Cosi's compatriots are getting a charge out of the fear they stoke in the villagers. They're all starving and pilfer as much food as they can eat from the market stalls. When the notary is found, he's pulled out of his house and a noose is put around his neck. They drag the old man through the streets to the main fountain. Volpe reads out the charges. In Firenze, this man helped the Fascists round up Jews for deportation. He stood on the train station platform and ticked off names as people were forced onto death trains. Here on the mountain, he told the Nazis the identities of families with partisan sons. The notary is defiant. "I had no choice! None of us have any choice!"

Volpe slaps his face. "Only the weak collaborate!"

The man's knees buckle as the rope is thrown over a tree branch above the fountain. Holding a Nazi Beretta by the barrel, Volpe walks through his men to choose an executioner. Cosimo stops breathing when his father pauses in front of him, but instead of testing his son, he hands the gun to the man next to him, a baker named Gigo. Cosimo knows his face is as red as it was when he was wearing the blue dress.

Gigo steps forward, places the muzzle against the old man's temple, and squeezes the trigger. Cosimo has to bite the inside of his cheek to stop the tears. The rope is yanked hard and the man's bloodied body is left dangling from the tree. Filtering back into the woods, the men slap Gigo's back and congratulate him. Cosi looks back and sees an old woman kneeling below the body. He wishes he had known his father before the war.

That night, around the campfire, Cosimo is surprised when Volpe announces his son will take part in bombing a railway trestle.

chapter 22

THE BUTTON

Lucia trips on a root and her startled cry echoes off tree trunks. She lies still, cursing her clumsiness and listening for movement. She has no idea where Cosimo is but surmises the partisans will be moving north ahead of the Allies. She is close to the German line, so she's avoiding rivers and roads and hiding when she hears vehicles. She stands and brushes pine needles and pebbles off her palms.

"Halt!" Two German soldiers, just steps away. One points his Luger at her heart and the other motions for her to approach. The blood drains from her legs. Can she walk? One soldier holds out his hand to help her descend the last few steps to the road's grey surface. "Documenti. Adesso!"

She blanks. In her panic to find Cosimo, she left their papers in the dugout. She only has her sewing kit in her bag. "Si, si." She makes a show of going through her purse, to buy time and think up a story. The key is to be charming, and not too cocky. They raise their weapons, and she removes her hands slowly, showing her palms and smiling sweetly. "Scusi signori, li ho persi."

"Lost them? Not having your papers is a jailable offence. Name?"

She tells the truth. "Lucia."

"I am Hans, and this is Jürgen."

She nods, uncomfortable with such familiarity.

"And where are you coming from, Lucia?"

She lies. "Bologna."

Hans is not much older than Cosimo. "And where are you going?"

"Sasso Marconi. My grandmother asked me to do some mending."

Jürgen tugs at her purse. His efforts expose the shoulder strap of her brassiere. Hans says something in German and Jürgen laughs.

"You are going in the wrong direction."

"I'm not used to these mountain trails," she lies.

She pulls her coat closed as Jürgen extracts items from her purse. Hans steps too close. His breath is sour. "What does your granny need mending?" he asks.

"Her winter coat needs new buttons."

Jürgen breaks the fragile spine of the family bible and tosses the papers in the dirt. Hans cocks an eyebrow. "Your dear grandmother's name?"

"Diavoletto. Maria Diavoletto."

She hopes invoking her grandmother's good-luck charm out loud will get her through this alive. Jürgen paws through her sewing kit. Hans grabs her chin roughly. There are poppy seeds at his gum line. The nose of his machine gun knocks against her shin. "How old are you, Lucia?"

"I am . . . thirty-two."

He grabs her between the legs and tries to push his fingers inside her. "Not so old," he growls.

Jürgen hisses he's found something. Hans pulls her closer, the front of her dress balled up in his fist. "Sweet Lucia. You're in trouble now."

Jürgen thrusts a shiny object between their faces. "What's this then?"

"I don't know," she says.

"Slut. This is a British officer's button. It seems you will mend for anyone—even the enemy."

Lucia would never carry such a dangerous item. How did it get in her kit? Jürgen kicks the sewing tin across the roadbed, sending needles, thimbles, and spools spiralling in bumpy, broken circles. The corkscrew of violence tightens. They grab at her limbs and clothing. Expose her breasts. Push her down onto the roadbed. She attempts to cover herself, but her movements are slow, like she's underwater. Splayed palms, sour drool from Hans's mouth drips onto her neck. His knee pries at her thighs. He fumbles with his belt. Gravel digs into her shoulder blades. She arches her back and tries to twist away, but Jürgen pulls her ankles apart. Cloth rips. The mountain's energy lifts her above the violence. There is no way he will enter her. She will die fighting. A flash of red. A jolt of hope ripples through her limbs. Brambles part. Hans rolls away. Jürgen swivels his machine gun and aims at the trees. Lucia covers her face. Shots ring out. Her heart stutters. Jürgen's gun falls first, and he crumples next to her. His flat eyes mere inches from her nose. She rolls the other way. Crawls. Her breathing is stifled. Hans's arm is tight around her neck. He hauls her to her feet, knees her lower back, and curses. He whips her around to face the bushes where the shots came from. She wants to cover her body, but she can't. A pinpoint of pain against her temple. He yells, "I'll shoot the bitch!" A branch cracks behind them. Hans swivels and falters. His grip loosens just enough so that Lucia is able to jab him hard with her elbow and push away. A shot grazes the tip of her ear as she stumbles forward into the ditch. His body hits the earth with a thud and there's one, two beats of silence. Men. Stella Rossa. Scramble out of gullies and drag the bodies back in. Shovels clang the earth. There's blood on her ear. They strip uniforms, weapons, and IDs. Lucia sits up to right her brassiere, dress, and hair.

She lurches to her knees and crawls to collect needles, pins, scissors, and thread. She stands and picks up the pages of the family bible.

A man named Massimo hands her the diavoletto and says, "Signora, andiamo. The gunshots will bring more Germans." The devil's tail is bent. Could it be what Hans stumbled on? She kisses it and kicks the brass button away.

At a stream, Lucia asks Massimo for a few moments of privacy to wash. He agrees, retracing their steps to sweep a branch over their tracks. When he returns, he says, "I apologize, Signora Capponi, but I must blindfold you."

He knows who she is! "Are you bringing me to Cosimo, to my son?" Massimo nods and she accepts the filthy blindfold and his callused hand. He's a farmer like her father. He guides her down, up, and over rough paths for about an hour. Water from streams soaks through her shoes. Sometimes the birdsong is muffled, and the air is cool and damp. Are they in caves or shaded thickets? They walk over lumpy drills in farmer's fields and stumble over loose shale. Finally, he turns her around in circles as if they were children playing a party game. When Massimo removes the blindfold, she feels off balance and blinks.

The road north to Bologna is a sea of Allied jeeps, artillery trucks, infantry units, tanks, and motorcycles. Barbara does a double take when she spots a bandaged Arch Fisher sitting on a roadside rock amid the chaos. She asks Jon to stop and waves Arch over. He climbs into the ambulance gingerly and starts in on a story as if the three of them had been chatting for hours. "They put it in the bog for a drink and the funniest thing is, it looked just like it belonged there," he says. "An elephant! In the bog. It was the craziest thing. A guy with lipstick on his nose threw things in the air and caught them. First it was crab apples, then empty beer bottles. I'd like to know where they found those in the citadel."

Barbara glances at Jon. He'd agreed to give her a lift to Salvaro with some medical supplies but certainly hadn't signed on to take a loopy patient back to his post.

"Are you feeling okay, Arch?" she asks.

"They gave me a shot of morphine just before I left and it's hard to tell if I'm thinking or talking."

Barbara offers Arch her canteen and he drains it, wipes his wet lips on his sleeve, and stares out the window.

Lucia is standing in the cool shade of a huge pergola weighed down with vines and branches. There are a dozen or more camouflaged tents. Men in a mishmash of uniforms and civilian clothing eye her shyly. Was she expected? She supposes they know she is Paolo's widow. She nods at the only other woman present, a young girl of about seventeen pinning socks to a clothesline. The men pepper Massimo with questions about the shooting. They're agitated, fearful that it will bring more Germans up the mountain. They are worried about something happening at a bridge. She scans the camp for Cosimo's mop of golden hair. Massimo leads her to the mouth of a cave and gestures for her to enter. It takes a few moments for her eyes to adjust to the dark.

"Welcome to our camp, Luci."

Her mouth opens.

"I'm glad you still recognize my voice," he says.

"P-P-Paulo?"

He steps into the light. Scruffier and thicker than when she last saw him. His jawline is muddled and there's sadness around his eyes. She flies into his arms, and he whispers into her hair. "I've dreamt about this for years." He smells like wood smoke, tobacco, and something familiar that she can't name. They kiss and she recalls everything they once shared.

"Mama and Papa. They're gone, Paolo. They're . . ." She can't finish the sentence.

He shushes her. "We don't know that."

"You know, don't you? Where are they?" she asks.

She searches his eyes for answers, but he is unable to hold her gaze. He doesn't want to tell her yet. She asks, "Why, Paolo, why did you leave us to fend for ourselves?"

"Luci, I got you here. I got you both home. It took longer than I would've liked, but the prison in Bologna . . ." he says. "You didn't think it was the priest, did you?"

"Lino? I did. I—he took good care of Cosi."

"He put him in danger."

"How is that different," Lucia asks, "from what he is doing here?"

Paolo bites his lip and looks at the cave floor. She steps out of his embrace. "I don't mean to be rude, given that your . . . our . . . men risked their lives for me today, but I need to see him. Where is he?"

The ambulance rumbles over the lip of a bomb crater and Arch picks up his tale. "Then the clown started throwing hatchets. Not one, but three! There wasn't a sound in the whole hall. He didn't know there's no doctor on our coast. No Brazilian nurses either. When he bowed, we all exhaled together. And that's when Garl bust in through the double doors with three flaming torches. He and the clown threw them back and forth, higher and higher. It's just like Garl to get up to devilment like that. The higher the torches spun, the paler the Salvation Army Captain got. When the clown caught all three and blew out the fire, no one applauded harder than Captain Tucker."

Paolo flicks his head and a couple of men emerge from deep within the cave, startling Lucia.

"Lucia, this is Dante and Armando. They're my right hands."

They nod. Dante gestures at his watch and Paolo asks for a moment. They converse at the cave's mouth. Lucia is annoyed. She used to be his right hand and now he won't speak in front of her.

"We are brothers," Paolo says, by way of apology. "We share everything."

"Then how is it that you don't know we've been here for months?" she asks.

"I knew where you were," he says. "We were keeping an eye."

"Why didn't you want to be with me? To meet your son? Why was it necessary for me to believe you were dead, Paolo?"

"Cosi didn't believe I was dead," he says flatly.

Blood rushes to Lucia's cheeks. Does Paolo know about the spring with Arch? He says, "Having you and Cosi here would've put these men at risk."

She says, "I founded this with you. Remember?"

"I would've been worried about you." His voice drops to a whisper. "You were safer with the invaders."

"Safer? When I was being raped at the border?"

He studies his hands. "This is war, Lucia. Your dignity is not the priority. What we're fighting for is much larger than that."

Wounded, she stands and paces. Promises have been broken. Her stomach growls, but she will not ask him for food. She demands once again to see Cosimo. Paolo pauses as if calculating something, then admits he's on a mission. Her rage bubbles over. "You sent our only son on a mission?"

"He is like everyone else. Every man here is risking their lives for a better future."

She glares at him. "He is not yet a man, you fool."

He attempts to calm her, saying Cosi will be back soon. But she won't let it go. He pounds his fists on the table and yells, "I'm your husband and you vowed to obey me."

She laughs. "You've forgotten who you married. I'm not some simple-minded casalinga."

Massimo coughs dramatically and enters the cave. He tells Paolo it's time. Paolo stands and orders Massimo to keep Lucia here.

They used one of the circus torches to light the coastal path home to Turk's Cove. Garl was running ahead playing at being a Viking marauder. Arch found the light disorienting and was asking him to snuff it out right before they got jumped and the light was stamped out. Arch was heaved into the goowiddy where someone sat on him and smacked him around until he lay still. They railed on Garl for what felt like hours. Kicks. Bites. Punches. Grunts. Throughout the beating, Garl called them pansies, cowards, and mama's boys. For that they boxed his ears, gave him a shiner, tore the arm from his coat, and split open his lip and forehead. When they were finished, the biggest one kicked Garl in the guts one last time and growled at him to stay out of the cod tongue trade on the Winterton wharf.

Two young partisans roll a gun to the mouth of the cave. Massimo stands, curses, and demands to know why it isn't at the trestle. The young men say it's broken. Massimo kneels to assess the problem. Lucia inches towards the cave's mouth. She hopes they'll have to cancel the mission. Armed men are streaming out of the camp and into the woods. Massimo is getting increasingly distraught. He tells the young men the mission will fail without the gun. When he lies on the ground and rolls under it, Lucia slips out and follows the fighters moving swiftly through branches and over roots. She is flying. Breathing in the mountain's energy.

On the edge of a cliff, overlooking a train trestle, they drop to the ground and wriggle forward. She follows, paying no mind to the pine needles and pebbles worrying her belly and breasts. Through vines and branches, she sees Cosimo, sitting in the middle of a train trestle with a fishing rod and a basket. She pushes against the earth to stand and scream out, but Massimo has landed next to her and he puts his hand over her mouth.

––––––––

Once the brutes ran off and Garl had caught his breath, Arch was his crutch for the last half hour home. Leaning on each other, they worried about how Skipper would react. Even though Garl wasn't sleeping in the house, it would only be a matter of days before the old man heard about the beating. There were no secrets in the cove. He might laugh it off and tell Garl he deserved it for taking money out of the Winterton boys' pockets. But he might not. By the time they got to the Turk's Cove bridge, Arch was convinced Skipper would fly into a rage and blame him. It would be an excuse to beat him for being soft and useless, so Arch begged Garl to rough him up, figuring if they were both in a state Skipper would be less tempted to even the score. Garl mustered a slap and a punch in the guts that winded Arch but didn't do any visible damage. Arch stuck out his chin demanding a shiner. Garl moaned that his arms were too tired and his head hurt. He reckoned Skipper would be even more furious if he caught on that he was being tricked. Garl started to leave and, overwhelmed by fear, Arch grabbed the back of his brother's coat, spun him around, and demanded that for once Garl act like a real big brother. He saw the flash of anger, but not the beach rock in Garl's fist. When the smooth granite shattered his gob, Arch stumbled backwards, gagging on blood and shards of enamel. He can still see

Garl standing there with the orb in his hand. Loud enough for the whole cove to hear, Arch cried out, "My teef?! Why did you do dat?"

Limping up the stream to his tilt, Garl said, "Just looking out for you, little brother. Wouldn't want you to have to deal with Skipper on your own."

From that night on, whenever Arch's tongue touched his false teeth, he remembered Garl's terrified expression through the stair spindles the night he and Min came back from town. His mouth was a constant reminder of the shame Min and he shared that they'd left Garl on his own to absorb Skipper's rage.

———

Massimo warns her with his gaze before releasing his hand from her mouth and puts his index finger to his lips. Lucia watches him signal the partisans on the German side of the ravine. Is he telling them that the gun is broken? She wishes she could soar off the cliff, catch a draft, descend onto Cosi's shoulders and lift him away in her talons.

She whispers, "He's too young."

"He's fast," Massimo whispers back. "If Cosi succeeds, we'll get the arms we need from the Allies and Bologna will be liberated."

The *if* clangs in the chambers of her heart.

———

Arch bites the skin around his fingernails as he tells Barbara and Jon about the raking. He is silent for a long time after that, prompting Barbara to ask about his crew. He tells her tales about Slade and Tombstone and the elaborate dugouts they built. Their extra messing adventures and card games. They both lurch forward as Jon slams on the brakes on a sharp, walled corner. A motley group of men step out from behind a stone church, blocking the way. Jon curses. He's about to lose some, or all, of his precious medical supplies to these bandits. Guns are pointed at the ambulance's front wheels as two of the men go around the back and flip up the canvas. Barbara hides film rolls in her pant cuffs.

The leader signals for his men to lower their weapons and politely asks Jon, Barbara, and Arch to step out of the vehicle. He steps forward and grasps Arch's arm. Barbara tries to stop him. "Signor. This man is injured. We're bringing him back to his post to recuperate."

The leader shakes his head. "There is no post. His regiment are cowards, they've gone home."

Arch says, "They're gone?"

The leader extends his hand. "Yes, Private Fisher, they're gone. Allow me to introduce myself. I'm Paolo. Paolo Capponi."

Arch rears back. "Paolo? I . . . Cosimo's mother, er, Lucia . . . she believes you were killed. That you're dead."

"As you can see, Private Fisher, I'm alive and well and regret not letting my loving wife know."

There is a heavy silence. Barbara holds up her camera and asks for a group shot to break the tension. Paolo stands off to the side, but the young bandits puff out their chests and tilt their chins towards the sun despite their grubby mix of uniforms. Most wear berets, there's one fez and even a World War One helmet with a spike on top. They all sport red handkerchiefs around their necks and place their right hands on their rifles, pistols, and pitchforks. Arch stands at the outer edge of the frame as Barbara's shutter snaps. She hasn't heard any of her colleagues bragging about meeting partisans. She's certain she'll be able to sell these shots. She asks Paolo to pose with his men.

"Regretfully, I must decline, Signora."

He flicks his head towards the woods and says, "Andiamo tutti."

Barbara calls out, "Arch, you can stay with us."

Paolo pauses. "It's okay, we'll look after Private Fisher."

Arch asks Barbara not to send any pictures of him to the St. John's papers. "I'm pretty sure I look like hell. It will give my poor mother a heart attack."

―――――

Armando and Dante climb up from the underside of the trestle just under Cosi. Massimo whispers that the Nazis won't be able to get any petrol or ammo to Bologna without this bridge. They hand something to Cosi and run the length of the exposed tracks, back to the cover of the forest. Massimo says it's Cosi's job to string the fuse to the German side and light it. Before the bridge blows, he's to climb down into the valley and make his way back to the camp. Lucia asks, "What about the gun? What was the gun for?"

―――――

Arch runs back to the truck and hands Barbara her precious pencil and the pages from her notebook. He says, "One last favour for a fellow Newf. Can you deliver this letter to Lucia Capponi, via a Father Lino in Bologna? I'm sure you'll be there for the liberation. His church is called Saint Paolo di something."

Barbara leans out the window and kisses Arch's cheek. "I'll see you on Water Street, Arch."

He waves as he walks into the woods with the partisans. Jon pushes the stick into drive and says, "You won't be seeing him again."

―――――

A jeep of Germans appears on the north side of the trestle. Their captain yells, "Halt!" Three soldiers kneel and aim their rifles at Cosi.

Lucia is on her knees, about to scream out his name. But she's flattened to the earth by Paolo. Where did he come from? She tries to squirm away from his grip. "Tell the men to shoot. We've got a big gun. We'll fire on them." Paolo looks to Massimo who shakes his head.

————

"Where is everyone?"

The young partisan with the World War One spiked helmet ties me to a chair. So, that's it then. Tied down like that circus elephant chained to the spruce stump.

"Jeez, b'y, you don't have to be so rough."

"Volpe told me to keep you here."

"I'm not going anywhere. I'm here to find Cosi. You've seen him, hey? The young fella, Paolo's son."

"Si, he's here. He'll be back soon"

That's what I gets for believing following orders would set me free. For tapping my trunk and standing on one foot and spinning around in hopes of applause and extra treats from the ringmasters. Not Garl. He's always done what he wants. Takes what he needs. He could care less for love or approval. Maybe that's the way to go. The way to survive.

————

The fuse is already lit in Cosimo's fish basket. If the Germans see it they will kill him on the spot. Two soldiers walk towards him. Lucia squirms. She feels nauseous and desperate. How could the plan go so wrong? They will kill him or the trestle will blow with Cosi on it. He stands slowly and, hands in the air, walks towards the Germans. Just before he reaches them, he flicks his left hand like he's flagging a taxi. She's seen him do this before. When he believed in magic. He's trying to make himself invisible. This desperate gesture signals his terror. They grab his arms and drag him towards the jeep. Paolo's grip tightens. "They won't kill him, Luci. They'll try to get our location out of him first," he says.

They watch Cosi point down to the valley, drawing the Germans away from Armando and Dante's hiding place and the explosives. A few soldiers follow his direction. Massimo taps his watch and Paolo's eyes lock onto the bridge. Lucia wriggles out of his grasp and is kneeling when the trestle blows. She feels the heat on her cheeks and screams, "Cosi! Ti amo!" Through the falling rubble and smoke, Cosi is silhouetted by the jeep headlights. He's hugging his knees. She watches the German captain draw his pistol and shoot her son in the head.

chapter 23

CUTTINGS

Lucia freefalls through oblivion. Hours? Days? Weeks? She wakes in Paolo's cave with no memory of coming back to the camp. Paolo sits at the foot of her straw mattress. It is dark. She can hear him smoking. It smells like his university apartment. Paolo says, "It was like he believed he was invisible. His bravery was astonishing."

When she opens her eyes again, it is day. Paolo is sitting at a nearby table. She sits up. "I need to be with him."

He extracts the silk map from his chest pocket and passes it to her. She clenches it in her fist, holds it to her face, and breathes in the scent of sunshine on sand. The coarse texture of his hair. His delight, as a baby, tasting his first peach. Juice dribbling over slick lips and chin.

She bolts to her feet and lunges at Paolo. He is taken by surprise but doesn't fight back. She gouges his weathered cheeks with her nails. Trying to draw blood or emotion. Trying to reverse time. He seems anxious to get this over with so he can do something else, be anywhere else.

"We are moving towards Bologna tomorrow, Luci. We'll mourn him properly later," he says.

He tries to pin her arms, to embrace her, but she bats him away and stands alone.

"He took the partisan name Diavoletto," he says.

This is a gut punch. Her knees twinge.

"We've notified the CLN about our wish to rename the brigade. We'll be called Diavoletto Rosso so that he will be remembered."

Lucia chokes out, "Remembered?"

Paolo chews his bottom lip. She'd forgotten he does this when he is stressed.

He is miles away from her. A whole decade. Longer. He's a stranger. There is no longer any ease between them.

"The Germans are guarding him. His body," Paolo says. "He's at Porte Lame. They've hung him from a tree as a warning to others."

He catches her as she crumples to the ground. "Lucia, they know the people are readying to revolt and they're trying to scare us. When we liberate the city, he'll have a hero's funeral."

Lucia can think of nothing else but wrapping herself around her son, touching his hair, kissing his cheek, sewing her grief into his shroud with her own stitches. She stands and tells Paolo she is going to get him.

His head snaps back. "They'll shoot you."

"Let them try."

As she walks to the mouth of the cave, Paolo calls after her, "What about your British private, Luci? He will be heartbroken if something happens to you."

She turns and reads the loss on Paolo's face. "You made a choice, Paolo. You let me believe you were dead. You could've chosen to have me fighting at your side."

He doesn't follow when she leaves. Hours pass before she finds a familiar path to her family's olive grove. Using her sewing scissors, she takes young cuttings from the most ancient trees. She wants Cosimo to have something from his land in his shroud.

The rumble of male voices seeps through chinks in her sleep's armour. She flattens herself over roots, to hide behind a large, knobby trunk. The men are speaking about revenge in Italian. Fascist soldiers complaining about how little time is left before the Allies arrive. They're headed towards Paolo's camp. Once they pass through the grove and are out of earshot, she runs back up the mountain to warn Paolo and his men. Out of breath and barely able to speak, when she reaches the camp, she pushes through a tight circle of fighters to raise the alarm. The men surround a blindfolded British soldier. Her steps falter. Weapons point at her heart, stopping her from wrapping her arms around Arch and telling him about Cosimo. Paolo glares.

Her voice wavers, but she manages to say, "Arch is a good man. It's not his fault. I told him you were dead. I believed it."

Arch swivels towards her voice. "Lucia? Oh, Lucia, I've just written you a letter. I'm so sorry."

"Silence!" Paolo makes a motion and the guns are lowered. "So you've come back to save your Brit?"

She finds her voice. "No. I came back to save you and your men. There's Fascisti. They're headed here."

Rifle bolts are cocked. Paolo signals for the guards at the periphery to investigate, then addresses the remaining men. "This soldier was bringing a photographer to our camp. He was putting all of us in danger."

Lucia steps forward and puts her hand on Arch's shoulder. "Arch would never do anything to put you at risk."

Paulo frowns. "Thank you, for singing your lover's praises."

Her face reddens. Some of the men snicker. She takes her hand away from his shoulder but addresses the entire group. "Let me remind you all. I am more than Paolo's wife. I am the co-founder of this brigade."

Garl breaks into the circle and no one raises their weapon. He seems shocked to see Lucia. Paolo says, "Garl? I thought you left?"

"I stayed to look for Archie here." He assesses the group. "And I've scrounged up the parts for the rocket launcher."

Paolo looks skyward. "It's too late."

Bursts of gunfire are heard nearby. Garl steps forward. "Arch may have shagged around with Lucy here, Paolo, but he can absolutely fix the Nebelwerfer."

The colour drains from Paolo's face. "If you ever speak of my wife like that again I will shoot you both."

"C'mon, Volpe b'y, you can trust me. Let Archie fix it. You can use it for Bologna. Then we'll be off. You won't ever have to lay eyes on him again and you'll have your little missy back."

"I don't trust you, Garl." says Paolo. "The flour you sold us was full of bugs."

Lucia digs her nails into her palms. More than once, Garl accused her of supplying food to the partisans when all along it was him. Paolo orders the brothers tied together and adds, "Not to mention all your broken promises of gun air drops, radios, and parts?"

"That's HQ," Garl squeaks. "That's not our fault!"

Paolo says, "And because we didn't have the rocket launcher parts you promised, we lost our son."

Arch angles his head towards Lucia. "What does he mean? What happened to Cosi?"

Lucia whispers, "He's gone, Arch. The Germans shot him."

Tears run down under the silk blindfold and collect at Arch's jawline. More than anything she wants to cry in his arms. But she steps away, worrying if she touches him again, it will cost him his life.

Garl pleads, "Volpe, I kept you and your men fed throughout the winter. Yes, the flour was the shits, but it was the same flour we ate."

She backs him up. "That's true, it's all they had. Cosi and I ate it too."

More partisans leave the camp with their guns drawn. Garl says, "I've got a couple of extra revolvers in my kit bag to fight those fuckers."

A young partisan unbuckles Garl's bag and takes out the pistols and a long object wrapped in a tea towel. He withdraws the blade from its sheath. The metal is dull and flat. Lucia gasps and tells Arch, "It's the sword."

"Lucia? Take my blindfold off."

"I can't, Arch. Paolo is angry. I've never seen him like this."

———

Garl chuckles and says, "Yeah, it's Archie's sword. But he couldn't use it when push came to shove. He chickened out and the German officer who owned it almost got away."

Lucia's hands shake. Paolo will see Arch's humanity as a sign of weakness. Garl says, "Lucy here can polish this right up. A man of your stature, Paolo. You can have it for the big day."

Paolo frowns. "Liberation day will be the first day of the new Italy. We've fought to destroy these crass symbols of oppression. I'd be ashamed to carry that. As ashamed, Garl, as you should be for betraying your brother."

———

"Lucia, lean in a little closer. You said once that we've got to tell those we love how we feel."

"Arch, not here. Not now. The guards are back."

There's a frantic conversation in mountain dialect. Men scatter. Arch wonders if they're alone.

"What are they saying? What's going on?"

Lucia says, "Someone needs to move this man or untie him.

Untie them. It's not right to leave him here like this."

Why is she calling me this man? "Where's Garl?"

"He's here, Arch. Paolo hasn't decided yet. He's . . . there's too much going on."

Gunshots and machine-gun fire. Closer than ever.

"Paolo, untie my brother. Garl will help you. You can't fail now we are days away from liberating Bologna." He won't like we. "You are days away from driving the intruders out. Garl can help. Let him help."

Men drop to the ground.

"Lucia, Lucia. I love you and I loved Cosimo."

"Arch. Me too. I love you too. Paolo, please. Please. Let them help."

———————

Garl is untied. Paolo orders Massimo and another partisan to get Lucia to safety. As she's being spirited away, she's convinced she hears a single gunshot ring out above the chaos and her knees buckle. The men keep running and the toes of her red shoes gouge the earth. They leave her in a hollowed-out tree and run back to assist. Lucia stays hidden, watching the skies over Bologna flash with artillery fire. The fight to break through the German line is on.

When the sound of gunfire from the camp has died off, she crawls out of her hiding place and follows the route to the grasshopper cave knowing Arch would go there too. The large boulders that formed the cave entrance are blown apart, shattered. Lucia feels her way through the splintered rocks in the darkness to find the entrance. She picks through rubble and branches, to the main room where furniture is smashed and the ceiling has partially fallen in. She curls up with her back against the wall to wait out the dawn. When there's enough morning light, she moves small boulders, smashed table legs, and broken wood looking for the coffee pot. There's water in her canteen and she still has the tablespoon of coffee grounds from her parents' grinder all those months ago. Digging through the debris, her fingertips graze wool. A blanket? No. No. A uniform. She claws through earth and leaves and sees her own stitches. No. No. No. Not now. His neck is as cold as the stones in her fists. She's too numb to cry as she clears debris from Arch's face, kisses his stone-dusted eyelids and the wound above his ear. His blood tastes like the sea. She remembers his whale story. How he wanted to slide down their gullets. If she could, she would swallow him whole, repair his wounds within her body then swim to Cosi and devour him too. They could then float forever in a sea of grief.

Did he escape and die here when the cave was bombed? Was he waiting for her? Was it the Fascists? Paolo? Garl? Who knew that this was one of their special places? Her hand covers his still heart. The chest pocket she repaired three times because he always carried too many nails, springs, washers, pencil nubs, and letters. Letters? He said he wrote a letter. She unbuttons the pocket, but the envelopes she finds are worn. One is three years old and sealed with censor's tape. She hesitates and whispers, "Forgive me." The letters are from Anna. The child is Garl's. Arch wasn't marrying Anna for the sake of appearances, but to help her find her daughter. The truth sits on her chest like a stone. If Lucia hadn't doubted him, he would be still alive and on his way home to find Bridget. Cosimo might still be alive, and their dreams of a future together in Bologna might still come true.

The mountain trembles with the movement of armies. The cave is no longer safe. She places Anna's letter back in Arch's pocket along with the olive cuttings. They are all she has, a gesture of love and contrition. She kisses his cold lips before leaving to pick her way out of the wreckage.

At the cave's entrance, a bomber fractures her thoughts with a starburst that gathers and swoops in the wind like a murmuration.

Glinting and shimmering, the sheen transforming from wave, to boat, to whales, and into something that looks like a tree. Absorbed in the shiny leaves of chaff fluttering between her fingers, she fails to notice the bomb that knocks her to her knees. Treetops ignite. The mountain heaves against her bloodied palms, urging her to run.

chapter 24

TWOJE ZDROWIE!

Black smoke mushrooms from mountain ridges. Barbara fiddles with her camera strap as Thunderbolts and Typhoons hammer napalm and gunpowder into Sole's German hideouts. She won't waste film on puffs of smoke knowing the real gold will be in Bologna. If only she can get there. At a South African canteen, four Polish soldiers drinking brandy hand her a glass. She toasts them. "Twoje Zdrowie."

"You speak Polish?"

"A little. My neighbours in St. John's were Polish dock workers."

"Yah, many dock workers. I'm Stan. What's your name?"

"I'm Baldwin, er Barbara. It's nice to meet you, Stan."

"Barbara, you take our picture?" he asks hopefully.

Stan and his friends pose with their arms draped loosely over each other's shoulders. They look relieved. She snaps their photo, and they all knock back their drinks. Stan leans in to commiserate. "We're going to reach Bologna before the goddamned Yankees. Our guys, they're almost at the city gates."

With her throat still stinging, she asks, "Do they have a photographer?"

Stan laughs. "That's not going to help."

"But the Americans have photographers," she says.

One of the other Poles spits on the ground. "So what?"

"Even if the Polish Army gets there first, the American photographers will take pictures of US troops at the city gates and will send those photos to *The New York Times*. Tomorrow's headline, all over the world, will be *Americans Liberate Bologna*."

They have a rushed conversation in Polish and Barbara finishes the dregs of her brandy knowing she has snagged a ride.

"Promise to take pictures of Poles for all the newspapers."

She nods.

———

Caroline's taxi pulls up in front of an unassuming building in a working-class neighbourhood. While she's paying the driver, a woman steps out of the Museo della Resistenza and takes in the sandwich board. Barbara checks her watch. Siesta! No matter how long she lived in Italy as a student, she never got the hang of siesta and would find herself locked out of cafés, art galleries, bakeries, and bookstores every afternoon. She bangs on the museum's door while the driver retrieves her suitcase. He points to a brass buzzer on the inside door frame, and she presses it for a rudely long time. The lock turns and the wooden door opens just wide enough for the curator to say firmly, in accented English, that the museum will reopen in the evening. Caroline pleads, "Sono canadese." She forgets the word for grandfather. "My grandfather and zio hanno combattuto con i partigiani. Terra Nova."

The curator's face emerges from the door. "The 166th?"

"Si!" Caroline says. "They were stationed on Mont Salvaro near Sole."

The door opens wide and the woman gestures for Caroline to enter. "Si, si. I'm familiar. Come in for a minute, but only a minute,

I must pick up my son at school."

She shakes Caroline's hand. "My name is Irma Falchini. I'm the part-time curator here."

"I'm Caroline Fisher. An artist. I'm here researching a project."

"Bene, maybe you can solve a mystery for me." Irma walks ahead, motion sensor lights illuminating rooms as she passes through them. In the main exhibition space, there's a blown-up image of a caribou on a red badge. It's the size of Caroline's head. "This moose," Irma asks, "it's from the Newfoundland uniform, no?"

"It's like a moose," Caroline says, "but it's a different animal. It's called a caribou. The 166th had pins and badges like that."

Irma gestures to an even larger wall-sized photo. A caribou pin holds together a red scarf worn by a striking man in a white shirt. "This is Paolo Capponi. A partisan leader they called the Fox."

Paolo is handsome. His eyes are bright, and he has one arm up in victory and the other cinched around the shoulders of a serious, dark-haired woman. There are armed guards, with their guns ready, all around them on the tank.

"Who's the woman?" asks Caroline.

"We think it's his first wife, Lucia. Unfortunately, we don't know much about her. We are only beginning to research the role of women in the resistance."

Irma tells Caroline the story of Paolo's son Cosimo and how, after the young man's death, Paolo renamed his brigade Diavoletto Rosso in his honour. She points to a small devil in Lucia's hand. "I'd really like to know why Paolo wears the caribou on Liberation Day. The partisans were very conscious of what their uniforms signalled."

"Who took the photo?" asks Caroline.

"Ah, yes, you may know her. A famous Canadian photographer, Barbara Kerr."

"A woman? I've never heard of her."

Caroline searches for Pop in the photo, but background features are blurred. If only she could step into this scene and walk around the tank to finally know if he was there. If he was telling the truth that he really did stay behind to look for Arch.

———

Barbara presses herself tightly into Stan's back as his motorcycle weaves across ruts, around trucks, jeeps, bulldozers, Shermans, quads, and tractors. She doesn't care if she has flies in her teeth, she can't stop smiling. If she survives this ride, she'll be one of the first photographers in Bologna. They dodge a column of South African tanks with open hatches. Their radios are all tuned to the BBC and the men are singing along with the Andrews Sisters. *Drinkin' rum and Coca-Cola, Go down Point Cumana, both mother and daughter, Workin' for the Yankee dollar!* In time with the beat, soldiers on the tanks pretend to row using their rifles as paddles. If they weren't in such a hurry to get to the city, she would demand that Stan stop so she could take some shots. Plumes of smoke and aeroplanes blot out the sun. The Poles told her fifteen hundred bombers are on the way. Flying Fortresses and Liberators drone above them, accompanied by the buzz of hundreds of Spitfires. While the sky belongs to the Allies, the retreating Germans are not giving up without a fight. There are occasional artillery explosions near the road, burned-out tanks and vehicles smoke in ditches. Infantry units cleave off to attack targets. A Liberator is hit by enemy fire and corkscrews backwards towards them. Tanks and trucks veer off to avoid the flaming fuselage. Stan steps on the accelerator to take advantage of the open road. Barbara ducks as the plane spins over their heads and slams into a farmer's field just behind them. The shockwave throbs in her shins, but Stan doesn't slow down.

They enter Bologna through Porte Mazzini. The Allies have been bombing the city in advance and the streets are clogged with smoking rubble, broken timbers, collapsed walls and abandoned German vehicles. Propaganda posters and wanted signs offering rewards for partisans cover windows and doors. There's no sign of Germans, but the air sizzles with tension. A boy runs out of a doorway and throws something. Stan skids to a stop and Barbara almost falls off. When she catches her balance, there are yellow mimosa branches in her lap. The boy's grandmother has caught up with him and is twisting his ear. She apologizes and tells them the party is in Nettuno. The woman threads some of the blossoms into the webbing on Barbara's helmet, kisses her and Stan on both cheeks, and tells them to be careful. The Germans left only two hours ago.

Slower now, they wind through alleys and streets until they hear strains of music and singing from the famous piazza. Stan parks his bike and holding hands they step into the flow of people from surrounding streets, doorways, and alleys. Everyone is laughing, crying, and embracing. The pull of joy and relief is irresistible. At the mouth of Nettuno, Italians and Polish soldiers have linked arms to dance in wide circles. An old man plays accordion. Young girls in white dresses wind a long red and white banner through the crowd. One of the circles opens for a Polish tank. Wine bottles are handed up to the soldiers as children climb on for rides. Barbara takes Stan's picture, kisses him, and thanks him for getting her here safely. He reminds her to get photos of the Poles and she nods. She takes a shot of a man holding a baby up to receive a kiss from a Polish gunner. The crowd cheers whenever a Nazi banner or flag is torn from a building and trampled, but the euphoria is also tinged with violence. She gets a couple of photos of a bloodied man being dragged away by an armed trio and a knot of people hissing and spitting on two young women with shaved heads. A small column of men attempts to march into the mayhem and there are screams of "Fascisti! Fascisti!" The men retreat when their leaders are roughed up. A waiter lifts a radio out onto the patio and adjusts the antenna.

BBC Newsflash, April 21, 1945. The liberation of Bologna has begun. The first troops in the city are Polish. Full surrender of Germany expected in weeks.

A hastily sewn Polish flag unfurls over a balcony to cheers and what Barbara guesses is the Polish anthem. Bologna's famous bell towers clang but are barely audible over the euphoria. She lets the surging crowd carry her forward to a tank smothered in mimosa flowers. Men in suits, ammo belts, and a jumble of uniforms guard a man in a brilliant white shirt standing on the turret. He has a red bandana pinned at his throat and he's holding a dark-haired woman wearing red shoes and trousers. It's Paolo, the partisan who took Arch Fisher into the woods. She snaps a couple of wides of the couple at the eye of this exuberant storm and moves in to grab tighter shots with their upper bodies filling the frame. The brunette's despair is striking. People climbing onto the tank, to greet Paulo, crowd the woman off. She lands a few feet away and Barbara grabs her arm. "Is that Paolo? The partisan leader?" The woman nods. Barbara lifts her camera and captures the woman's grief framed by reaching arms. "What's your name?" she asks.

"What's important is my son's name. Cosimo. He died defending Italy. He was just sixteen. I'm going to find his body now." The woman slips into the frenzy and it hits Barbara that this must be Lucia. She grabs Arch's letter from her pouch and calling out, she pushes through the melee. More and more people are spilling into the piazza from every direction and she quickly loses sight of Lucia.

On the opposite side of the piazza, a large American flag is draped over a dais. One of her press buddies, Dan, is taking pictures from the stage. Barbara frames Dan nicely with the flag and the crowds, knowing he'll thank her for the negative later. US soldiers plug in microphones and chairs are being arranged. The Americans arrived hours after the Poles and the Brits, but they'll try to stage manage this liberation as their own. Dan sees her and climbs down. "Babs. How the hell did you get here?"

"I hitched a ride with a lovely Polish motorcycle driver. Who would have thought the Poles would get here first?" She laughs, but his brow furrows and before she can slap his hand away, he reaches out and grabs one of her breasts. Barbara jumps back and yells, "What the hell, Dan? I got here without doing any favours for soldiers."

Dan's CO strides towards them. He's seen everything. When she opens her mouth to complain, he cuts her off. "Sergeant Kerr, what are you doing here at the front?"

She says, "Sir, I believe the front is northeast of here now."

"We have not given clearance for females to enter this zone."

Before she can point out the thousands of women in the piazza, the American CO signals for his MPs. "Get this broad out of here!"

———————

Irma leaves Caroline to consider Paolo and Lucia's dichotomy of joy and grief. The curator returns with a large cardboard box.

"She used a pen name during the war. Baldwin. She published her photos as Baldwin Kerr."

No wonder Caroline hadn't been able to find much information on Kerr's work.

Irma says, "We have her entire Italian war archive, all her papers, journals, letters, and photos, but no one has had time to go through it."

Caroline dons white cotton gloves. Her hands are shaking as she carefully opens one file folder and then another. There are nurses in a jeep, hospital scenes, Allied soldiers on a tarmac, what looks like an abandoned post in the mountains, soldiers leaning against tanks, a group of armed men and a soldier with a bandaged head. "Oh my God, I think that's my great-uncle. I'd know that smile anywhere."

Irma turns the photo over and reads. "*Private A. Fisher (Nfld). With a group of partisans on the road near Tudiano church. Not pictured, but present, partisan leader, Paolo Capponi (Volpe). He would not let me take his portrait.*"

Time stands still. Was Pop there too? Maybe he stood to the side with Paolo? She takes a photo of the print with her iPhone and says, "Irma, you may be one step closer to knowing where he got the caribou pin."

"Was your uncle missing his caribou when he came home?"

"Unfortunately, he didn't come back. He died here, somewhere in the mountains, just before Liberation Day."

"I'm sorry for your loss, Caroline. So many people died on Monte Sole and Salvaro. Maybe the Kerr archive can help you piece the story together." She returns the photos to the box, looks at her watch, and claps her hands together. "I really must go. I am officially late now. Can you come back this evening?"

Caroline peels off the cotton gloves. "I can't. My flight home leaves in a couple of hours."

"Then you must return to Bologna soon. You are part of our story."

As she locks the museum's front door, Irma says that too many Italians have forgotten the sacrifices of the war years. Caroline blurts out what she witnessed in the enoteca, and Irma shakes her head. "It is shocking, isn't it? After the war, so many, Italians left for America, Australia, Brazil. Everyone has at least one refugee relative and yet so many are drinking the poison of Fascismo again."

Irma gives Caroline her card, tells her to come back soon, and kisses her on both cheeks before peeling off on her bicycle.

———

Half a day later, Caroline drags her suitcase through a snowdrift in her St. John's driveway. It's past midnight and she's famished.

She finds a bagel in the bread drawer, taps it on the counter, and deems it edible. She wishes Min was still alive so she could tell her how beautiful Monte Sole is. It would mean so much to her to know that Arch's body rests in such a tranquil place. Barbara Kerr's photos may hold more answers about Arch's last days, but it hardly matters anymore. She chews and runs her fingers along the tiny leaves sprouting on the olive. She will never fully understand the impossible decisions Pop and Arch faced in Italy, but she no longer feels any shame around Arch's disappearance, Pop's role in it, and the burning of the letters because their story didn't end there. As Irma said, we are part of Bologna's ongoing story. She takes another bite and sifts through unopened mail: gym and fried chicken coupons, a power bill, and a postcard of a surfer. She turns it over.

Hello Caroline, I sent you the olive tree. I hope you don't mind. It was in desperate need of care as I'm sure you saw. I read a news story this week that gave me the courage to reach out to you and would love to meet when I return to Newfoundland. My summer place is in New Melbourne, not far from Turk's Cove. Would you be able to meet me there on July 1st weekend? I have a book I'd like to show you. Harrison

chapter 25

HARRISON

The biting wind whipping off Trinity Bay has not deterred a dozen or so surfers. Harrison answers the door in jeans and a Memorial University hoodie. His eyes are kind and his feet bare. "Come in, Caroline! It's such a pleasure to meet you in person."

He smiles easily, his dark, curly hair flops back and forth when they shake hands, and Caroline likes him immediately. He offers her a beer and she asks how he ended up in New Melbourne. He tells her he came to Newfoundland to do his doctorate in history, that he surfs for fun and shares the cabin with friends.

He asks about the olive as they stand at the picture window watching the surfers paddle out to catch a new wave. She tells him about the tree guru who taught her how to repot it and that now there are tiny green buds and even some leaves on the branches. He tips his beer to his lips. "I'm so glad to hear that."

She waits a couple of beats before asking him about the book he mentioned in the postcard. When he pads up over the stairs to retrieve it, she takes in the main room. Pine walls, floors, and ceilings. A graffitied picnic table. Damp wetsuits drying on the back of a black leather couch, opalescent surfboards stacked under the window, two large dog kennels in one corner, and a small hydroponic greenhouse lit by pink light in the other. When he comes back, they sit at the picnic table. He extracts a leatherbound book from a Ziploc bag and unbuckles the child's belt holding it together.

She says, "The movers you hired to bring the tree said you had a family bible with a note for me."

He lifts the cover and says, "It's not really a bible. It's more like a family archive. Look at these endpapers. My grandmother made them when she was a little girl."

There's a child's exuberance in the pink and purple swirls. He turns pages of tissue and rag paper, vellum, and newsprint. There are garden plans, plant and seed dissections, pressed leaves, a family tree that folds out, and many pages of columns of figures written in nib pen. He says, "This is a record of the crops and family births and deaths since 1675 or so. Some of the pages are written in mountain dialect, but sometime in the 1800s, everyone had to learn Tuscan Italian, even the farmers on Monte Sole."

Her heart leaps. "Sole? I was just there!"

He tilts his head. "You were on Monte Sole? Why?"

"I was in Italy researching an art project. My grandfather and great-uncle were stationed in the mountains near Sole during the war. Have you been?"

"My grandmother lived there. And . . . she wrote to your great-grandmother from there."

"What? She wrote to Min? I don't understand."

"Remember, I mentioned in the postcard. A news story that inspired me to reach out. Some archaeologists found a skeleton of a partisan in a cave in Cyprus. He'd been missing since the war. He died in the cave, but there was just enough light in there for a tree to grow from his body. From the figs he'd eaten before he died. From the seeds in his stomach," he says, spreading his hands.

Caroline wonders what a Cypriot fig tree has to do with her.

"Unbelievable, isn't it?" he says. "It took them seventy years, but the tree led them to the body. That story convinced me that an old family tale could actually be true." He extracts an envelope from the crumbling bible and says, "My father, Rafael, recited this to me over the phone and made me promise to read it to you someday. It's too precious to send in the mail and when I first came to Newfoundland, I didn't know how to find you or how to bring all this up. Can I read it to you now?"

She nods as he flattens the creased paper with his palms. He clears his throat.

In 1953, when I was nine, your grandmother took me to Monte Salvaro across the valley from Sole. We walked for an hour or so on paths to a place where a small olive tree was growing. It was a funny place for an olive. It was surrounded by oaks and large boulders and grew out of a place she called the grasshopper's cave. We spent the afternoon clearing away debris and cutting back vines to give the olive more sunlight. She took some cuttings that she wanted to send to a place I'd never heard of. A place called New-found-land. On the way home, she told me that the olive grew on my father's grave.

New-found-land sounded like a place out of Peter Pan. She never spoke about it again and I was so young, I began to think I'd imagined it. But on her deathbed, she told me the story again. She said that just before Bologna's liberation, she found my father's body in that cave. She didn't know how he died nor did she know at the time she was pregnant with me. She was unable to bury him, but she left olive cuttings from the family grove with his body. As you know, her marriage to Paolo did not survive the war, and she was devastated by your uncle Cosimo's death. Cosimo was my half-brother.

In 1944, when Lucia and Cosimo went back to Sole to look for the family, she fell in love with and became pregnant by a British soldier named Archibald Fisher. She believed Paolo was dead and she was working as a laundress at Arch's artillery post on Salvaro.

After the war, because she'd lived in England while Italians suffered, because she'd worked with the partisans, and left her husband to have a child with a soldier, she was shunned. Women who worked, who defied the church, who dared to make their own decisions, were considered unclean—even in the so-called 'new Italy.' When she made it back to the mountains with Cosimo's body after the liberation, the family house had been sacked and burned, not by Nazis or Fascists, but by neighbours who did not want her to return. You might remember a kind old lady, but Lucia was as tough as a mountain goat. She rebuilt and worked for decades alongside people who made her life difficult. She did that to make a home for me and to honour her family. She buried Cosimo in the family olive grove and stayed in the mountains to tend his and Arch's grave. She tilled the fields by herself, harvested olives and kept chickens, cows, and goats. She also raised silkworms, spun silk and sent it to a buyer in England. She did all that with her own hands, without any help from neighbours, without Cosimo, Paolo, or Archibald. She was an incredibly strong and determined woman.

Someday, I hope you will find a way to connect with Archibald Fisher's family as they are also your family. Lucia wrote in the bible that they live in a place called Turk's Cove in New-Found-Land. It doesn't matter that Lucia and Arch weren't married. She loved him and their love gave us both a future.

Amore, Rafael

Harrison pauses and wipes his eyes. Caroline's head is spinning. She stands and paces around the room. She asks Harrison why Lucia or Rafael never contacted Min to say Arch had a son.

"I don't know. Maybe Lucia was too proud to ask for help. Maybe she worried your family would think she was lying or trying to get something from them. Not all the Newfoundland soldiers had been kind to her, so maybe she was worried about how the news would be received. My dad was a solitary, shy man, probably because of how they were treated after the war. I wish he'd had the courage to reach out because he would've loved it here. I often think of him when I'm on my surfboard. This rocky coastline, the whales, the meadows, the berries, the little cove where Arch grew up, would've made him so happy."

Caroline's eyes cloud over with tears for a cousin she's never met. Harrison tells her they moved to California when Lucia died. That's where he was born. He says the only thing Rafael brought from Italy was a pincushion and this book, the family bible. "During the war and after, Lucia scribbled notes in here," he says. "You might want to read it."

"This is so much to take in, Harrison."

"I came to Newfoundland for my studies because I wanted to know more about the place where Arch grew up. I started surfing on weekends here in Trinity Bay. One summer, a bunch of us rented a place in Turk's Cove. When I walked into the kitchen and saw the olive tree, and the soldiers' portraits on the wall, I knew. I had to sit down. It was like I had been pulled into that room, across continents and time, by an irresistible force. I know there was at least one letter between Lucia and Min. The one with the olive cuttings from Arch's tree," Harrison says. "And I've always wondered if Lucia mentioned Rafael."

"I don't think so. Min would not have been able to keep that secret. She would've been overjoyed. But I can't tell you for sure because Arch's brother, Garl, burned all the letters."

A squall passes over Harrison's face. "I didn't know Garl was Arch's brother."

"Yes, he's the other portrait on the wall in Min's house. He's the officer and he's my grandfather."

His eyes widen and he turns away from Caroline to stare out the window. When he turns back, she can tell he's choosing his words carefully. He says, "Lucia wrote in the bible that Garl tried to have her killed. He planted a British officer's button in her sewing kit. Two German soldiers found it and attacked her. If Paolo's men hadn't intervened, I wouldn't be here talking to you."

Caroline's voice shakes. "How? How did she know it was Pop?"

"He came onto her, and she turned him down and she suspected it was his revenge. As you say, he was an officer, so he would've had a button and he would've known how dangerous it would be for her."

Down on the beach, the surfers are warming themselves around a fire.

"I'm sorry, Caroline," he says. "That must be difficult to hear. We all think of our grandparents as heroes."

She nods. "I no longer believe in heroes. Not in the traditional way. Researching the choices they faced during the war has given me a more nuanced understanding of Pop." She explains to Harrison that Arch and Garl's childhood was difficult. Min said their father had been abusive and after the war Garl spent months, sometimes years, working in mines and remote oil camps. Using alcohol to deal with the trauma of whatever happened in Italy. "When I was growing up, he could be gentle and funny, but also quite mean after a few drinks. I'm sorry he put your grandmother in danger."

"You shouldn't apologize for him," says Harrison.

"I guess not," she says. "Speaking of heroes, I've just seen a picture of Lucia in Bologna. Do you have a photo of her?"

"Really? Dad had this photo from a magazine on his bedside table."

He extracts a black and white print from the back of the bible. Lucia's head and shoulders are framed by open window shutters; she's beaming with her face tilted towards the sun. It is undeniably the same woman who radiates grief from the wall at the Partisan Museum.

"She looks like she's in love," says Caroline.

"Yes. Arch and Cosimo were probably still alive when this was taken. Where did *you* see a photo of her?"

"At the Partisan Museum in Bologna. Have you ever been to it?" He shakes his head.

"She takes up a whole wall. She's on a tank with Paolo on Liberation Day and looks a decade older than this photo even though it would've been taken only a few weeks later."

He says, "I'm writing my dissertation on her contribution to the resistance."

Caroline gives Harrison Irma's card and suggests he reach out to her about the Kerr archive and the connections between the partisans and the 166th. They stand shoulder to shoulder, watching the surfers' hopeful struggle to capture the energy of the sea. Harrison says, "I'll reach out and tell her I'm interested, but I can't go right away. My girlfriend Tracy and I are having a baby in a few months. She's out there today." He gestures towards the water.

"Harrison, that is amazing news. Congratulations!"

A swell lifts the surfers to the shoreline, and Caroline feels Min's presence. She says, "Your great-grandmother Min would be thrilled by that news. She'd make you a cherry cake and tell your future. I can't read palms like she could, but I have her recipe and will make her cake for you both when you join us for supper."

He nods in the direction of the surfers. "I'd love that. Let's walk down to the beach. I'll introduce you to Tracy."

———

276 | ANGELA ANTLE

Caroline rubs Min's key between her thumb and forefinger. The lock is stiff, but when she opens the front door, Min splays her paperback, gets up from the daybed, and rushes towards Caroline with open arms. She feels loved and secure until the wind grabs the door from her hand, slams it shut on the past, leaving her stranded in the present. The kitchen looks bereft without the olive. She texts Leo. *I'll drive back in the a.m., good meeting. Late supper. Min's for tonight.*

She builds a small fire in the wood stove and unrolls the quilt and pillow Harrison lent her. Inside the bedroll, he's thoughtfully included a can of beer, a saran-wrapped hamburger, and an expertly rolled joint. She wraps the quilt around her shoulders and takes the joint outside. Shrieks of laughter and a bass beat carry across the bay from a party on the bridge as she smokes. A hurricane down south is pushing heavy tropical air north. The humidity and weed make her sleepy and she goes into the house and tries to get comfortable on the daybed.

She is startled awake by a crash a few hours later. The house is shaking in the wind and the main room is bathed in bright orange light. When she fell asleep there were just embers, but now, voracious flames lick at the stove's window. She gets up. Arch's military portrait has fallen off its hook and the floor is littered with shattered glass. She stuffs her feet into her shoes and grabs the broom. She sweeps and gathers up the broken sections of the frame. Pulling large shards away from his face, she's careful not to scrape the emulsion. She tugs at a large piece near Arch's smile and when it comes free, folded paper that had pinned the portrait to the frame falls out and she unfolds it.

———————

November 29, 1955

Dear Min,

I'm so sorry to hear about the letters. God only knows what was up with Garl. The war, and his inability to find Arch, it all left a wound. And he was a hard case before that, wasn't he? But on those last days in the mountains, he tried to do the right thing. He got right up in Knox's face, yelling, forgetting he'd been demoted to private, and demanding that we all stay to look for Arch. Knox had lost his own brother in the war, so he let Garl rage on for a while until he couldn't take it no more. I'll never forget the spray of spittle when he let Garl have it. "Private Fisher, ten Allied armies are blasting through here on the way to Bologna and we have orders to get out of the way. So, get your kit together. You're going home. For Christ's sake try, just try, to find an ounce of joy in that."

On our last night, he snuck away to find him on his own. He lost his pension for that move, but he probably got to attend the big party in Nettuno. Truth be told, we all would've loved to have been there. It would've helped make sense of all those months of waiting, starving, and freezing. I wish I could've helped him, but I had to bring Tombstone home. He was in a fine state by then, talking to people who weren't there, yelling out for no reason and refusing to wash, saying the whole war was a waste of humanity. His wife had died, and we couldn't tell him. He kept asking why no one was writing him, but at the end we were hiding all his letters. I did walk down to Pistoia with him to look for Arch. Oh My! What a place! A tent hospital over-run with gorgeous Brazilian nurses. I was tempted to shoot myself in the foot just to have one of those babes lean over my bed every morning. Arch had been there, but no one knew where he was cause they were upping sticks and moving north.

When we left Italy, I hoped and prayed that Arch was off shagging Lucia somewhere. Not a theory we shared with Knox or Garl, now mind ya. I never told you about her before, but I want you to know that Arch was in love when he died. He was absolutely smitten and so was she. They practically glowed when they was together.

Once we got home, Tombstone found out his wife was dead and the brass disbanded the regiment. Tombstone went straight to the Waterford. And before they could sort out what to do with the rest of us, the armistice was signed.

That's around the time I came out to thank you for all the letters, socks, and cherry cake for my birthdays. Do you remember when you first told me about Anna? We were digging your potatoes. You could've knocked me over with a feather when you told me Arch was engaged. That he'd promised to marry Anna and help her find Bridget. Even though the kid was Garl's. That was just like him. God love him.

I don't know if I've ever thanked you for setting us up. Even though she arrived at Gin's Restaurant, with her hair up in curlers under a scarf, she was still gorgeous. I never wrote you after that, but I want you to know, I waited a year, just in case Arch came back. After what her folks did, she didn't want to go home, so we moved out to Alberta and got married here. We got a sweet spot in a little place called Elnora.

Anyway, old girl, I knows after the letter bonfire you're probably convinced your eldest is an arsehole or worse. And yes, he had his moments, but he tried to find Arch. I'd swear on the bible if he hadn't burned it! In his own way he loved his brother and sometimes he even did the right thing. After we'd been in Elnora for about a year, Garl showed up one day unannounced. We'd had no luck with the mucky-mucks back home and the last person Anna wanted to see was your Garland. But bold as brass, he unlatched our front gate and walked up to the front door with a little girl by the hand. He came into the kitchen and apologized to Anna. It's a job to say who was more surprised by that. Then he kneeled in front of Brid and told her Anna was her real mommy and I was her daddy. She was about to start kindergarten, and she had red curly hair and freckles. We didn't ask him where she'd been or how he found her. We didn't even ask for proof it was her! But by da Jesus, Brid makes everything right. She has love to spare and makes us a real family. Come up and visit. I'll send you money for the ticket. Brid would love to meet her nan. I'm going to sign off now with the last thing Arch said to me. He said, it's not killing that's heroic, it's love and forgiveness. Hey b'y? They're the only things worth fighting for.

Much Love, Slade

ACKNOWLEDGEMENTS

Lisa Moore's generosity and passion for teaching is creating a whole new generation of writers and I'm so grateful to have attended her creative writing classes at Memorial University. Thanks to the WritersNL Mentorship Program, I was able to work with writer Trudy Morgan-Cole on my very rough first draft. Shed Writers Deb Hynes, Shelly Kawaja, Tena Laing, Monica Kidd, and Lindsey Bird gave me feedback on many rewrites and I am thankful for their keen ears and wise words. I'm also appreciative of savvy editing magicians Sharon Bala, Kate Kennedy, and Jocelyne Thomas, as well as Julie Liger Belair for the stunning cover. Thank you to Major General Peter Williams for answering my questions about all things military and Dr. Nancy Pedri for advice on Italian text.

Thanks to MUN librarian Joanne Cole who showed me the World War Two silk map in the QEII Library Collection, Pauline Cox of MUNFLA for allowing me to listen to the voices of the 166th in archives of the radio program *Calling Newfoundland*, and MUN librarian Joan Ritcey who gave me a copy of Harold Lake's *Perhaps They Left Us Up There*. Harold's experience in Cassino inspired

Arch's harrowing drive down the mountain. Thanks to Andy Jones who lent me his copy of Daphne Collins's *Crossing the Narrows*. I learned about the Canadian Film Unit through Dan Conlin's *War Through the Lens* and Edward W. Chafe's *Gunners* captured the friendships and indomitable spirit of the 166th despite the difficult conditions and their lack of leave while in Italy. Reading *La Resistenza, Il Fascismo, La Memoria Bologna 1943-1945*, edited by Alberto De Bernardi and Alberto Preti, introduced me to the incredible bravery of the regular people in Italy's resistance—many of them women.

Thanks to Rebecca Rose and the Breakwater team. I'm so proud to publish with this venerable fifty-year-old Newfoundland company.

Writing a novel is a funny thing. There are long bouts of slow time spent alone in rooms and in your own head and then magical chance meetings and discoveries propel you forward at warp speed. Meeting the lovely (now deceased) Reverend Wesley Oake at the Gander Legion and receiving letters and photos from him encouraged me at a time when I was losing my way. Sitting across a plane aisle from Tom Godden who happened to be reading a copy of Harold Lake's book was another one of those moments. He generously shared his father's treasured 166th documents including a detailed mimeographed map that helped me structure the story. Gerry Whelan and his brothers heard about my project and shared their father's precious World War Two journal. And John O'Dea and his wife Margaret generously shared World War Two-era letters written by their fathers.

The Saltbox Olive never could've been written without un-interrupted time and creative space of the Banff Writer's Retreat, the Lemon Tree Residency at Camporsevoli (where I saw the diavoletto), and the generosity of friends' writing cabins in Small Point-Broad Cove-Blackhead-Adam's Cove.

Much love to Mark Quinn for driving me from the Apennines to the Adriatic and back to Bologna. We may still owe some road tolls, but it was worth it to stand on the ground where the 166th stood and to walk the paths of the Monte Sole Park. Thanks to my choir girls and Friday gang for their encouragement, and to Patricia and Barbara for their support during the absences necessary to research and write this novel.

Although the structure of *The Saltbox Olive* loosely follows the battles and travels of the 166th in Italy from 1941–45 and some of the stories are inspired by actual events and people, this is an entirely fictional account with fictional characters.

My great-uncle—the real Arch Fisher—died on November 29, 1943, establishing a forward observation post just below Mozzagrogna, before the Battle of the Sangro. Harold Lake wrote of seeing his Newfoundland shoulder patch in the mud, just before his body was bulldozed. Arch is buried in the Commonwealth War Graves Commission cemetery at the Sangro alongside fifteen other 166th members: Ron White, E. Williams, W. E. G. Hopkins, J. Murray, E. L. Bowen, J. J. Veitch, J. C. Conway, S. Moore, J. P. Kent, L. G. Burton, H. Greenhalgh, H. M. Thistle, R. G. Childs, R. Bursey, and J. J. Hanlon. The Newfoundland graves are among 2,500 others from England, Scotland, Ireland, India, Pakistan, Nepal, New Zealand, Canada, South Africa, and Australia—men who gave their lives to fight back the tide of fascism.

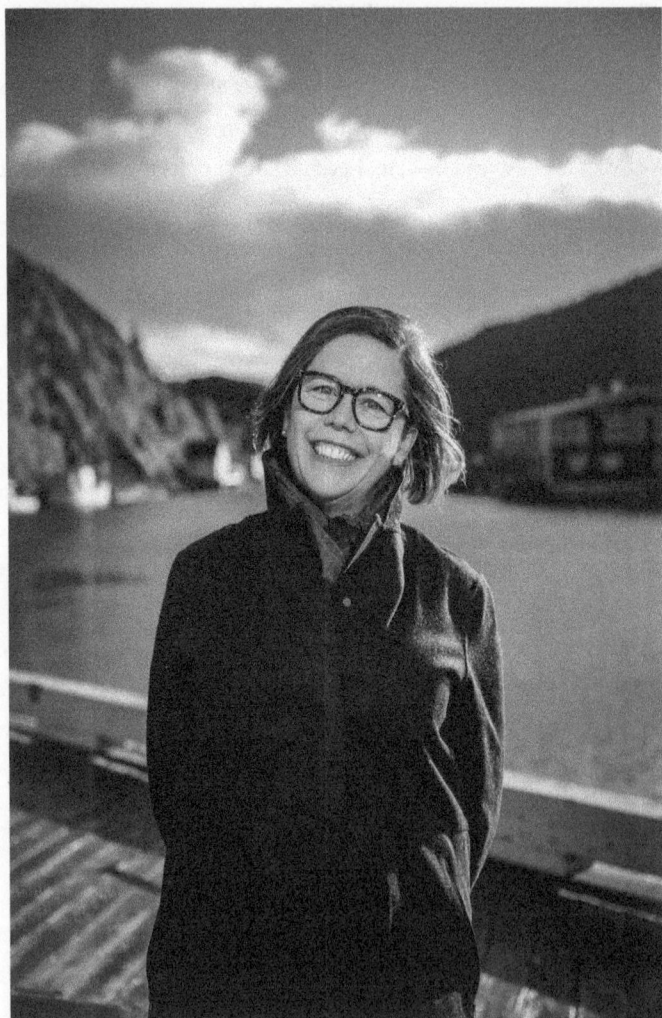

THE AUTHOR

Angela Antle is a writer, artist, and documentary maker based in St. John's, Newfoundland. Antle's writing has appeared in *Riddle Fence, Newfoundland Quarterly,* and CBC.ca. She wrote and directed *Gander's Ripple Effect: How a Small Town's Kindness Opened on Broadway,* and wrote the feature-length Irish-Norwegian-Canadian documentary *Atlantic: What Lies Beneath.* Narrated by Brendan Gleeson, it was the winner of best documentary awards at the Dublin, Wexford, Nickel, and Chagrin Film Festivals. As a journalist, Angela has rowed a dory through the Narrows, covered the subculture of Florida's Spring Break, taken bumpy komatik rides on the coast of Labrador, hitchhiked from France to Newfoundland on a fishing boat, interviewed a Prime Minister on Broadway, and recorded Ron Hynes singing "Sonny's Dream" in Ireland. She is an interdisciplinary PhD candidate at Memorial University, a member of Norway's Empowered Futures Energy School, and was recently named the 2025 Rachel Carson Writer in Residence at Ludwig-Maximilians-Universität München.